Echoes of the Heart

Secrets of Scarlett Hall

Book 2

Jennifer Monroe

This book, *Echoes of the Heart*, can be read as a standalone story, but it is best read as a part of the Secrets of Scarlett Hall series. If you have not yet read *Whispers of Light*, I would highly recommend you do so.

Jennifer

The Defiant Brides Series

The Duke's Wager

The Spinster's Secret

The Duchess Remembers

The Earl's Mission

Duke of Thorns

Regency Hearts Series

The Duke of Fire

Return of the Duke

The Duke of Ravens

Duke of Storms

Prologue

Eleanor Lambert awoke with a start from a horrible nightmare concerning her middle daughter, Hannah. In the dream, the girl was in trouble, and Eleanor had been unable to rescue her. From what danger Eleanor did not know, but it sent her heart into a rapid flutter and left her breathless, nonetheless.

Just enough moonlight filtered through an opening in the drapes to allow Eleanor to light a candle that sat in the brass holder beside her bed. Although it was silly to believe anything was wrong, she felt the need to check on the quietest of her three daughters. Therefore, she donned her dressing gown and, with candle in hand, made her way down the chilly hall toward Hannah's bedroom.

The house was quiet, as it should have been past the midnight hour, but she paused at the door to Juliet's room to listen to the faint snore coming from within. She smiled. Her youngest daughter would be mortified if Eleanor was to tell her she snored, faint or no.

The next door led to Hannah's bedroom, and Eleanor listened for any sounds coming from within but heard nothing. It was common for Hannah to sleep quieter than her sisters, but with the fright Eleanor had endured, she knew she would never sleep if she did not check on the girl.

Girl? Eleanor thought with a clenched heart. Hannah was nineteen and therefore a woman. How could Eleanor still consider her a girl?

She turned the door handle and entered the room. The figure of her daughter wrapped in a blanket on the bed warmed Eleanor's heart. Memories of coming in at night and reading the child a story, or telling her one of her own, flooded her mind, and it was early on when Hannah wanted to do the reading. The girl had remarkable abilities in reading and storytelling, even from a young age, and had not given up on either even as a young woman.

Isabel, Eleanor's eldest daughter, was now married and made her home in Camellia Estates. At least she was not far from Scarlett Hall. Soon, Hannah and Juliet, a year apart in age, would find gentlemen and be off to new homes, as well, leaving Eleanor alone in a house much too large for one person and a slew of servants. Alone, that is, until Nathaniel, the youngest of Eleanor's children, returned from boarding school.

Sadness pressed down on Eleanor, but she pushed it aside. It was what children did; they grew to adults, married, and started their own families. Is that not what she had done herself?

She made her way to the bed and frowned at the body hidden by the blanket. Hannah was curled up into a ball, and Eleanor could not blame her; the chill of the winter air seeped through cracks in the windowpanes, and she shivered in response. With a smile, she leaned over and pulled the blanket back enough to allow Hannah more air to breathe.

However, it was not her daughter's blond tresses she saw but instead an old dress rolled into a ball resting on the pillow and other clothes bundled together to create the body.

Panic overtook her as she sat on the edge of the bed. How could it be that her sweet innocent Hannah had slipped out of the house? And, where would she go?

Eleanor had been spending her time worrying over Juliet and her mischief that it never occurred to her to also keep an eye on Hannah. The girl had never done anything to give her cause to worry, unlike Juliet, who lay in the room next door, her snoring audible from here. Poor Juliet had taken a terrible fall two days earlier in the stables, injuring her foot.

Poor girl, indeed! Whenever Hannah was caught in some misdeed, Juliet was oftentimes not far behind—or rather in front. However, with Juliet unable to move about, Eleanor could draw only one conclusion: Hannah had slipped away of her own accord.

Oh, there had been rumors amongst the servants, but Eleanor had dismissed them when she had thought they were speaking of Juliet. That girl sneaking out of the house would not have surprised her one bit. But Hannah? That did give her pause.

She sighed, for she had no one to blame but herself. The last year had been a trying one, and in the process of working through the problems, she had neglected her daughters, and Hannah had sought solace elsewhere.

The signs had been there all along, but she had ignored them. Hannah had withdrawn from her, their hugs and conversations less over the past year. Eleanor could not stop the guilt that washed over her, and the voice of her late husband came to haunt her. Charles had warned her that Hannah, like all women according to him, could not be trusted. It was one of the few times Eleanor had stood up to the man, a decision she had never regretted, even today.

Letting out a sigh, she gathered her thoughts. If Hannah sought company this night, Eleanor hoped it was not with a man. She shivered, dismissing such ideas. Hannah had told her she had no interest in courting, and she certainly was not in love. However, what if that had been a lie?

With a heavy heart, Eleanor rose from the bed and made her way down the stairs to the foyer. She was so caught up in her worries, she did not notice the butler standing beside the front door until she was nearly upon him.

"Forbes," she gasped, her hand moving to her breast. "You startled me."

The tall man emerged from the shadows. Although he was just a few years older than Eleanor, his hair was a cap of silver and made him appear older than he was.

"Forgive me, my Lady," he said with a deep bow. "I heard footsteps and wished to make certain all was secure. Are you all right?"

Eleanor began to nod but then stopped. "No, I am not all right. Hannah is gone, and in her bed is a decoy to hide her escape." She narrowed her eyes at the man. "Do you know anything about her whereabouts?"

"No, my Lady," he replied with eyes wide with shock at the mere suggestion of him participating in such a conspiracy. "Shall I search the house?"

"Thank you," Eleanor replied. "I will be in the study. Please tell me if you learn anything."

Forbes gave a quick nod and then disappeared into the shadows as candlelight lit Eleanor's way to the study. She used the single candle to light others and took a seat at the desk before taking a quill in hand. Writing letters had always been a way for her to release worry, and now she would pen two, just as she had eight months earlier.

Taking a deep breath, she released it, but her worry over Hannah did not subside. Where could her daughter have gone? The girl's love of books and stories would be her undoing if she was not careful.

When she had gained some semblance of calm, she began to write:

Charles,

You would be pleased to know that Scarlett Hall was saved due to the sacrifice made by Isabel. Her strength of enduring the death of her husband and accepting a marriage of convenience has provided Hannah and Juliet with a chance at a better life. I believe you would be proud, for the strength Isabel possesses is admired by many.

However, Hannah is the main subject of this letter. The most innocent of our daughters, the one who would prefer to remain home and read than to attend parties, the one who dreams of writing a book rather than marrying, has surprised me. In just a few days, she is to leave for her first season, but she has told me she does not wish to attend. If I force her hand in this matter, will she run away? And if so, into whose arms? This is a great concern for me, for I understand all too well that a woman can be easily led astray, and Hannah can be much too trusting for her own good.

4

My hand will be forced, and although I can think of many reasons not to stop her from following her heart, I must do so, for her own sake.

I am aware that this letter is quite unpleasant, but I must do what I must. I only hope that Hannah forgives me.

Your Wife,
Eleanor

With a sigh, Eleanor placed the parchment to the side and took another. Now, she would have to write to Isabel and once again ask for her strength. Although few options existed, the help of her eldest daughter would be needed, and she had no doubt the woman would rush to her aid.

A knock at the door made her turn to see Forbes enter the room.

"My apologies, my Lady. The servants who are awake know nothing. I searched outside in hopes of finding her, and it led me to find a horse missing from the stables."

Eleanor nodded. "Thank you, Forbes. If a horse is missing, it is clear she has left the property. I will wait up in hopes she will return by morning. It is too late to do anything until then, anyway. That is all. You should rest now. We have a long day ahead of us tomorrow."

"If you require anything, my Lady," he said with another of his deep bows.

"I will not hesitate to ask," she replied with a smile.

Forbes nodded and left the room, closing the door behind him.

Eleanor dipped the nib of the quill in the ink and began the second letter as the candles flickered beside her.

My Dearest Isabel, ...

Chapter One

Although Miss Hannah Lambert had sneaked from her home after everyone was fast asleep on several occasions in the past, the fear that overtook her each time she did so was not easy to endure. It was the fear of someone catching her or of being set upon by highwaymen, both reasonable rationales of which to be fearful. However, she had one fear less rational, and for whatever reason, she found it frightened more than the others.

The fact of the matter was that her younger sister Juliet, one well known for her fantastical stories, had included amongst the possible horrors of being out late at night tales of men who roamed the night in order to kidnap women and force them into marriage.

The idea of being kidnapped was terrifying enough, but to be forced into marriage was what caused her to shiver as her horse trudged down the road. In her mind, marriage was for the simpleminded, and Hannah was much too intelligent to be tricked into such a relationship.

For one, a woman would have to fall in love in order to be married, and she had yet to experience such an emotion—not outside of the love she had for her family. She had read extensively on the subject, and although Isabel, her elder sister, had found love for the second time, that did not mean Hannah was meant to find it for herself. It was true she had shied away from any men who attempted to call, and last season—which was to be her coming out season—she had feigned illness in order to remain home rather than join others her age in London. Even her mother did not suspect deception, and although it hurt Hannah to deceive the woman she loved dearly, the cause was worthy of such dramatics.

The truth was, Hannah had a dream to publish a novel, and that dream would never be realized if she were to fall in love. No man would allow his wife to become a writer—a woman writer was frowned upon, married or not, as it was. Even if she found a man willing to allow her to do such a thing, she knew love would keep her from writing. Had love not consumed Isabel over the past month? The woman would sit and stare at her husband with a grin so wide it was almost silly. Well, seeing such things were nice from afar, but they were far better when one wrote about them.

Every Thursday at the same time there was a cottage where likeminded men and women gathered in order to share and learn the craft of writing. Hannah had learned of the place while eavesdropping at a party she had attended and soon found her way to the cottage of one Mr. Albert Moore. He was a sheep farmer who had never married, which was an oddity for a man forty years of age. However, his love and knowledge of reading and writing, a strange ability by a man of his station to be sure, intrigued Hannah. More importantly, he helped guide her in her endeavor.

She recalled her third time at his home, when she had read an excerpt of her novel to the group. Although many had complimented her, it was Albert who later came to her privately.

"I must say," he had whispered to her, "you are a far better writer than any of these others."

She could not help but beam at his words, for they had boosted her spirit, as well as her confidence that she was making the right decision for her life.

He lowered his voice further. "However, I would caution you to keep my observation to yourself. We would not wish to upset the others, now, would we?"

It was that continued kindness and support that Hannah had accepted a personal invitation this Monday night to join Albert in a special meeting. At first, she had been excited. It was to be only the two of them, and he promised a worthy surprise if she agreed. Of course, she had agreed readily. How could she not?

Now, however, she questioned her judgment. It was one thing to sneak away to join a group and quite another to agree to meet a man alone. She had confided in no one about this meeting, so if anything went awry, no one would know her whereabouts. If the *ton* learned about this, her name would be ruined forever. If her mother found out, it would crush her. And what if the man had other intentions?

Juliet had spoken often of men who wooed women with words. Was this what Albert was attempting to do?

Well, it is too late to turn back now, she counseled herself, *for if I do, I may very likely miss the opportunity of a lifetime.*

She guided the horse down the small path that led to the cottage, and her mind turned to Albert. Her worries were unfounded and silly; the man was like her, forsaking love in order to dedicate his time to the love of books. This brought her a sense of relief as she tied the horse to one of the trees as she had done on so many evenings before.

However, as she walked toward the cottage, she could not stop a tentacle of doubt from tickling her mind once again. Perhaps it would be best if she returned home.

Before she could change her mind, the door opened, and Albert appeared in the doorway. There was no turning back now.

"Miss Hannah," he said with a bow. "You decided to come after all. I worried you would give into the fear with which so many new authors are struck." He wore a simple white shirt and waistcoat and tan breeches, all well-worn, and she was embarrassed to realize that even Daniel, the stable hand at Scarlett Hall, had better clothing.

However, it was not the wealth that defined a person but his or her heart, and Albert had been nothing but supportive of her desire to write. And his smile was as inviting as it always was. Why had she been so concerned? The man, though a watcher of sheep by trade, had always behaved like a gentleman.

"Not at all," Hannah replied, glad her voice did not expose her lie. "I am not like other authors, for I shall complete my novel one day. And have it published."

He stepped back to allow her to enter, and with renewed confidence she moved past him into the now familiar interior of the cottage. The house was small, consisting of only two rooms. One room was a bedroom Hannah had never seen, and the other was a sitting room combined with the kitchen and dining room with space large enough to host the weekly meetings without making participants feel cramped. Few pieces of furniture included a sofa with worn cushions, three small tables, and several simple chairs, all of which would remain empty this night.

The sound of the door closed behind her, and Hannah's heart thumped and she let out a small yelp.

"What is wrong?" Albert asked as he brushed back his dark hair speckled with silver. He placed calloused hands on her arms. "Are you all right? Was your journey safe?"

She swallowed hard, but the worry behind his eyes made her chastise herself inwardly once again. "I am well," she replied. "I believe my concern comes from my fear of being caught. Forgive my skittishness."

Albert sighed as he dropped his hands to his side. "It is expected that you would be afraid of discovery."

"It is?" Hannah asked with surprise. "I thought you would think me a coward."

"Not at all. You stand far above those of the *ton*. The truth of the matter is, they would be jealous if they were to learn about your gift."

Hannah giggled. Albert was always encouraging her and lifting her spirit. Many times after the group was dismissed, she would share her heart and the problems at home. Each time, he would comfort her, assuring her that she was strong and would achieve her dream despite the complications of her life. It was those compliments and his willingness to help that had always made her feel wanted, a feeling she had not experienced at home for some time.

"Thank you," she said. "You are always so kind."

He smiled and took her elbow. "Please, sit. I have a surprise for you."

Hannah nodded and walked over to one of the chairs, but before she could sit, he said, "On the couch, if you will, please."

Thinking nothing odd in the request, she sat on the sofa as Albert went to the area designated as his kitchen. When he returned to the seating area, he carried with him two glasses of wine. "I believe tonight will be a night of celebration."

"Celebration?" Hannah asked. "What will we celebrate?"

"I have done much thinking over the last few months," he replied as he handed her one of the glasses and sat beside her on the sofa. He nodded at the glass. "Take a drink. I believe you will like it."

She did as he requested. The wine was good with a bold fruity flavor that rolled on her tongue. "This is lovely."

"I saved up to buy it especially for this special night," Albert said with a wide grin. "However, that is unimportant. What is important is you and your happiness."

Hannah could not help but smile. He really was a kind man. She took another sip of her wine. It was good enough to have sat on the table in Scarlett Hall.

"I imagine you are wondering why I asked you over tonight."

"I must admit that my curiosity is piqued," she replied.

When Albert placed his glass on a nearby table and reached over and took her hand, her heart skipped a beat, and she had to fight the urge to pull back her hand.

"I would never hurt you," he whispered.

"I know," she said before taking a deeper drink of her wine. "What is it you wish to share with me?"

He smiled, and for a brief moment, Hannah swore she saw desire in his eyes. She dismissed it almost immediately. For one, she had no idea what desire truly looked like and by believing she was seeing such an emotion was an unfair judgement. For another, it could have been a reflection from the candlelight and nothing more.

"You have shared your heart with me many times," he said, still holding her hand. "Do you regret doing so?"

"Not at all. It is wonderful to have someone to whom I can confide."

He placed his other hand on top of hers so hers was now enveloped in his. "And you have spoken of concerns for attending the London season, have you not?"

Her mouth went dry, and she took another drink of wine in an attempt to add moisture to it. "Yes. I must leave in three days, but I have no desire to participate in a ritual to find a man to marry." Such a thought was more worrisome than being found in this man's house alone. "I do not wish that."

"And neither do I," Albert said. "I have come to respect you as the strong and intelligent woman you are. It is true; you are far too wise to be married off to some gentleman who will never understand your love of the written word."

Hannah nodded. This man truly did understand her. "That is my greatest fear. Unlike my book, where I shall choose the ending, I will have no choice in marrying or continuing my dream." She struggled to keep the sadness at bay, and she emptied her wine glass and set it on the table beside Albert's.

"If you close your eyes," Albert said with a smile, "I will tell you your surprise."

She could not help but return his smile. "Very well," she replied as she did as he bade.

"Imagine publishing your first novel. The people will love it and want more. The publisher will ask you to write other novels. Can you see it?"

Hannah nodded. In her mind's eye, she saw people reading her novel at every street corner. "I can see it," she whispered. "I shall walk around the streets of London as people speak of my book, not knowing it was I who wrote it."

"Yes," Albert said. "Now imagine you are married to a man who cares not for your talent. Instead he has you attending parties and doing his will."

The thought of that frightened her. "Then the world will never know my book," she whispered. "For my husband would never allow it."

"Most men would not," Albert said, his voice now so quiet she could barely hear him. "But there is one who would. A man who would support you and encourage you. He would work from the rising to the setting of the sun while you wrote. His happiness would come from knowing that you did as your heart desired."

Hannah smiled. "That would be lovely," she said. "If only it were true and such a man existed."

"It is true," Albert said. "For I am that man."

Confusion coursed through Hannah. What did he mean, he was that man?

Then, to her shock and dismay, she felt something press against her lips, and her eyes flew open with alarm to find Albert kissing her. It was nothing like the kisses described in books, for the feeling was unsettling. There was no passion, no flutter of her heart, but instead a cold and bland sensation.

She pulled her hand from his and pushed him away. "Albert?" she said with an angry gasp. "What has come over you? We are friends, and I would never have expected such behavior from you!" What she wanted to do was weep and, even more, to return home. It had been a mistake coming here! What had she been thinking? She stood to leave, but Albert blocked her path. Was that anger in his eyes now?

"For over a year, I have helped you. Now I have devised a plan to save you, and you are angry with me?"

"That does not mean you can take liberties! What is it you want?"

"Marry me," Albert said to Hannah's astonishment. "We shall have a life together. I will work to provide for you, and you shall continue to write. You will be happy, and so will I."

Hannah's jaw dropped. She did not want to marry anyone, but certainly not a man she did not love. "I...I do not..."

"Listen for one moment before you decide. If you were to marry me, think of the life you could lead! It would be spent writing and following your dreams. I just want to be there with you to support you in this endeavor of yours. I do not have the riches others who seek your hand possess, but I can give you my heart."

Hannah was overcome by the kindness the man demonstrated, and she could not stop her anger from turning to compassion. The man, who by all accounts was poor, had a rich heart. "I do not know," she whispered.

In truth, she did not, for what he offered was everything she wanted. To be able to write her books and have a husband who supported her was a dream come true.

However, she knew her mother, nor anyone else in society, would never approve such a union. Although she did not care what society thought of her, how her mother and sisters viewed her was important. "This is a very complicated decision; one I shall need time on which to think."

"I expected nothing less from a mind like yours," Albert said. "And I will be here waiting for your reply as your friend."

"Thank you," Hannah said, overcome with emotion. What emotion had yet to be determined.

He opened the door for her and followed her outside. "Hannah."

She turned to face him, fearing he wished to kiss her again.

"Your dreams are right here," he said with his hand open, palm up before him. "You may choose to take them." He paused for a moment. "Or put them away forever." His hand closed. "That is for you to decide."

"Thank you," she whispered and then hurried to her horse.

As she rode away wanting nothing more than to return to her home, new fears entered her mind. She had kissed a man she did not love; what did that make her? Would accepting his proposal to have her dream fulfilled be worth having to kiss him again? She did not know what she was to do, for the answer to have her dream fulfilled resided in a man she did not love. The one thing she had vowed to never accept.

***

After returning the horse to the stables, Hannah made her way up the steps to Scarlett Hall. She loved her home and the feeling of security it provided and could not wait to return to her room to consider the matters of the night. Usually, she would climb the trellis that led to her bedroom window; however, tonight she decided to risk going through the front door. She was unsure if she had the strength to make that climb.

Slipping inside the house, she let out a breath, relieved that the night's events were over.

"I am glad you decided to return," her mother said, startling Hannah. She looked up as her mother came down the stairs with a candle in her hand. "I have always expected this of Juliet but not you, Hannah."

Shame came over Hannah as her mother came to a stop before her. "Mother," she said not wanting to tell the woman the truth. "I was only…" her words trailed off as guilt washed over her.

"Let us go to the study and speak. I am afraid our whispers will carry through this house, awakening more than people."

Hannah found the comment odd, but she followed her mother without speaking as her mind churned. Should she tell the woman the truth? Or would it be best if she attempted an elaborate tale as Juliet was prone to do? Neither choice eased her mind.

As her mother lit other candles from the one she held, she said nothing, which only increased Hannah's concern. When the veil of darkness retreated, her mother walked over to the large desk that had belonged to her father.

"Sit," her mother said as she indicated the wing backed chair in front of the desk. "I believe we shall be talking for some time."

Hannah did as her mother bade and was alarmed when her mother sat behind the desk. When she spoke from her father's chair, it did not bode well for the receiver of her speech.

Hannah cleared her throat. "What should I say?" she asked, a defiance rising inside her. "What is it you wish to know?" She almost laughed. Of course, she knew what her mother would ask, but she had to keep an air of innocence about her for as long as she could.

"This is not your first adventure out at night, is it?"

How did her mother know? Yet, the woman seemed to know everything no matter how much Hannah tried to hide her tracks.

"No," Hannah replied.

"How many times have you sneaked out?"

Should she lie? No, truth would be best at this moment. "At least twenty." She shifted in her chair. "You see, there is a group…that is…"

"A society of writers," her mother finished for her, and Hannah could not help but gasp. "Where the members share their thoughts on a variety of books. Where one goes to improve his or her craft."

Hannah stared at her mother in shock. "How did you know? The society is secret. No one outside of it is to know."

Her mother gave a laugh that held little mirth. "I imagine I learned about it in the same way you did." She sighed. "One thing you will learn in life is that secrets have a way of finding new ears to hear them. Not all, mind you, but that is of no consequence. What is of consequence is that you must stop this immediately."

Hannah wrung her hands. She did not wish to argue with her mother, but the woman did not seem to understand the importance of her meetings. "I am sorry, but I cannot."

"You will," her mother stated firmly. "You are to leave in a few days for London. There, you will enjoy whatever balls and parties for which you receive invites. If all goes well, you will meet a gentleman. You are a woman now; far too old for these childish antics."

A gnawing in the pit of Hannah's stomach made her feel ill. "You do not understand…"

Her mother raised a hand, and Hannah clamped her mouth shut. "I understand better than you realize. However, it is my responsibility to look after you, to guide you in life. I cannot, and will not, allow this."

Anger rose in Hannah. "You care for me now?" she demanded as a hot tear escaped her eye. "I have not seen much of you in the past year, for your time has been consumed with Juliet and Isabel. I was left alone with no one to care for me!"

"I…" Her mother's voice broke. "I have been consumed with problems that do not concern you. I have failed you, and for that I apologize. However, that does not change the fact that in three days, you will be leaving here whether you want to or not."

Hannah had heard enough. Only one thing would allow her from being forced to endure the London season. "I have met a man," she said with a jut to her chin. "A man who supports my dreams of one day having a published novel, and tonight, he asked for my hand in marriage."

Never had Hannah seen her mother move so quickly as she rounded the desk and stood before her. "Who is this man? What did he tell you?"

Hannah had witnessed her mother's anger only a few times before, but never had she seen it this strong. What she wanted to do was lie, to tell her mother that he was a noble baron and that she had agreed to his request. However, she had done enough deception to last her three lifetimes. "His name is Albert Moore, the man who leads our society meetings."

"That tells me nothing," her mother said.

"He is forty years of age and is poor by any standard. Yet, he has led the group for years, and I have become his favorite. He sees the world differently from others." She sighed. "I will not lie; I do not love him, and I told him I needed time to consider his proposal."

Her mother gave her a stern glare. "This man? He compliments you?" Hannah nodded. "I imagine he also comments on your beauty, your mind, and your strength."

"He does," Hannah said in surprise. "How did you know?"

"I also suppose he has promised you everything you ever wanted, even to allow you to write while he sees to supporting the home."

"Yes. You see, my novel is not complete, but with his help, it has improved. He promised that he will do anything to see me happy, even if it means me spending my time writing."

"I have no doubt that he promised you these things," her mother said as she took Hannah's hand. "You are strikingly beautiful and possess a great mind. However, it is easy for a man with nothing to promise everything. You are innocent, my child. He wishes to have a beautiful woman at his side, but I fear he does not, and cannot, love you. You deserve a man who can provide for you, not one who does not have your best interests at heart."

Hannah might not have loved Albert, but what her mother said angered her even more. "You do not know him," she said. "He is an honorable man who only wishes to help me!"

"Not all men who give aid are honorable," her mother said, her voice rising. "I may not know this man, but I have known those like him. You will keep away from him." The last words were said with a finger pointed at Hannah.

"What shall I do then?" Hannah demanded. "Is it not my life and my choice? If I do as you wish and I go to London, chances are I will find a man who will never allow me to pursue my dreams."

"And if you remain here?" her mother asked. "Will you marry this man? This Albert?"

"Perhaps," Hannah replied, although the truth was, she did not wish to marry Albert. "He is a simple sheep farmer, and although I do not care for him, he does care for me. If he provides a way to allow me to write, then I may consider his offer of marriage."

Her mother pursed her lips and returned to the desk chair. "Here is what will happen," she said in that matter-of-fact tone that brooked no argument. "We will speak of this matter and of this man no longer. You will leave for London in three days. When you arrive, you will be in Isabel's care and will do as she says. You will soon catch the eye of a gentleman who is more appropriate for you. Then you may begin to think of the life ahead of you."

"My life is here," Hannah said as she approached the desk. "Scarlett Hall is my home. If I cannot be allowed to marry Albert, then I will become a spinster and remain here."

"You will do as I request," her mother said. "This house is not the end of your story. And it certainly is not in the arms of a sheep farmer who has wooed you with false promises."

Hannah crossed her arms over her chest. "I will not," she said firmly. "I shall leave tonight and tell Albert that I accept his proposal." As the words left her lips, she knew they were not true. She needed more time, but the fact she was leaving soon did not allow her such luxuries.

"If you leave tonight," her mother said, "or the next, or if you refuse to attend the season, I shall reveal to all the secret of your society. All will know it was you who revealed and broke their trust."

Tears streamed down Hannah's cheeks. How could her mother do this to her? "You would ruin my name in order to get your way?" she asked as she tried in vain to wipe away the wetness from her face. How she hated her mother at this moment. "All these years you favored Juliet and Isabel while I was left alone with my books. Now that I have found happiness, you wish to take it away from me?"

Her mother sighed. "I wish to save you."

"Save me from whom?" Hannah demanded.

"From yourself." Her mother stood once again. "Perhaps you will meet a gentleman who will allow you to pursue your dream. However, you must understand that I do this because I love you and wish only for you to be happy."

Her mother opened the study door, and Hannah stepped through. Although she loved her mother with all her heart, she was angry and saddened by her words. Therefore, without thought, she spun around and glared at the woman. "You care nothing for me," she said through clenched teeth. "When I find happiness, you wish to take it away. I wish Father was alive and that you had taken his place!"

Her mother's eyes went wide, and Hannah thought her heart would break. She wanted to apologize but found the words caught in her throat.

"I have always wanted the best for you," her mother said, her voice breaking. "Sometimes, in love, we must hurt those around us in order to do what is best for them. That is the cost of love." Without another word, her mother closed the door and left Hannah standing in the darkness of the hallway.

Hannah returned to her room. She felt disgusted by the horrible words she had said to her mother. Her anger was not only with her mother, however. Albert had placed a kiss on her lips without her permission, and that was how this anger began. How could she have taken it out on her mother in such a horrible manner?

The truth of the matter was she had two choices. Either she could defy her mother and run away with Albert. They would marry, and she would become the wife of a sheep farmer, but at least she would be able to write.

Her other choice was to accompany Isabel to London for the season. There she would be forced to attend boring parties and endure the boorish manners of men who would see her as a choice cut of beef rather than as the woman she was.

Lying in bed, her eyes grew heavy. She had no idea what choice to make, but whichever it was, she had only three days to make it.

Chapter Two

There were two things expected of a marquess. The first was to secure a healthy bride who would produce an heir. The second was to act and remain a gentleman at all times in order to maintain a powerful standing and gain the respect of those in society.

Unfortunately, at the age of one and twenty, John Stanford had failed in both. It was not that he did not try to find a bride, for, in fact, he had attended the season for the last three years in order to do just that. However, with the numerous women who smiled his way, it was difficult to choose just one.

As to the second expectation—to be a gentleman—he was, in fact, such a man, contrary to what those in Cornwall said. If a gentleman happened to be taking his leisure in a pub and a fight ensued, whether it be over issues with gambling or some other disagreement, said gentleman had every right to defend himself.

His greatest challenge, however, was that more problems than normal came his way, unexpected ones like the one that now forced him to take a carriage to the home of his cousin, Laurence Redbrook, Duke of Ludlow.

Laurence, who in all reality was a second cousin to John, had married just a few months earlier, and John did not understand why the ceremony had been so small, or why it had been rushed. In truth, he was hurt he had not been invited, for he and his cousin shared a special bond. Not only had they attended the same schools, Laurence had gone to Cornwall in order to offer condolences when John's father died.

Regardless, it was not the affront over the lack of invitation to the wedding that placed John on this journey. No, it was something far worse. Trouble unlike any he could have imagined had come his way, and, unwilling to deal with the consequences of his actions, he ran.

The carriage hit a rut, and John sighed as he grabbed the inside walls. Hiring a carriage at the last moment had been a mistake. The driver was inept, and John wondered if the man had as many years' experience as he touted. His control of the vehicle certainly did not demonstrate it. Yet, there had been no alternative, for his departure from his home had been swift.

His plan was simple and, he thought, wise. He would arrive at the home of his cousin and find a way to join him and his new wife for the season. Laurence had never attended before, but John had received a letter one month prior that included the man's plans, which had surprised John that Laurence was leaving behind the life of a recluse for the gaiety of parties and balls in London. Yet, the manner in which the Duke spoke of his wife intrigued John. He was curious to see what kind of woman could make as dramatic a change in the man as she had.

Drawing back the dark blue curtain, John glanced out at his surroundings. It had been a few years since he had visited Camellia Estates, and he was genuinely looking forward to a visit. As the carriage made a left, a bit faster than John expected, his face slammed into the window, and he grabbed his nose to see if he was bleeding. Lucky for the driver, he was not.

He took a deep breath to relax himself. It was imperative he not draw his cousin's suspicions—or that of anyone else, for that matter. He had to maintain a cool demeanor, an air of unconcernedness, for if word reached Cornwall he was here, all would be lost.

The carriage stopped in front of Camellia Estates, much to John's relief, and he closed his eyes for a moment in order to collect himself. By the time the door opened, he was much calmer.

"We're here, my Lord," the driver said with a bow.

"So we are," John said in a clipped tone. "At least we arrived alive," he added in a mumble.

"What was that, my Lord?"

John sighed. "Never mind." He might need the man longer if things did not go well with Laurence, and there was the chance the man would return to Cornwall and reveal where he had taken John despite the fact John had paid him a hefty fee for keeping such information to himself. "Wait here. I shall return shortly."

The man bowed again. "Yes, my Lord."

Camellia Estates had not changed much since the last time John had visited. It still had its neat row of hedges that ran alongside the house and out to the stables to his left. However, no other extravagance was spent on the front gardens. If he remembered correctly, the former Duke and Duchess had focused more on the larger back gardens, which had always left John dumbfounded.

As he made his way to the front door, John rehearsed once more what he would say when he spoke to Laurence, but the door opened before he reached the bottom step. Laurence peered out as if not recognizing John, and then a woman joined him.

So, that must be his wife, John thought. The woman was beautiful with her blond hair in ringlets around her face and bright eyes filled with concern.

"There is no need to hurry to greet me," John called out with a laugh when they stopped at the top of the steps.

"John?" Laurence asked. "Is that you? What on Earth are you doing here?" Then the man laughed. "I'm sorry, it is good to see you. I was not expecting you."

"I'm pleased to see you, as well. I apologize for coming unannounced. I hope you do not mind."

Laurence came down the steps to greet John; his limp did not appear as bad as John remembered. "Let's have a look at you." He placed his hands on John's shoulders. "You have not changed much. A bit older, but we could say that about us all, could we not?" He turned to the woman. "I would like to introduce my wife, Isabel."

The woman came to stand beside Laurence and offered a kind smile and a bend to her head. She had a regal stance but lacked the haughty air of so many of the *ton*. He immediately felt relaxed in her company.

"Isabel, this is my cousin, John Stanford from Cornwall. I believe I have mentioned him."

"Second cousin," John corrected with a laugh. "But close enough to almost be considered firsts. My pleasure." He kissed the top of her hand, and she smiled again.

"The pleasure is all mine."

"Trust me, it is an honor to meet the woman about whom my cousin boasts in his letters."

Isabel blushed. "It is good to finally meet you, as well," she said. "It is true; Laurence has spoken of you often."

John glanced down to see a letter clutched in her other hand before she pulled it behind her back. That piqued his curiosity. He made no inquiry, nor would he, but it would be interesting to learn what secrets this lady held.

An awkward silence fell around them. Would Laurence not ask him in? They had not parted ways on bad terms, not that John remembered.

"Isabel," Laurence said, "you should be on your way."

"But your cousin. I cannot be rude…"

Laurence gave her an even look and she fell silent. "If you are not back by five, I will meet you at the house. Otherwise, please give my regards to your mother and sisters." He made a gesture to a man John had not noticed standing beside one of the hedges. "Your driver is welcome to rest either with the stable hands or he may go in through the kitchen. I am certain Mrs. Brantley can get him a coffee or some tea if he so desires."

"He is not my driver," John said. "That is, yes, I hired him, but my own driver took ill and I was forced to hire him for my journey."

"Where is it you are heading?" Laurence asked. "And what brings you this way?"

"London," John replied, his heart racing. The next few minutes would be crucial, and he needed to keep his story straight. "I have no friends who are able to attend this year, as most are otherwise already engaged or married." He let out a deep sigh. "I thought seeing you before I left on my own might lift my spirits. You know how I hate to be alone."

"You will be staying at your London house alone?" Laurence asked in clear surprise.

John nodded. "It will be fine. If I am lucky, I may receive an invitation or two for dinner."

Laurence clapped John on the back. "Well, no cousin of mine will be left alone, especially during the season. I have more than enough room for ten cousins—and their servants."

Laurence pulled John toward the door, but John stopped him. "I cannot intrude on you and your wife's first season together." He sighed again. Sighing always helped make a point. "No, I shall wait alone and pray that a friend might turn up. I will be no nuisance to anyone."

"Nonsense," Laurence argued. "Your friend is already here. Let us have your belongings brought inside. We have much on which to catch up, and I have many questions to ask."

"And I shall answer every one of them," John replied. Inside, however, he worried. What would he ask? Perhaps he would not be as forthcoming with some questions as he would others.

John paid the driver to bring in his belongings. "Well, I am glad to have that journey end. That driver was a bit callous in his driving."

"Many have little or no experience," Laurence said as they headed inside. "So, tell me, how is life in Cornwall?"

They entered the foyer, and John turned to face his cousin. "It is the same as it always is, I suppose. Between working and caring for Mother, I find little time for myself. And you? Forgive my curiosity, but is everything in order? Isabel seemed...distressed."

Laurence sighed and shook his head. "Isabel is well. It is her sisters who have caused us worry."

"Perhaps sharing over a glass of brandy is in order?" John said with a wide grin.

Laurence laughed. "You and your brandy," he said, although he headed to the study without pause. "At least I now have an excuse to have a few more drinks than I usually do."

***

John spent the next hour answering his cousin's questions about life in Cornwall. Although he did not inform him of everything—leaving out certain parts John did not wish to share—he told enough to satisfy the questions the man asked, or so he assumed by the smile Lawrence wore.

They were on their second brandy, and Laurence, being a light drinker, loosened his tongue and was sharing life as one married to a member of the Lambert family.

"So, let me see if I understand this correctly," John said. "There are two more sisters?" When Laurence nodded, John added, "And a cousin who is more a sister than a cousin?"

"Yes. In the manner in which I see you as a brother? That is how they see Annabel."

The kind words sent a spear of guilt through John's heart for the lies he had told his cousin. Well, not lies outright but more omissions. Regardless, he could not help the feeling of remorse.

"Juliet is the youngest of the three sisters and is prone to mischief. When Isabel told me this morning that it was Hannah who had left the house in the middle of the night, we were both shocked."

"She does not typically do such things?"

"Certainly not," Laurence replied. "Or rather, we would never have suspected such behavior from her. She is intelligent, well read, and far from one who would engage in that type of mischief."

John suppressed a smile. He had known many societal women who had done things such as drinking or sneaking from their homes at night. However, this Hannah, who by all accounts Laurence had described as a bluestocking without using the term, intrigued him much. Where would a bluestocking go at night?

"With the season nearing," John said after taking a sip of his brandy, "she will soon be married. Then her wild ways will be left behind. It will be good for her. In London, she will be far too busy to find trouble. This is her first season, I presume?"

Laurence glanced around as if someone would overhear before leaning toward John and lowering his voice. "Do not tell a soul, but last year right before the season was to begin, Hannah came down with a mysterious illness. The doctor could find nothing wrong but recommended bed rest. It was only recently that I learned she had fabricated the whole thing so she would not have to attend."

John laughed. "She feigned illness to escape the season? This woman is quite the mischief-maker!" When he took notice of the frown Laurence wore, he added, "My apologies. I meant no disrespect to the woman."

Laurence sighed. "Yes, I realize this. It is just that Isabel worries for her sisters as a mother would her children, and I find myself worrying for all of them. Hannah is a wonderful woman, and the plan is to see her find a husband. However, I fear her stubbornness and intelligence will make it much more difficult than it should. It is not her wish to find a husband from what I understand." He stopped and tilted his head at John. "Why have you not married, or become engaged at the very least?"

John, who had just taken a sip of his drink, erupted in a choking cough. "Sorry, it went down the wrong way," he managed to say. He cleared his throat and set the glass on the table before him. "These things a man must do in order to find a bride are such a cumbersome burden. But in truth, I have not found a woman to my liking." And that was the truth, for although many women sought his attention, and he theirs, he could never seem to dedicate himself to just one. Each woman had something to give that he enjoyed, but he had yet to find that one woman who possessed it all.

Laurence gave him a thoughtful look. "I thought I would remain alone," he said. "That is, until I met Isabel. Many women in this world possess strength, and a man is fortunate when he finds one."

"I truly am happy for you," John said, glad the conversation had moved on to a new, and safer, subject. "Perhaps you two shall provide the influence Hannah needs this season. When she sees your happiness, she might just put her wild ways behind her."

"That is our hope," Laurence replied. "However, she will need convincing from someone other than ourselves. If she could see that the season is indeed a festive time to celebrate..." his words trailed off and a smile came to his lips. "John," he said with a thoughtful look, "might I ask a favor of you?"

"Of course," John replied. "There is nothing I would not do for you." Laurence was the kind of man who had more than once given John aid, and if doing this man a favor meant John could spend the season with him and leave behind his troubles in Cornwall, he would do anything the man requested.

"Hannah. Would you make her feel...wanted?" Laurence shook his head. "My choice of words is poor. What I mean to say is...that is..."

"You are asking your handsome cousin to feign interest in her?" John asked with a grin. "Perhaps give her a boost of confidence so she will be more willing to accept further invitations from other men?"

Laurence laughed. "Yes, exactly that. I was hoping to say it in a more, let us say, delicate, manner."

"I would be happy to assist you in this endeavor," John said as he raised his glass as if to toast. "For the first few weeks, the woman will believe I cannot breathe unless she is in my presence. Her spirit will be lifted to such heights, every eligible man will gaze to the sky in order to see her."

Laurence shook his head. "You certainly have a high opinion of yourself."

"Not at all," John said with a chuckle. "I am simply the pedestal on which Miss Hannah will stand in order to be noticed by someone more...appropriate. I am handsome for a reason, after all."

"You have never been modest concerning your appearance. If it serves you well, then I believe you have the right to brag."

Although on the outside John wore a smile, inside he trembled. His handsomeness, as it were, was exactly the reason he was in his current predicament; it had caused him more problems than good as of late.

"You must understand one thing," Laurence said, taking on a serious note. "Isabel and her sister's happiness mean everything to me. You must not allow Hannah, or Isabel for that matter, to learn of this arrangement. It is crucial that Hannah finds a suitor this season, for Isabel and I both fear she may try to avoid doing so once again."

John lifted his glass once more. "Have no fear. There is nothing with which to worry concerning Hannah. She will suspect nothing, and, with my help, I may even be able to guide her to a gentleman worthy of marriage."

"Thank you," Laurence replied. "You have no idea how much relief this gives me."

The two men raised their glasses, and as John took a sip from his, his mind began to wander. It would not be difficult to get this Hannah under his spell, for all women were easily prone to it. Yet, there was more to gain than the gratitude of his cousin. Although he would honor his word and find her a gentleman by the season's end, he would also have the woman pay him for his generosity.

And as the plans began to develop in his mind, his smile widened all the more.

Chapter Three

Hannah sat on Juliet's bed listening to her sister explain to their cousin Annabel how she had injured her ankle. It had been Hannah's intention to seek advice for her dilemma with Albert and the upcoming season, but she was interested in how the girl—no she was now eighteen, no longer a girl but a young woman—had ended up in bed rather than readying herself for her first season.

Although Juliet did not admit why she had been in the stables, Hannah suspected it had something to do with the stable hand, Daniel. A blind man could see that her sister was enamored with the young man; although she denied that fact whenever anyone asked. However, it was Juliet's way; all extravagant tales and dramatics that Hannah had to admit aided her in the story she was writing. That story that had yet been completed.

"It was then, my dear cousin," Juliet was saying to Annabel, "that Daniel was too afraid to climb up into the loft."

Hannah rolled her eyes, but Annabel gasped. "But you suspected a highwayman had taken refuge there from the storm!" she cried. "Did you not fear for your own safety?"

Juliet gave a dramatic sigh and pulled her long black hair over her shoulder. She lay propped up on numerous pillows, her swollen foot wrapped in bandages and lying on a stack of blankets. "When the safety of one's family is in peril, a woman must take charge. Even when a cowardly stable hand is nearby and refuses to lend aid."

"You are brave," Annabel breathed. She took Juliet's hand in her own. "Such bravery is rare among men and unheard of in women."

"That is true," Juliet replied with a shake to her head. "Although, I will be the first to admit that I am no ordinary woman. I have been blessed with both beauty and courage."

Hannah rolled her eyes again. It was true that Juliet was beautiful, perhaps the loveliest of the three sisters, and Juliet, herself, would be the first to say so. She spoke so often about her own handsomeness that she tended to bore those around her.

"What happened next?" Annabel asked, clearly caught up in the story. "Did you see the man?"

Juliet sighed. "Unfortunately, he was not there. In fact, I found no trace except this bottle of wine." She lifted the pillow beside her, and Hannah could not help when her eyes widened in shock. "I wanted proof of an intruder, so when I reached out to grab the bottle, I slipped on the rung of the ladder whilst calling out for help." Juliet wiped at her eyes although Hannah saw no tears. "Daniel, the fool, could not move he was so frozen with fear, and therefore I fell and injured myself."

Annabel shook her head. "To think that man stood and watched you fall. Does he have no honor? No dignity? Is this what I must endure next year when I attend my first season? Men with no backbone?"

Hannah wished nothing more than to leave so she would not be forced to listen to any more of Juliet's foolishness, but she still needed to speak with both Juliet and Annabel. The only way to do that was to remain patient until Juliet was finished with her story.

Juliet sighed again, but this time with less dramatics as before. "I suppose I should not lie further," she said. "Indeed, Daniel was consumed by fear, but I cannot say he is without honor, for last night, he came into my room and gave me the bottle of wine."

Hannah could not stop the gasp that sprang from her lips. She may not believe all the stories Juliet told, but it certainly explained how the bottle came into her possession. Highwayman, indeed!

"At first I thought he meant to have his way with me," Juliet continued, "for uncivilized men are prone to such actions. Even more so with women who possess my beauty, for it is exceedingly rare. I was afraid, for who would hear my cries for help?" Juliet gave a sad smile and Annabel patted her hand. "However, to my surprise, he offered the wine and then his life."

"His life?" Hannah asked. "What do you mean?" Advice or no, she was nearing the peak of her patience.

"My dear child," Juliet said, and Hannah wanted to slap her. The girl was younger than she by a year! "Daniel realized how dishonorable he acted when he allowed me to fall, so he came to bid me farewell. He said he would prove his honor by walking to the top of the hill behind our house and take his own life by falling on the end of a sword."

The manner in which her sister said this was so serious, Hannah was unsure whether to believe her or not. Daniel was kind, and she could imagine him being honorable, but enough to take his own life? That was suspect.

"He said that the guilt he carried was great and that no matter what he did in life, he would live in shame. Therefore, he asked if he could borrow Father's sword so he could die with honor."

Annabel wiped at her eyes. "That is so beautiful."

"It is," Juliet replied. "And so, I thought, what is the greatest honor? He, the foolish stable boy, taking his own life? Or me forgiving him for his shortcomings?"

Annabel gasped. "You forgave him?"

"I did. Of course, the man thanked me and said he would now dedicate his life to reclaiming his honor and to lose his fear. I took pity on him and have decided to teach him to read."

Hannah might not believe everything Juliet said, but she did find the last kind on her sister's part, and she told her as much.

Juliet smiled and put the bottle to her lips and took a drink. Then she held it out to Hannah and Annabel. "Ladies?"

"It would be best if I did not," Annabel said. "Although...it is tempting."

Juliet offered the bottle to Hannah, who shook her head. "No, I am in enough trouble as it is."

"I know," Juliet said. "I heard the echoes of your anger last night; they disturbed me from my sleep." She sighed and took another sip before hiding the bottle under her pillow. "Much like the ghost who kissed me."

"A ghost?" Annabel gasped.

Hannah considered taking away the wine bottle and drinking it herself.

"Oh yes," Juliet replied. "I hear noises in the night, and I have lain in bed whilst the ghost tells me I am beautiful. More than once he has kissed me."

Hannah hoped her sister would keep these stories to herself. If anyone outside of the family were to hear them, their family name would be tarnished for generations to come. 'The mad Juliet' they would say.

"However, that story can wait for another time," Juliet said, repositioning herself on the pillows. "Now, tell me, dear sister, what happened with Mother that caused me to awaken in the dead of night?"

"That is why I am here," Hannah replied with a sigh. "We made a pact to help one another in times of need." Both Juliet and Annabel nodded. Hannah smoothed her skirts in order to delay what had to be said. "You know I do not wish to attend the London season?"

Annabel nodded, but Juliet frowned. "I still do not understand why. Here it is, my first season, and I am stuck in bed with an injured foot. I should be going with you. I have waited my entire life for my first season." She sat with her arms crossed and a pout on her lips.

"Yes, yes," Hannah said. "But I believe I have found a way to not be forced to attend, but it requires me to…"

The door opened and Hannah drew in a breath before she realized it was Isabel, who stopped at the end of the bed and gave each woman a glare.

"With each report of trouble, I never find one, but three of you," she said. She walked over and placed a hand on Hannah's shoulder. "We must speak."

Hannah nodded. "I understand. If I am to tell you, then I may as well tell you all, for I need your wisdom in this matter."

Isabel looked about the room and then joined the three on the bed. This, of course, caused Juliet to beam.

"Tell us what made you decide to sneak out of the house last night."

This brought about gasps from the other two girls, but Hannah ignored them. "The very thing that caused me to leave the first time, a year ago, and many times since," she replied as she wrung her hands in her lap.

Isabel snorted. "And what would that be?" she demanded.

"The chance to have my dreams come true."

***

Hannah drew in a deep breath in order to control her emotions. "You all know I have always wanted to write a novel."

The others nodded and offered smiles Hannah found encouraging.

"I learned of a society that consists not only of men, but also several women, who meet in secret every Thursday. So, one day, I found the courage to leave Scarlett Hall late at night and go to this meeting place."

"Was it a cave?" Juliet asked in clear awe. Leave it to her to bring a mysterious cave into the story!

"No, it was not a cave," Hannah snapped. "They meet in a small cottage belonging to a sheep farmer by the name of Albert Moore." An image of the man kissing her the night before sent a shiver down her spine. "In his home, I found women like myself—women who love to not only read but also to write stories. It was that love of the written word we shared that had me returning as often as I could." She turned to Isabel. "I am sorry for causing you distress. It was not my intention."

"It is not me about whom you should be concerned," Isabel said. "It is Mother. She is troubled by your behavior, and I believe it has frightened her. And rightly so."

Hannah sighed. "She does not understand. I tried reasoning with her last night; to make her see what I do is worthy of my time despite that it is unbecoming of a lady."

Juliet shook her head. "You are not telling us everything," she said in light admonishment. "I heard your voice last night, and you are not one to yell."

"I did not yell," Hannah replied defensively, although she could not help the shame that bubbled up inside her. "I merely raised my voice..." Her words trailed off, and she thought of what she had said to her mother before returning to her room. They were cruel words, and she regretted them. The truth of the matter was she should apologize to her mother, but she could not face her again. Not yet.

"What happened last night?" Isabel asked. "Mother said she would not reveal it to me, for the secret is yours to tell."

Annabel reached over and took Hannah by the hand. "We are sisters," she said, "bound by our love and the pact we have made. You may tell us if you wish, without fear of any judgment."

"Yes, Annabel speaks the truth," Isabel said. "We are here to help. Speak your heart, and we will do what we can to assist." Juliet echoed agreement, and the four women once more joined hands, as was common whenever they made such vows.

Hannah could not stop the rush of love that welled up inside her. These women had always been there for her, and she had to trust them. "The man who runs the group, Albert, he is a kind man and loves books as much as I. He is also aware of my pain."

"What pain is that?" Isabel asked.

"The season. To marry." A great sorrow overtook the love in her heart at the thought of the expectations for her. "Do you not see? If I attend the season, there is a chance that I will meet a man. What if I fall in love?"

"Oh, Hannah," Isabel said with a light squeeze of her hand, "you should not be worried about falling in love. It is a new experience, but I promise, it is wonderful."

"But it is not only that. What man will allow his wife to write? To seek a way to have my novel published? That is my dilemma. If I go to London, I will be forced to say goodbye to that which I love—my writing."

She was surprised how quickly the room fell silent. What she had expected was to hear Isabel with her ready advice, but instead it was Juliet who spoke first.

"How does this man, Albert, find himself in your troubles? You said he knows your heart? Has he somehow offered you a solution?"

"He has," Hannah replied. "And that is what is causing the majority of my confusion. He offers to allow me to write, yet I do not love him. Nor do I find him handsome, if I were honest." She sighed. "I know it sounds cruel, for the man is by no means ugly, but I feel nothing for him, even when he…kissed me." The last was spoken in a whisper, but by the collective gasp from the other women, they had heard the words quite clearly.

Then Juliet put her head back and laughed. "Forgive me," she said after several moments of guffaws. "I do not mean to make fun, but you must understand. You? My sweet innocent sister engaged in a kiss with a boy?"

Hannah gave a derisive sniff. "He is no boy. He is forty years of age and has asked for my hand in marriage."

The gasps this time were not as pronounced as before, but her sisters' eyes grew wider. And, for the first time in recent memory, Juliet seemed to have no words to say.

"I know you think me a harlot, but I was not expecting a kiss. In truth, I did not want it, not from him nor anyone else. However, if his proposal allows me to pursue my dream, I may have to endure them to obtain what I want."

Isabel released her hand and stood beside the bed. Had she upset her sister so much that she could no longer bare to look at her?

"Isabel," Hannah pleaded, "do not hate me."

"I could never hate you," her elder sister replied as she rounded the bed to pull Hannah into her arms. In the comforting embrace, Hannah could not stop the flow of tears. "You are no harlot, and even if you were, nothing could break our bond."

"Thank you," Hannah whispered. "Will you help me? Help me find a way to escape this torment Mother inflicts on me. I cannot go to London!" If anyone could find a way to get her out of the mess she had made, Isabel could.

"I do not like to defy our mother," Isabel said. "However, in this case, I believe I shall make an exception. I will not have my sister marry a man she does not love. Now," she pushed back a strand of Hannah's hair, "sit and I shall tell you what I know."

"Please, do."

"The society you have joined is not the only one of its kind in this country. In fact, there are many."

This shocked Hannah. Why did she not know?

"I heard it mentioned that there is a group that meets in London where the best scholars come together in order to share their knowledge, and women hone their skills of the written word."

"Is this true?" Hannah asked, not wanting to build her hopes too high. "If so, there is a chance I can meet more people like me! And the best publishing houses are in London!"

"Yes, there are many. If you come with me, you would have access to one—or all—of them."

Hannah worried her bottom lip. "That would mean attending the season, the parties, meeting gentlemen..." Oh, bother! She would be forced to endure the cinching of the *ton* if she was to gain freedom from them. "Again, I am caught between two choices."

"I have heard enough," Juliet said from her propped pillows. "You are not seeing the possibilities in front of you."

"The possibility of what?" Hannah demanded. "To go to London and get married?"

"No," her sister replied with a sigh. "You must appease Mother, so you agree to go to London. You may even attend a few parties and dinners and speak with other like-minded women. However, if you remain yourself and keep your nose in a book as you typically do, what man would look your way? This will give you more time to complete your novel, for the chances of you being invited to more parties will dwindle each time you leave one without so much as speaking to a gentleman."

On most occasions, such words hurt, but Hannah welcomed them now. "You are absolutely right!" she exclaimed. "My younger sister has given me wisdom! I can please Mother and go to London. I can write anywhere, if truth be told. When I return to Scarlett Hall at the end of the season, I will be able to work on my next book. In fact, I can continue this cycle until I become a spinster!" The idea became more intriguing with each word.

Isabel leaned over and embraced Hannah. "You must apologize to Mother before you leave," she whispered in Hannah's ear. "She loves you and only wants what is best for you."

"I will. I promise," Hannah replied. She would do so, but perhaps not right away; she was still angry with the woman!

Annabel joined Isabel and Hannah in their hug, and Juliet clicked her tongue from the bed. "Do not forget about me! Your sister who injured herself and gave up the season in order to save your lives!"

The other three laughed and made their way back to the bed, where they pulled Juliet into their embrace. It was not an easy task with Juliet's leg bound and in the way, but that did not matter. Moments such as this brought joy to Hannah's heart, perhaps as much as writing did. The more she thought about it, the more she realized that attending the season did not mean the end to her writing. Furthermore, she would not have to marry Albert, or any other man for that matter.

And that was the best news of all.

Chapter Four

All too soon, the day arrived when Hannah would leave for London. Now, however, she was pleased to be going, not for the same reasons most as women—an excitement of meeting an acceptable suitor—but because she would be able to complete her novel. She had begun her manuscript a year earlier, but completing it had been a challenge, so she hoped a change of setting would bring about new ideas.

She kept her writing in an old ledger cover labeled 'Business' in order to keep it from prying eyes—mainly from Juliet—and thus far it had been the perfect hiding place. Now, it lay at the bottom of one of her trunks, which sat beside the front door.

Having already said goodbye to Juliet, Hannah was working up the courage to apologize to her mother. The family butler, Forbes, stood waiting with her, and his eyes seemed to follow her pacing. Quite often, he would offer a kind word or a warm smile, but today it was as if he studied her, which only increased her anxiety.

"Miss Hannah?" the man asked after some time. "You appear troubled. May I do anything to ease your worries?"

Hannah sighed. She wanted his advice, but she could not bring herself to tell him her problems. Perhaps if she asked without outright telling him...

"I must say something to someone, and although my vocabulary is strong, I must say what needs to be said."

Forbes raised his chin. "In such times, when words are needed, we have a tendency to overthink them."

Hannah was relieved the butler understood her dilemma, and she waited with rapt attention for whatever guidance he could give.

"Yes," the man continued, "one must consider if he should speak with civility and honor, or with common language found in the alleyways of London." He winked, which made Hannah giggle. "I find that when I am struggling to find the right words, such as you are now, the simplest and most honest of words are the best. If they come from the heart, their meaning will be understood."

So, he thought she should simply be honest. The truth was, he was correct in his advice, even if the words were a bit confusing. "Thank you, Forbes," Hannah said. "Your wisdom is appreciated."

The butler gave a bow to his head, and Hannah hurried away in search of her mother. Yes, it was time to speak from her heart, as Forbes put it, and apologize.

She paused at the door to the study. When she was a child, her father was often gone on business, and if he returned late at night after she had gone to bed, the following morning, she would rush to this room and find him there. He always had a waiting gift as a way to apologize for his absence. Then he would explain the necessity of leaving in order to provide for the family, even when Hannah did not ask for such an explanation. She understood early on that men had their responsibilities, and oftentimes they had to take care of them outside the home.

Despite his explanations, Hannah often wondered if her mother understood the sacrifices her father had made over the years. Hannah doubted the woman did.

When she opened the door, she found her mother standing by the window gazing out as she often did as of late.

"Mother?" Hannah said as she tried to ease her beating heart.

Her mother turned, and for the first time, Hannah noticed the tiny wrinkles at the corners of her eyes. "The day has arrived," the woman said as she walked toward Hannah. "Your first season. Are you ready?"

"Yes," Hannah replied. "However, I wish to say something before I leave." She thought of the advice Forbes had given her, and she did as he suggested. "My words the other night were cruel, and I did not mean them. Forgive me."

Her mother smiled. "Of course, I forgive you," she said, and Hannah was surprised to see her eyes glisten with unshed tears. "If I can arrange a proper chaperon for Juliet at some point, I may come to

London to see you. Unfortunately, Doctor Comerford has said she will not be able to travel for several months, so she will be unable to attend."

Hannah felt sorry for Juliet, for the girl had spoken of nothing but the London season since she was fourteen. However, Hannah was not certain she liked the idea of her mother joining her. It was not that she did not want her mother there, but her plans would be ruined if the woman accepted invitations on her behalf, which Hannah had no doubts she would.

However, now was meant for reconciliation, not more arguments. "That would be nice," Hannah lied. "I expect I will be very busy with the number of invitations I will receive. I am glad to be going now. What a horrible waste of one's time remaining at home."

With a raise of an eyebrow, her mother replied, "Indeed." She took Hannah by the hand. "The season is a magic time, and one does not know what she will find. Maybe a new friendship that will last a lifetime. Or perhaps a gentleman shall win her heart?"

Hannah nodded and forced a smile. No man would win her heart, for it was not a prize to be won. However, if her mother believed Hannah was willing, she would make her happy by acting the part.

"You know," her mother continued, "you may be surprised. Love comes when you least expect it, but when it does, it will be the most wondrous of feelings. Do not hide from it. Instead I council embracing it."

"I will, Mother," Hannah replied. She took a letter she had written the previous day from her pocket. "This is for Albert. It explains why I cannot accept his proposal of marriage and that I wish the best for him, but I can no longer attend the meetings."

"A very wise decision," her mother said, taking the letter and pulling Hannah in for an embrace. "You are much too intelligent and precious to make such a hasty decision."

Hannah could not stop the smile that spread on her lips, although she felt a twinge of guilt for lying about what was contained in that letter. She knew that if she shut out Albert completely, a bridge would be burned if the need to escape arose later.

Therefore, in her letter, she explained that she would need more time to consider his proposal, and when she returned from London, she would inform him of her answer. However, her mother did not need to know that.

"The hour is upon us," her mother said with a quick glance at the clock on the mantel. "Isabel should be arriving at any moment."

Hannah nodded and followed her mother to the front door. She stopped to take one more glance around. Soon, she would return to Scarlett hall, her novel in the expert hands of a publisher. Juliet would be overcome with jealousy, and Annabel would wish to be in her presence. Isabel and her mother would apologize for doubting her abilities. Yet Hannah would be kind to them all. Perhaps she would buy them all gifts, even Forbes, who always had a kind word for her.

And as she spent the off-season beginning a new book, she would attain such wealth from the sales of her first, she might even buy the grand house for herself.

***

As Isabel alighted from the carriage and Laurence spoke to the driver, Hannah waited on the stoop. She always admired her older sister, for she had everything any woman could want. She was bright, intelligent, confident, and handsome, and yet what Hannah admired most was her strength.

"It has arrived," Isabel said with a smile as she embraced Hannah. "My sister's first season. Are you excited?"

"Oh, yes," Hannah lied. "I am looking forward to the months ahead." That much was true.

Isabel smiled, and there was movement from the carriage as another person stepped out. He was dressed in an impeccable dark coat and well-fitted tan breeches. He pushed back a dark wave of hair from his brow, and a strange feeling came over Hannah, as if she were running a fever. Her legs became weak, and her heart began to race. The man, whoever he was, was devilishly handsome, perhaps the most beautiful man she had ever seen.

As the man walked toward them, panic overwhelmed Hannah, and she looked toward the winter sky wondering if the sun had brought on this warm feeling, or perhaps she had come down with some sort of illness. Would she be able to use illness as an excuse not to go to London two years in a row? It was doubtful.

"Are you all right?" Isabel asked. "You have grown quite pale."

Hannah turned to look at Isabel, but when she attempted to reply, she could do nothing more than croak, her throat was so dry. "I...I am feeling..."

The man stood beside them now, and Hannah clamped her mouth shut before she fainted from embarrassment.

"Ah, yes," Isabel said with a smile. "Mother, Hannah, may I introduce Lord John Stanford, Marquess of Greyhedge, and cousin to Laurence. He will be accompanying us to London."

Although her mother seemed able to greet the man, Hannah found the act almost impossible. Somehow, she had forgotten how to speak.

"Miss Hannah," the Marquess said, and Hannah thought she would indeed faint. The man possessed a voice that was strong yet gentle enough to call down the birds from the trees. "It is an honor to meet you. Isabel has spoken very highly of you."

"Thank you," Hannah managed to mumble. How could one man be so handsome? "It is nice to handsome you as well." She clamped her jaw shut. What was wrong with her? She glanced at the ground, wishing she could hurl herself into the bushes in order to hide herself.

"I beg your pardon?" Lord Stanford asked.

"I know of a cobbler by the name of Hans," Hannah explained, her mind pushing together whatever it could to devise an explanation that did not make her appear a madwoman. "You could be his son." She groaned inwardly and resigned herself to the hedges where she would live out the remainder of her days.

However, as so often in her life, Isabel came to her rescue. "You are right," she said as if studying the Marquess anew. "He does resemble him. He is a spitting image, in fact."

Hannah let out a sigh of relief, but when she noticed the wicked grin the man wore, she wondered if he believed their story.

"I shall take that as a compliment," he replied.

"Well, I suppose we should be on our way," Isabel said.

Her mother hugged Isabel and then Hannah. "Just a moment before you leave," she said to Hannah.

"We will wait in the carriage," Isabel said.

The Marquess nodded and followed Isabel toward the waiting vehicle.

"I want you to enjoy yourself," her mother said when the others were gone. "If for any reason you need me, I am here for you."

Hannah smiled. For all the woman's wish to see Hannah off and married, she still wanted to help. It eased Hannah's mind, but she would not be needing her mother's help anytime soon. The majority of her time would be focused on finishing her manuscript when she was not out pretending to enjoy herself. "Thank you, Mother," she replied. For a moment there was an uncomfortable silence, so Hannah added, "I should leave now."

Her mother smiled and hugged her once again. When the embrace broke, Hannah noticed the woman's eyes were brimming with tears.

When she entered the carriage, she paused. Isabel and Laurence were sharing a bench, leaving one space open beside Laurence's cousin. The man wore a wide grin, and when the door shut with a bang behind her, Hannah took the empty seat beside him. She would not be panicked! She would not, no matter how handsome he was!

What she found was that sitting beside him made it worse. She smoothed out her blue skirts and found herself wondering if he liked the color blue.

"I believe I am just as excited for this season as you," Laurence said, breaking the silence. "Like you, this is my first. I believe we will both have much to share about our newfound experiences."

"I agree, Your Grace" Hannah replied, feeling Lord Stanford's gaze upon her. "It will be very amusing."

Laurence sighed. "I have told you before; you must call me Laurence," he said with a smile as the carriage pulled forward. "We are family, after all."

Before Hannah could respond, Lord Stanford spoke. "That is true. And for that reason, you must call me John. After all, we are all part of the same family now that your sister has married Laurence."

Hannah found she could not look at the man, so she watched as her mother lifted her hand and waved just before she and Scarlett Hall disappeared from sight.

"May I call you Hannah?"

Turning from the window, Hannah focused on her hands in her lap. "That is fine...John." Saying the man's name caused a bead of sweat to trail down her forehead, which begged to be removed. However, a lady did not do such a thing in the company of a gentleman. What would this man think of her if she did such an unladylike thing?

The next thing she knew, a kerchief was placed in her hand. "Please, the sun is particularly hot for this time of year."

Hannah could only nod at John, and she quickly dabbed at her brow. When she went to return the kerchief, he shook his head. "No, it is yours. Consider it the first gift of many of the season."

Hannah looked to Isabel, hoping her sister would help her escape the conversation, but the woman was peering out the window.

"I realize one's first season can be distressing at first, but you have no reason to worry. I am quite experienced with everything in London, so if you are in need of companionship or have questions, please feel free to call on me."

"Thank you," Hannah murmured. She looked up to see him staring at her, and she thought she would melt right at that moment. It was as if his smile drew her in, and she lacked the power to fight against it. His cheekbones were high, and his jaw set just right. She had studied many of the finest sculptures and could imagine this man chiseled by skilled hands. Of course, those sculptures lacked clothing. Oh, why had she remembered *that*? Her cheeks had to be keeping them all warm!

"There is so much I want to ask you," John said. "You must forgive me, for I am a curious one."

Hannah could not help but smile. "Please, feel free to ask me anything." Amazingly, she meant what she said, for what she wanted was to share everything with this man.

"The cobbler of whom you spoke?" he said, his grin widening, "Tell me more about him and his son."

Oh, goodness! she thought. *Anything but that!*

43

Chapter Five

During the journey, Hannah was thankful that Laurence kept his cousin occupied with conversation. Her blasted tongue! What was wrong with her? When John had asked her about the cobbler—who did not exist, if the truth be known—she could not help but pretend to be Juliet and make up a story right there on the spot. The man seemed satisfied with her explanation, thank heavens, but that did not diminish the embarrassment she carried with her.

They traveled until an hour before sundown, stopping at an inn along the way. After seeing their things to their rooms and washing the dust of the journey from her face and hands, she met the others in the dining room of the inn, where they had a lovely dinner of baked partridge and yams. Although the other three engaged in conversation, Hannah picked at her food, as lovely as it was, and could not wait to have the meal end. Several times, she could have sworn that John was staring at her, yet when she turned to look, he was already speaking to Laurence or laughing at something Isabel had said.

Now, Hannah sat in a large comfortable chair, a book in her lap, beside a roaring fire in a tiny room that had a small collection of reading material. Laurence and Isabel had remained in the dining room to share in drinks—where John had gone Hannah did not know, nor did she care—and Hannah was happy to have the small sanctuary located between the desk where they checked in and the dining hall.

The fire crackled and cast its light on the only other occupant in the room, a much older woman, perhaps in her seventies, who wore a black dress. Her hands and neck were adorned with jewels, and she stared at the fire as if it held some sort of secret.

Hannah smiled, and the woman turned to look at her. "Off to London, are you?" the woman asked in a voice that was close to shouting.

"I am indeed," Hannah replied.

The old woman sighed. "I remember my first season. Well, not necessarily a season but more a local party hosted by some baron or another. That is where I met my Harold fifty years ago." She leaned forward. "And we have been married ever since."

"That is lovely," Hannah replied. "To be in love for that long is an amazing feat."

The old woman snorted, and Hannah wondered if she had offended her in some way. "It was love at first sight, if you can believe such a thing exists. Then it became a chore. At least I have my jewels." She fingered one of the many necklaces she wore and sighed. Then, with a grunt, she pulled herself from the chair. "Be sure you get plenty of jewelry. It is the least a woman should receive for a life of servitude."

Hannah could not help but stare at the woman in shock as she left the room. So, her fears concerning marriage were justified. There was no hope for those who gave into what their heart might feel. At least she would never become one of those women!

Once again at peace with her life's choices, she returned to her book, but it was not long before her mind wandered back to John. He was so dashing and his smile was so warm. She giggled at a thought that perhaps his smile held some magical element, for it seemed to brighten a room and warm her heart.

She sat up in shock. What was she doing thinking of the man in such a manner? She had a task before her, a novel that was in need of completion, and she had no business wasting her time on some man who would more than likely leave her in an emotional heap. However, despite her desire to push him from her thoughts, she could not glean one word from her book, and with a sigh of frustration, she closed the book with a *snap*.

"I see that I may not be welcome to join you."

Hannah turned to find John standing beside her, a glass of amber liquid in his hand, his towering figure intriguing but not as intimidating as she would have expected. What if this man, like the hero in the book she had been attempting to read, were to grab her and kiss her by the firelight? Would his lips be cold and hard or warm and soft?

Her cheeks burned, and she scolded herself for such thoughts. She was an intelligent woman, not some daft ninny!

"I apologize for the intrusion," he said. "Enjoy your evening."

He turned to leave, and she could not stop herself from saying, "Wait! My apologies. It is not you with whom I am frustrated but rather this book."

He arched an eyebrow, and she fought to breathe.

"Please, join me." *There, that was not so bad, was it?* She almost laughed. The result of her invitation remained to be seen.

"I would like that," John said. He flashed her a smile so beautiful Hannah felt herself melting into the chair as he took the seat in the blue high back chair across from her. "Do you read often?"

"Yes, I do," Hannah replied. It suddenly occurred to her that a gentleman such as this man would not see a lady reading as a positive attribute, and for the first time, she was uncertain how she felt about that.

However, John did not seem to have that opinion, for he replied, "That is good. Too many are consumed with subjects that are, shall we say, trivial in nature? They do not take the time to read."

His response shocked, and pleased, her, and when he winked, she felt that same heat she had earlier. "Y-you?" she stammered. "You enjoy reading, as well?"

"But of course," he replied as if it was the most logical thing a man could do. "A true gentleman must have a library in order to read, and he also must be willing to allow those around him to share in its splendor."

A dizziness grasped Hannah. He was dashing *and* he enjoyed reading?

"That is enough about me," he said, crossing a foot over the opposite knee. "For I am all too boring."

"Not at all!" Hannah said, much louder than she had anticipated. She swallowed and made another attempt, this time with better moderation of her voice. "You are not boring at all. In fact, I find you intriguing." Her throat went dry as he lifted his glass and took a drink from it. How a man could make a simple motion so interesting was beyond her.

"Intriguing?" he said with a laugh. "I suppose I am at that. So, tell me, when you are not reading, what do you enjoy doing for entertainment?"

Hannah glanced toward the door and then back at him. Would the man laugh if she told him the truth? She did not know him, but for some reason, she felt her secrets safe with him. "Butterflies," she replied. "I find myself watching them in the garden and then sketching them and reading about them later."

His jaw dropped, and Hannah braced herself for his taunt. *Well, you did it to yourself, you know.*

"That is amazing," he said, yet again surprising Hannah. "May I share something with you? You must promise you will never tease me or tell another soul."

"Never," she whispered as she leaned forward in her chair. "I would never do anything to hurt you." Her heart fluttered as she said the words, and she realized they were the truth.

"I have no skills in drawing, but I am fascinated with winged creatures as you are. However, my interest lies with the birds. The freedom they possess and the manner in which they rise above us all, to journey through the skies to undiscovered faraway lands..." He sighed. "It is as the poet MacArthur once said. 'To be as the bird is to be free.'"

"So beautiful," Hannah said, although she had never heard of the poet. "You also read poetry?"

"When I am not writing it."

Hannah had to take a drink of her wine in order to cool herself. She had to learn more about this man, thus the wine could lend aid in that arena, as well.

However, as she set her glass back on the nearby table, a woman of great beauty entered the room. Her hair was a darker blond than

Hannah's and her blue dress emphasized a nearly perfect figure. The woman was indeed lovely, far more so than Hannah could ever hope to be.

"My Lady," John said, rushing from the chair and smiling a broad smile that showed dimples Hannah had not seen before. "This is the finest chair in this establishment. Please, take it." He moved aside and offered her his hand to allow her to sit.

"Thank you…"

"Lord John Stanford," he finished for her as his eyes looked her up and down with appreciation.

"It is a pleasure," the woman said. "I am Miss Catherine Oakley." She batted her eyelashes at him, and Hannah could do nothing but stare as John brought a chair and set it between her and Miss Oakley.

Was the woman so blind that she could not see that she and John were sharing a special moment? Then, as the woman answered yet another question John had asked, the realization of what had occurred came over her. The woman had seen John's smile and wanted it for herself. Caring nothing for Hannah's feelings, she arrived to steal him away from her.

She wanted to laugh. What a foolish thought. Who was John to her anyway? They were merely traveling companions and nothing more. Furthermore, John would never be fool enough to be led away by any woman, let alone this Miss Oakley. He was clearly more sophisticated than to allow such a thing to happen.

"Alas, another season," John said with a laugh. "Perhaps it will be my last; although, I suspect this may be the best season yet."

"Why, that is my hope, as well," Miss Oakley replied with that titter men seemed to find delightful. "Though I grow bored of the endless parties, at times. It is my dream that one day life shall be much simpler." The woman sighed and looked past John to Hannah. "Do you not agree?"

"It is her first season," John replied for her. "It would be unwise to make a judgment before experiencing it, would you not say?"

Miss Oakley giggled. "Oh, then you are but a babe just out of swaddling? I shall speak no more of the season, then." She leaned in closer to John, and John turned so his back was to Hannah. "I must know someone you know. In what businesses are you involved?"

John laughed. "Too many of which to speak," he replied. "Although, I can assure you there is nothing on which I do not have my hands."

Hannah's jaw dropped. Was he being crass? From the tiny giggle Miss Oakley gave, she assumed he was.

"This is good to know," the woman said as she rose from her chair. "I should find my father before he drinks every bottle of spirits in the inn."

"He sounds like a man I would like to meet one day."

"I will arrange that," Miss Oakley replied. "In fact, I shall leave my father's address with the innkeeper. Do send a card when you arrive in London. I believe my father would be most eager to do business with a man such as yourself."

Hannah could not help but glare at the woman. How dare she disguise pleasure as business!

John went to speak, no doubt to tell the woman that he would not be able to meet because he would be much too busy, but Isabel entered the room before he could say anything more.

"Hannah," Isabel said in a chastising tone, "it is late. We should be off to bed."

With burning cheeks, Hannah clasped her book to her breast and stood. "It was a pleasure to meet you," she said to Miss Oakley, although the lie burned on her tongue. What she wanted was to throw her book at the woman!

"Good night," John said, and Hannah let out a sigh. She had nothing about which to be concerned; John was much too intelligent for this woman, and he would not be led astray.

Once in her room, she found herself staring at the ceiling, her mind once again thinking of John. As many peculiar thoughts had raced through her brain that day, two in particular pushed their way above the others.

Why was she concerned with whom John spoke? And why had that concern made her want to hurt Miss Oakley, a person with whom she had just been acquainted?

***

When Hannah left with her sister, John let out a sigh of relief. Not because the woman had left but rather for the string of tales he had told through the day in order to appease her. He had no interest in birds or reading, nor had he ever read a line of poetry outside of what had been required at university, and even then he found it dull. However, he saw the effect his words had on Hannah by her smile. She had seemed fascinated with his every word, and his progress with her was bound to please Laurence.

Yet, a peculiar feeling had come over him as she left the room, for a part of him had not wanted her to go.

"I should retire, as well," Miss Oakley said, interrupting his thoughts. "Father wishes to leave at sunrise, and the hour is late."

The woman was pretty, like most other women with whom he had made an acquaintance, but that made her much too typical for his tastes. However, he could not resist making a woman, any woman, smile. He was not the rogue many believed him to be, but neither was he a prude, and he justified his actions by remembering the smile he gave them.

"Such a travesty to miss another moment of your company," he said with a bow and a secretive smile that had never let him down when it came to women. He was not disappointed when she honored him with a deep blush. It was not the same pinkness of the cheeks he received from Hannah, but rather a more knowledgeable reddening that said she was accustomed to such attention. However, he enjoyed the game as much as most men enjoyed playing piquet. "Perhaps fate will allow us to speak again one day."

"That would be lovely," Miss Oakley replied, that blush deepening. "My father has many businesses, and I am certain when I tell him what a gentleman you are, he will be pleased to invite you to dinner and share in some of his fine brandy as you engage in business dealings together."

John smiled, but his mind raced. The fact of the matter was he was in need of some new business connections, and if this woman could initiate such a connection, it might be exactly what he needed. If it meant pretending to find her interesting in the process, then so be it.

"That would be wonderful. I am eager to meet him."

"Then I will await your card," she said before turning and leaving as gracefully as she had entered.

John returned to his chair. On most occasions such as these, those occasions where he piqued the interest of some woman such as Miss Oakley, he felt a sense of pride in his accomplishments. These encounters typically were followed up with him sending a card, calling over, and engaging in conversation. It was a ritual much like a hunter stalking his prey. There was a thrill in the game.

In the end, when he had completed his task, he found such women boring. Oftentimes they would speak of embroidery or other mundane tasks that held no appeal to him. That was when he would break their hearts. He never set out to hurt anyone, but as he continued to play his game, he no longer saw the woman but rather a conquest of sorts.

The problem now was that, a month earlier, he had sworn off the game.

He trembled at the memory and grabbed his glass to take a swift drink. Not only had he met his match, but it had not ended as he would have liked. For that reason, he had left his home in Cornwall and sought refuge with his cousin.

The room was now empty, as was the seat beside him. The woman who had occupied it earlier intrigued him. He did not feel a bit guilty for lying concerning his love for nature and books, but he had done it for a noble cause. Regardless, something about the woman caused him to pause. By all appearances, she was a bluestocking through and through, but she lacked the plainness of many of the women he knew who preferred books to men.

When he had first laid eyes on her that morning, he had to exaggerate his bravado lest he be consumed by her beauty. When she spoke, it was with authority no matter how quiet her voice was.

And then there was the mention of the cobbler, Hans, and his son.

John was no fool. He had heard quite clearly that she had called him handsome, but he enjoyed teasing her in the carriage by inquiring more about this supposed cobbler. The more she tried to explain, the more improbable was her story, but as she spoke, he found himself drawn in by her voice.

"It is the drink," he mumbled into his glass. "You can have any woman you choose, and it will not be a bluestocking, I promise you that." He finished off the rest of his drink and then gazed into the fire. Although he was intrigued with Hannah, they had nothing in common.

That was not true; they both were equally handsome.

He chuckled. No, he would have to find a different woman by the end of the season, one he could finally marry and put the troubles he left behind in Cornwall away for good.

"You have not retired to bed?" Laurence asked as he stepped into the room.

John smiled at his cousin, who took the seat Hannah had vacated earlier. How strange that this recluse—made so of his own doing because of his embarrassment over his leg—was going to London. John wanted to know what Isabel had done to make such great changes in this man.

"No, I have been thinking on a few things," John replied to the question Laurence had asked.

His cousin chuckled. "Fires tend to do that with men."

A server entered the room with a tray that held two mugs. He placed them on the table, bowed, and then left the room. John looked down at the ale and smiled.

"Indeed, fires can bring about many thoughts," he replied as he picked up one of the mugs. "Thanks for this." He lifted the mug as if to toast.

Laurence lifted his in reply. "It has been some time since I have enjoyed a good mug of ale."

John chuckled. "Indeed. Concerning that, and I do not mean to be rude..."

"We are family. Speak freely."

"You were never one to leave your home, and now you are on your way to London for the season? What has changed that made you decide to do such a thing?"

Laurence pursed his lips in thought. "There are many factors, but in truth, I must admit it was all due to Isabel."

"She is making you attend?" John asked in surprise. Was the man so in love that he would allow his wife to dictate his comings and goings? If this was the case, the dukedom was in dire trouble.

"No," Laurence said with a laugh. "Isabel, she has the strength many women, and perhaps even men, lack. It was in that strength that I confronted my past."

"That is good news," John said, thinking about his own past. "I am pleased for you. I have not seen you this cheerful since…"

"Yes, since before my parents' untimely death. I am at peace now, as much as they are."

John considered the man's words. To be at peace was something for which he longed, but he doubted the existence of another woman such as Isabel for himself.

"How was your conversation with Hannah?" Laurence had a twinkle in his eyes John was unsure if he cared for or not.

"Intriguing." He glanced to either side to assure himself no one could overhear. "The woman loves to read. I must admit that, although I care nothing for such activities, she did make it sound interesting."

"She is a good woman, but I fear she has become so engrossed in her books, she has forgotten the outside world. I did the same, but for different reasons, and I believe this season will force her out into the world."

"I will do what I can to help," John said. "Judging by our conversation tonight, she is excited about the season. I have no doubt that she will find the perfect suitor before she is to return home."

"That will make Isabel and myself, and her mother, very happy," Laurence said with a smile. "But what of you? This is your fourth season. Will you come away with a woman you believe is worthy as a bride?"

"Oh, yes," John replied. "By the end of the season, I will have a bride-to-be."

"Then we shall drink to luck, for both you and Hannah." He raised his mug. "May you both find what you seek."

John raised his mug in agreement. He was unsure about Hannah, but he knew he needed as much luck as he could get.

Chapter Six

As Hannah followed Laurence and Isabel through their London residence, a townhouse much larger than she had expected with its nine bedrooms, a ballroom, and a library, as well as the typical drawing and other necessary rooms. Granted, it was not as large as Scarlett Hall, but it was impressive, nonetheless.

Scarlett Hall. Just the thought of her childhood home gave her a longing to return there, to return to a time when these heavy burdens to attend the season were not forced upon her. A time when she was allowed to read whenever she liked, wherever she wished, and rarely called upon to pretend to be someone she was not. She also missed the open fields, but the small park nearby would have to do.

Hannah perked up when she went to the bedroom assigned her and found she had been assigned a lady's maid, Sally by name. To most women of the *ton*, having a lady's maid was as common as owning a pair of stockings. However, Hannah's mother thought the cost of such a servant was unnecessary, especially when one had three daughters.

"You may have a lady's maid when you marry," she had told her daughters often. "Until then, rely on one another for aid in dressing."

To be honest, Hannah could not have cared less if she had a maid or not, but the fact she had one now, she had to admit, was a bit exciting. Juliet was not a patient companion when it came to dressing, especially on those nights when full-dress was required.

After an early dinner of which Hannah ate little—traveling did that to her—she gained permission to visit the library. Laurence did not seem surprised at the request; Hannah wondered if she was that obvious and realized she should not be. Regardless, she was glad for the distraction.

The sun had yet to set, and it streamed rays through a grand window that brought light to the otherwise dark room. Bookshelves filled two of the walls floor to ceiling, the rich dark-stained wood crafted with intricate lines. Two large club chairs sat before a fireplace, a dying fire popping from time to time in the grate. To some, the room had a stuffiness that would have sent them running to the open airiness of the drawing room. However, to Hannah, it was like a comfortable blanket.

She would have enjoyed it much more if a problem were not gnawing at the back of her mind. Thoughts of John and the night before persisted, and although she did not wish ill will on Miss Oakley, Hannah could not help but wonder how long the two had spent talking beside the fire after she retired.

Against her will, her imagination took root. She could picture them, their chairs pushed close together, Miss Oakley seducing John with her beauty and wit and leaving poor John to cower in fright when the woman made an attempt to kiss him against his will. He was a gentleman and would never strike a lady; however, Hannah would be happy to do it for him. With steps as quick as lightning, she would give the woman a right slap for her forwardness, and Miss Oakley would beg for forgiveness. Then, when the woman ran away in shame, Hannah would allow John to hold her.

A loud pop from the fireplace brought Hannah back to the library, and she placed a hand on her cheek in horror. What was wrong with her? Never in her life had she ever thought of striking a girl—or a woman—because of a man! Juliet, yes, for her moments of foolishness, but never had she grown so jealous she wished to strike someone. Then again, she had never had any interest in a man before....

"You have a guilty expression."

Hannah turned to see Isabel enter the room, a wide grin on her face.

"Have you been caught in something you should not?"

Is she so strong and wise that she could read my thoughts? Hannah wondered in a panic. No, that was ridiculous.

"Do I need to inform Laurence?"

She did know!

"I..." The words stuck in Hannah's throat. What would Laurence do when he found out she had found an attraction for his cousin?

Isabel came to stand in front of Hannah, her arms crossed over her breasts. "Imagine his horror in learning you have stolen one of his books."

Hannah sighed as her body deflated with relief. She would not have to confess the truth to her sister!

"This is so exciting," Isabel said as she plopped herself into the chair beside Hannah. "Our first season together! I do wish Juliet was here to share in it with us, as well."

"Yes, I do, too," Hannah said. "I never thought I would miss her, but I truly do."

Isabel nodded and looked around the room as if in search of something. "John seems a nice man."

"Yes," Hannah said, unable to keep an image of his smile from appearing in her mind. "Very nice."

"Do you enjoy his company?"

Hannah nodded.

Her sister seemed to study her for a moment. Did she know the extent of interest Hannah had in the man?

"We have made several plans, including taking a carriage ride through St. James Park. I have never been, but I hear it is a marvelous place to meet others. On Friday, I believe we shall go shopping for a new dress."

Hannah understood that it was a part of the season to engage in numerous activities; however, she had come for a specific reason. She leaned forward and lowered her voice. "What of the society?" she asked with a glance toward the door. "The one of which you spoke?"

"From what I heard, they are to meet in a fortnight on a Tuesday late in the evening," her sister replied. "I have already sent word that they should expect your arrival."

Hannah bounded from her chair and embraced her sister. "Thank you for that! My dreams will come true this season, I can tell. And although my book will be discussed often once it is published, I will never forget your help in this matter."

Isabel took Hannah's hand. "You are more than welcome. And to be honest, it was Laurence who told me about this group. However, you must never tell anyone else."

"Oh, you have my word!" Hannah said, liking her brother-in-law even more.

"And do not forget your promise," Isabel said with a pointed look. "You are to genuinely attend whatever functions come your way and be open to meeting gentlemen who approach you."

The price she had to pay in order to see her book completed, and published, was well worth the inconveniences as far as she was concerned. Although she had no desire to meet any gentleman, nor to fall in love, she agreed, nonetheless. "I will attend so many balls you will scold me for never being here. In fact, when is our first?"

"Laurence has a good friend, Mr. Hugh Elkins, who is hosting a party next Saturday. His parties are known to be the best for starting the season off right, and his invitations are highly coveted, even if he is the younger son of an earl and not an earl himself." She patted Hannah's hand. "Now, I would advise you to prepare for bed soon. We will be busy tomorrow and every day that follows. You will need sleep when you can take it." She stood just as John entered the room and stopped upon seeing them.

"Oh, forgive me for interrupting," he said.

Isabel smiled. "Not at all. I was just bidding Hannah a good night."

"I promise to be in and out in a jiffy. I have been wanting to read for the last few nights, and I simply could not put it off for another day."

A flutter in her heart left Hannah a bit breathless, especially when John smiled at her before moving to one of the bookcases.

When Hannah looked at Isabel, she could not help but notice the tiny smile that played on her lips, as if she had some sort of secret. Yet, it was there only a few moments, and Hannah wondered if her mind was playing tricks on her.

"Well, goodnight," Isabel said, and she left the room, leaving Hannah alone with John.

Then a thought came to Hannah. Was it appropriate for her to be alone in a room with the man? In all reality, they were not courting, and he was a guest in the house just as she was, after all. They were bound to run into one another from time to time, were they not?

Yes, it is fine, she assured herself.

"Ah, here it is," he said as he pulled a book off the shelf. "'The Gentleman's Guide to Africa'. I was recommended this book some time ago, but I have not had the chance to find it. When I learned Laurence had a copy, I could hardly believe it."

Hannah could do nothing more than nod—her voice had somehow left her once again. John took the chair Isabel had vacated and sat gazing at her, and Hannah had to fight the urge to shift in her seat.

"And what is it you are reading?" he asked as he leaned over to look at her book.

"The...poetry of Rice."

"Rice?" John asked with a small frown. "How would one write about such a food?" He shrugged. "If you enjoy it enough you might fill a whole book, I suppose."

Hannah could not stop herself from closing her eyes and laughing, but when she opened her eyes once more and saw him staring at her with a worried look, she stopped and covered her mouth. Had he been serious in his statement? She wished she could pull the cushion over herself and hide.

"I see I am not caught up with the latest poetry." He sighed as Hannah struggled to contain her laughter, even as it horrified her that she wanted to laugh. "There is no need to poke fun at me. I shall write a poem concerning pudding."

She could no longer hold in her mirth, and tears streamed down her face as she laughed so hard her stomach hurt. Finding her breath was difficult, but she wiped the tears from her eyes and took a deep breath to bring herself back under control.

The poor man wore an exasperated look. "It is something many people enjoy..."

She could not allow the man to suffer any longer. "It is not rice as in the food; it is the man's name. Bartholomew Rice."

John cleared his throat, his cheeks a bright crimson. "I see. I was only speaking in jest, you know. Of course, no one would write about rice—the food."

Hannah suppressed another giggle and did her best to regain her composure. She studied the man as he opened the book before him. Even his eyes were handsome, if such a thing were possible, and his lips moved as he read, which she found an enthralling action, perhaps the most arresting thing she had ever seen.

"We are to take a carriage ride in St. James Park. Did your sister tell you?"

Hannah, who had been sitting gazing at him with her chin resting in her hand, her elbow leaning on the arm of the chair, sat up straighter in the chair. "Yes. Before you arrived she informed me."

"I have been to St. James Park many times," he said as he closed his book. "It is nice, but you must endure countless greetings and pretend you are fascinated with everything you see."

"Oh, you are accompanying us?" she asked stupidly. Had he not included himself in that 'we' he mentioned?

He nodded. "I am."

Well, that made the outing seem that much more appealing than it had been when she first learned of it.

"I imagine we will see each other quite often throughout the season," he continued. "We will more than likely attend many of the same functions and parties. If you do not mind my company, of course."

Hannah shook her head so quickly, she thought it might leave her shoulders. "Not at all," she blurted before she could restrain her response. "You must not...I mean, you should remain with us the entire season." Why had she said that? Was she concerned he would find others with whom he would rather spend his time? Why should she care? It was all so confusing! She would not fall in love with anyone, this man included!

However, when he rose from the chair and smiled down at her, she knew she was lying to herself. "I look forward to that," he said. "For you, Hannah, have already made my season better than all the others combined. Goodnight." He bowed and left the room, leaving Hannah staring at the closed door.

She released her breath and sank into the softness of the chair. He thought she would make the season better? He wished to spend more time with her?

Setting her book to the side, she rested her head into the back of the chair, her mind bringing forth images of what the time they spent together would be like. Some of them even made her blush.

Chapter Seven

A pair of feet moved quickly through Scarlett Hall, although they produced no sound. To take such careful steps was a mastery long practiced and had never failed. The house was large, much too large for a single family—even if they had four children who inhabited it at one time.

Now, another bed sat empty, and it was as if the walls spoke of the loneliness left behind. Not everyone listened to the walls, but some existed to do just that.

The figure stopped outside Juliet's room and, as was done many times before, opened the door without a sound. A smile formed on lips—just as they had before—and a few steps later eyes soaked in the innocent figure of the youngest of the Lambert daughters.

She slept in her shift, her body atop the heavy blanket. With each rise and fall of her breath, her bosom moved ever so gently. The figure sighed as it reached out and brushed back a long strand of dark hair from the girl's face. Although she was beautiful, the young woman was prone to mischief. That was a shame, for she would have made a worthy bride, but she would never change. A shame, indeed.

The figure placed a hand to her cheek and relished in the smooth skin. Although tempted to kiss her head as was done many times before, it was not worth the risk of waking her. Juliet needed her rest, and waking her would serve no purpose.

A sigh escaped as the figure left the room, closing the door as quietly as when entered, and the figure moved to the closed door that led to the bedroom of the Lady of the house. The woman was a striking beauty matched only by that of her daughters. The matriarch who controlled not only the vast home and wealth, but the women who resided within it.

Like Juliet, her mother slept soundly, although blankets covered her form. Many nights had been spent watching this woman as she slept. For hours, the figure stood in the darkness contemplating how to proceed with the plan.

Lady Eleanor shifted in the bed, and tension seized the figure as the woman sighed and turned to face the window, her back to the watcher. It was too great a chance standing here, not when the time to complete the task was so near.

Therefore, the figure left the room and made its way to the room belonging to Hannah. The feeling of being in her room both thrilled and excited, and there was a longing for the woman. For he had desired her longer than she would ever have suspected. He walked over to her bed and ran a hand over the soft blanket before leaning over and inhaling the sweet fragrance left on her pillow.

"Soon we will be united," he whispered as if she were there. "And we shall kiss as lovers do."

He went to her vanity table where several bottles of perfume sat side by side. She was far too beautiful to need such fragrances, so he would rid her of them soon enough. She was for his eyes only, and he had to be careful lest another man try to steal her from him.

However, before he could worry about another man stealing her, he needed to find a way to gain her trust. Over time, he had gained much, enough that she confided her secrets in him. However, that was not enough. She would have to see him in a different light, and now that she had left for the season, he needed something to move his plan into action.

He was to entice the woman, lead her away from her childhood home, and once she was his, they would return to Scarlett Hall as man and wife. Lady Eleanor would not be happy, for he was far older than her daughter, but it would not matter, for once they were wed, he would finally take control of the house and the wealth that accompanied it. He and Hannah would commandeer the set of suites the mistress of the house currently occupied, allowing him to work his way through the coffers, changing his life from a humble man to one who was elevated in the *ton*.

Yet, how could he gain that last bit of trust that was needed?

Standing in the shadows, he thought the task impossible, but then an idea came to him as he spotted an intricate hair pin. By all accounts, the object was innocent enough, but as a plan formed in his mind, he realized that the pin would be the key to his success. It would unlock the heart's desires, and Hannah would trust him like never before.

His enthusiasm was so great, he considered shouting out with joy. However, he could not do such a thing. If he did, he would be revealed, and it was much too early to have that happen. Therefore, he placed the hairpin into his jacket pocket and left the room once more.

As he passed by Juliet's room again, he stifled a laugh. Her mischievous ways would soon be over, for once he took control of the house, she would be sent far away. If Lady Eleanor took it in her mind to attempt to stop him, he would make sure she was sent packing, as well. The woman had no right to run a house when a man was willing and able to do such things.

Moving down the stairs, he peeked into the library and smiled. Hannah had spent many hours of her life in this room, and he would indulge himself in sitting where she had sat so often.

After all, who was there to stop him?

Chapter Eight

In the past, Hannah cared little for dresses and the other feminine things Juliet and other women of the *ton* found important. However, she could not help but admire the silky white dress as she viewed herself in the full-length mirror. It had a high waist, flowing skirts and light blue lace at the cuffs and down the front. Over it, she wore a blue Pelisse coat that reached to her knees. Although she loved the coat, she hated the idea of covering the beautiful dress, but with the weather still cool, she had little choice. The fact was, she wished to look her best for the carriage ride through St. James Park.

"Is it your hair?" Sally asked. "I'm sorry if it doesn't meet your approval. I can do much better if you'd like."

Hannah smiled at the nervous lady's maid. The woman was kind and always seemed to fret over whether she had displeased Hannah or not. "Not at all," Hannah replied. "The style is well done. I must admit, your work is always wonderful."

The woman beamed at the compliment and seemed to relax.

As Hannah turned her attention back to her reflection, however, she frowned. "My dress is adequate, but I must admit, for the first time I see myself as rather plain."

"You are far from plain, Miss Hannah," Sally said, her eyes wide with shock. "You are beautiful, in fact. I'd expect you'll need to buy an extra bag for all the cards you'll receive this season."

Hannah could not help but laugh, feeling a bit better. She cared not for any cards, but for some reason she had an overwhelming urge to please John, and that fact nettled her. Why should she care what he thought? They were merely friends, or at least that was what she had come to consider him—as a friend—based on their common interests.

That aside, however, she *had* spent last night and this morning fretting over her dress. The truth was that she did not want John whisked away by some woman for the remainder of the season. If a woman such as Miss Oakley used his good nature against him, the poor man would only be made to look the fool. The more she considered it, the more she realized it was up to her to take the initiative and entice John to stay near her. Yet, how did one go about doing such a thing?

"Sally?" Hannah said, turning to the maid. The woman was nearing thirty, and over the past few days, Hannah had felt comfortable enough to share some of her secrets with the woman. "I must ask you for some advice."

"But of course, Miss," Sally replied. "I'll do my best to help."

"Suppose a woman has a friend, a gentleman friend. She has no intentions of romantic notions with him, of course." An image of John kissing her as they stood beside the fire came to mind and she pushed it away with heat in her cheeks. "At the same time, she finds a need to keep him nearby. Shall we say, out of the hands of other women? To protect him, of course."

"I see," Sally replied.

"How would you advise her to proceed in keeping him safe?"

Sally walked over to the vanity table. "Well, a woman must use both her mind and heart to do such a thing," she said. She picked up a bottle of perfume. "The first step would be to entice him with a scent. May I?"

Hannah nodded. "Please do."

Sally added a dab behind each ear, on her wrists, and in the hollow of her throat. "Does this gentleman in question enjoy conversation?"

"He does," Hannah replied, remembering the night at the inn—before Miss Oakley had arrived, of course. "He enjoys the same activities as I...that is, my friend. Do you believe one should continue engaging him in conversation?"

"Yes, Miss. There is one more thing." She bit at her lip. "I'm afraid it might offend you. It's not very becoming of a lady such as yourself, but I've heard women in your position speak of it."

"You will not offend me," Hannah replied, now curious as to the advice this woman was to give. Unbecoming of a lady? "What do you suggest I do?"

Sally glanced at the closed door and then took a half-step toward Hannah. "You may feign a fall or illness, either one will do the trick, it doesn't matter. What does matter is that he will then want to help you. My sister did that to a man. She pretended she was faint and fell against him, and of course he had no choice but to hold her or she would have fallen to the ground."

Hannah's eyes went wide. "Oh, my! That is quite…"

"Bold?" Sally said, finishing the sentence for her. "That might be true, but when the man held her, something changed between them, like a spark ignited that lit a fire that burned deep. It came as no surprise when they were married within the year."

Hannah considered Sally's advice. She had no plans to marry John, but what the woman said made sense. She had to keep him safe from those women who would use him for their own gain. This was not solely an attempt to gain his attention; she already had that.

"Thank you," Hannah said and then gave the woman a hug. "I shall consider your advice."

The door opened and Isabel entered the room. "I would expect Juliet to make everyone wait, but I would not have expected such behavior from you."

Hannah gasped as she looked at the clock. "I'm sorry," she said. She glanced once more at the vanity table, but she had nothing more to add to her ensemble. "I'm ready."

Isabel gave her a stern glare but laughed to show she was teasing. "Good. The weather is too poor for an open carriage, unfortunately. However, it will still be an experience to remember."

Hannah nodded, and they made their way downstairs. She cared not if the carriage had but one wheel; as long as she was near John, that was all that mattered. How strange it was to find interest in a man, especially when she had not been expecting—or wishing for—it.

When she stepped outside, she looked to the sky. Gray clouds threatened rain. It was not yet raining, for which she was glad, but she wished she could have experienced this outing in an open carriage. Unfortunately, English weather could never be trusted during this time of year.

Then she spotted John waiting near the carriage. Did he realize how tight his coat drew against his broad chest? Or how the muscles in his arms were clear under his sleeves? When he laughed as he did now while speaking to Laurence how radiant his smile was? Horrible weather or not, the familiar lightheadedness returned as she approached the carriage. And John. It was as if all semblance of sense had left her, and she could not help but feel a twinge of excitement at sitting beside him.

"Hannah," John said with a deep bow, "it is wonderful to see you again."

Hannah concentrated on her balance as she smiled at him. It would be just her luck to topple from the step and land on her backside in front of the man! She doubted rather highly that such a fall was what Sally meant when she gave her advice.

Laurence glanced upwards. "I am hoping the weather holds," he said as a footman opened the door for them. "No matter. We will continue our excursion regardless. I had Weber add a few blankets to keep us warm."

Hannah followed Isabel into the carriage, and then John took the seat beside her, much to her delight.

"That storm looks as though it might become fierce," he said as he looked out the window. "Those clouds look quite menacing."

Hannah could not take her eyes from the man's arms, for the sleeve of his coat had drawn tighter, and when he pushed back the curtain further, she wondered what it would be like to touch his arm.

A feeling of shame washed over her, and when she turned to Isabel, she saw a small smile playing on the woman's lips. "You look beautiful in that dress," her sister said.

It was strange, but Hannah found she rather enjoyed the compliment, for in the past, her appearance was never of any great importance. If she brushed her hair and wore clean clothing, that was enough for her.

What she did find was that she hoped John would agree or make a similar comment. However, he did not. Instead, he began a conversation with Laurence about business matters, and Hannah leaned back into the cushioned seat. Well, what did she expect? He was a man, after all.

***

Hannah drew back the curtain on the carriage window and looked outside, amazed at what she saw. Two paths, one for those on foot and the other for carriages, snaked through the park. She pulled down the window and poked her head out to see that their carriage was in the middle of one long line that branched out in front of and behind theirs. However, it was the canal that fascinated Hannah, especially the birds gathered near it, large and white with the largest beaks she had ever seen.

"Is that…a pelican?" she asked with a gasp. She had heard of them, but to have the experience of seeing one was enthralling.

"Indeed," Laurence replied. "A gift from a Russian ambassador nearly two hundred years ago. They continue to thrive here and have made it their home."

Hannah sighed as she moved away from the window and turned her attention to the man who sat beside her. He seemed preoccupied and content with gazing out his own window, and Hannah wondered about what he could be thinking. The truth of the matter was, she knew very little about him to even guess at his thoughts.

"Are there any pelicans on your side?" she asked in an attempt to grab his attention.

"No." At least he had replied. He had become unusually quiet and her question did nothing to draw him from his thoughts.

"Have you seen the pelicans before?"

"Many times."

That explained his disinterest, but she found his inattentiveness frustrating. Isabel and Laurence, still newly married, whispered and giggle to each other. Strangely, that was what Hannah wanted.

Then Sally's advice came to her. She would need to time the perfect moment to feign illness and fall against the man; that would gain his attention, especially in such close quarters. Once in his arms, he would have no choice than to look at her—and hold her tightly.

As these thoughts came to her, the carriage made a sudden left, sending Hannah towards John. Although the turn was not all that jarring, she exaggerated it by falling against John.

"Oh!" she said as she pushed herself against him. Unfortunately for her, the carriage came to a stop at that precise moment, and he had turned toward her so that her head rested against his chest. That was not what she had planned! It was one thing to be jostled against his side or back and quite another to find herself cozying up to his front, even if it was a broad, hard chest....

"Hannah?" John asked in shock. "Are you all right?"

She looked up into his eyes and batted her eyelashes like she had seen Miss Oakley do back at the inn. "I believe so," she replied demurely. "A moment, please, to allow me to regain my composure."

"Of course," he said. Then he frowned and his face puckered. "That scent..."

Hannah fought to suppress a smile. The plan Sally had suggested had worked! Although Hannah knew men were simple creatures, she could not believe how the perfume had confounded him. She suspected that the smell had provided a stirring of desire and interest within him. She prayed she had not applied too much, for the man might become an uncontrollable wild beast because of it.

"Oh, my perfume?" she asked with an air of innocence.

Laurence and Isabel had been watching something outside the carriage, murmuring to one another excitedly, and Hannah was relieved they were not taking heed of the exchange between her and John.

"Yes, your perfume..." He closed his eyes. "It is much too..." He turned his head and released a loud sneeze and then another. "It is very strong."

"I am sorry," Hannah whimpered as she righted herself.

"No apologies..." Sneeze. "Necessary." Sneeze. "If you will excuse me; I must get some air."

Horrified, Hannah moved away just as Laurence and Isabel exited the carriage, followed immediately by John, who threw himself from the vehicle as if escaping a fire.

Hannah sat staring out the door, a sense of shame blanketing her. The poor man had suffered because of the perfume, and she vowed to never wear any again. Taking a deep breath, she exited the carriage and glanced around to find a group of people gathered to the right of the line, two carriages before them. The driver was squatted down beside one of the great wheels.

"We should see if they need any assistance," John said as he sniffed and then wiped at his nose with a kerchief. "They may be stranded."

Hannah followed behind, the sense of dread thickening in the air around her, but for the life of her, she did not know why.

"May we be of any assistance?" John asked.

Hannah had not noticed that the carriage's occupants, an elderly gentleman with silver hair and a younger dark blond woman—both with their backs to them—stood outside the carriage.

"No, thank you," the older man replied. "Apparently the bearings seem to have caught. My driver was afraid we would cause an accident and therefore pulled over to the side. Is everyone in your party well?"

"Quite well," Laurence replied just as the woman turned.

"Miss Oakley!" John gasped. A smile spread across his face as he bowed to the woman. "It is an honor to see you again."

"You know this man?" her companion, more than likely her father if Hannah was to hazard a guess, asked, eying John with disapproval, much to Hannah's delight.

"Yes, Father," the woman replied, returning John's smile. "We met, was it just two nights ago? At that little inn we stopped at when we were on our way to London. Do you recall the gentleman of whom I spoke concerning business? Lord John Stanford, was it not?"

The older man's frown disappeared. "Ah, yes! Forgive me." He put out his hand, and John gave it a firm shake. "Stanford, yes, it is a pleasure to meet you indeed. Miles Oakley."

Introductions were made, and Hannah had never felt more ill in her life. How could this woman, out of all the women in London, happen to be just ahead of them in the park? What was worse was John smiling at her and how Miss Oakley reacted with that prim pinkness to her cheeks when he did.

Lord Oakley clapped John on the back. "Well, young man, it cannot be simply chance that you met my Catherine and have now met again with your willingness to lend us aid. I request you join us for dinner at your convenience in celebration for your nobleness."

Hannah could not calm the racing of her heart. Of all the things that could possibly have gone wrong! She prayed that John would say he was much too busy or make some other excuse.

"It would be an honor," John replied. "Please send a card with the date and time that is most acceptable to you."

Hannah's heart sank, and she held her stomach as she returned to the carriage. Miss Oakley could spend the remainder of her life stranded in St. James Park as far as she was concerned!

Brooding in her sadness, she flopped onto the bench and crossed her arms in vexation. That was what she got for having an interest in a man! Perhaps this was a sign that she should return to her books and leave the idea of men behind—for good!

When the others returned to the carriage, Laurence said, "The luck you have! To meet a woman whose father is one of the largest importers of wine? Tell me, how do you do it?"

"It is a matter of being irresistible by making certain everyone receives a smile," John replied, much to Hannah's ire. "For who can resist a smile?"

Apparently that awful Miss Oakley cannot, Hannah thought. Well, she would not give up! She would do everything in her power to stop that horrid woman, for she certainly was *not* an appropriate match for John!

The first party of the season was the following day, and if she failed in winning over John, then she would lose him forever.

And that was something she realized she was not willing to allow to happen.

Chapter Nine

The ballroom was crowded with a sea of people, the women in dresses of all colors of the rainbow with hair in elaborate chignons that differed as much as the dresses. Hannah, herself, wore a deep blue gown of velvet with white lace at the hem and a white satin belt at the waist. On her wrist hung a simple gold bracelet, and she forewent the perfume; there was no reason to worsen her chances of drawing John's attention. It had been a costly error, and she vowed to never do it again.

They had arrived at the party, the first of the season, hosted by a school friend of Laurence, one Mr. Hugh Elkins, and although Hannah had attended a few parties in the past—none in London, of course—she had never seen one as grand as this.

A small orchestra played in a far corner of the opulent room, a massive fern creating a lush backdrop. Along one wall sat a line of tables with every type of food imaginable, and footmen walked around offering various types of drinks they carried on trays balanced on their hands. More than once, Hannah worried a guest would turn and bump into a tray, but the footmen seemed to anticipate the movement of everyone around them, managing to keep their trays from toppling to the floor.

The chatter of people smothered the sounds of the stringed instruments at times, and although many of the guests wore wide grins and laughed, Hannah felt alone. Isabel and Laurence were making their rounds, and much to her dismay, John had also disappeared into the crowd. She had circled the room twice but had yet to find him.

Frustrated, she grabbed a glass of wine from the tray of a passing footman and took a sip. She was not all that interested in drinking it; she simply wanted something to do. An older woman smiled as she walked past, and Hannah returned it, but the woman did not stop to speak with her, which was perfectly fine with Hannah.

Blast him! she thought about John leaving her alone; although, in all reality he had no reason to report his doings to her.

She went to take another sip of her wine when she spotted him speaking to two women across the room. It was impossible for her to make out what they were saying from this distance, but they seemed to be having a quite enjoyable conversation, much to Hannah's chagrin. Granted, she had no cause to be jealous; however, she did find it rude that he would leave her alone to go speak to other women. Furthermore, what type of women stood tittering over a man they barely knew?

Well, perhaps they knew him more than she suspected. He had attended the London season for the past three years, had he not?

She sighed, finished the remainder of her wine in one gulp, and grabbed another glass from a passing footman. One of the women stood with her glass empty, and John smiled and took it from her. He stopped a footman and took another glass to hand to the woman.

Hannah narrowed her eyes at him. Fuming, she devised a plan, and with confident steps, she made her way to where John and his two *hussies* stood, stopping to glance around as if she had not seen him. Then, she just so happened to bump into his arm. Well, perhaps not just so.

"Oh!" she said with a gasp. "My apologies, my Lord! I did not see you there."

"Hannah," John replied, and she feigned surprise. "Please, I would like you to meet some people I know." He turned to his companions. "Miss Margaret Tambling," he said of the taller dark-haired woman, "and Miss Penelope Wellington," she had raven locks and plump cheeks, "may I introduce Miss Hannah Lambert of Wiltshire."

"My pleasure," Hannah said with a quick curtsy. It did not escape her that Miss Tambling seemed to struggle to keep her eyes off John, and that only added to her dislike of the woman.

"Is this your first season?" Miss Tambling asked. "I do not recall having seen you before." The words were said with the utmost snobbery, and Hanna had the urge to reply in kind.

"Indeed, this is my first season. My brother-in-law, the Duke of Ludlow, is a very close friend of Mr. Elkins. As a matter of fact, it was at his personal request that I attend this evening as an honored guest." Hannah held back her glee as the smug smiles of the women fell.

Miss Tambling gave her what Hannah assumed was a tolerant gaze and turned her attention back to John. "Will you be attending the ball given by Lord Montgomery three weeks from tonight?" she asked in a tone that was sickeningly sweet. "It is always one of the best of the season, and Penny and I will be in attendance."

Hannah felt a wave of panic come over her. She *had* to do something! Before John could respond, she brought her hand to her forehead and gasped. "Oh, my!"

John turned to her, his face alarmed. "Hannah?"

"I-I am so sorry," she said in a weak voice. "I believe I need a bit of fresh air. Please, continue; I will find my way out...unless I faint before I get to the door."

Miss Tambling's eyes narrowed, and Hannah smiled inwardly.

"I will accompany you," John said, his voice filled with concern. "Ladies, enjoy your evening."

With John at her side, Hannah felt some strange sense of victory. As they moved through the crowd, she had never felt prouder at the looks of admiration she received. It was only over a week ago that she had wanted nothing more than to remain at Scarlett Hall and have nothing to do with London; however, now that she was here, and at John's side, she found she never wanted to leave. She did not understand the reason for it, but she welcomed it all the same.

They exited the ballroom and came to a large door, which John held open for her.

"This way," he said.

She walked past him and inhaled the fresh air. She could not have the man grow suspicious. Torches had been set out along the path in order to allow the guests to see, and to bring a bit of warmth to the cool night.

"How are you feeling?" John asked. "Is there anything I can do?"

The moment had arrived, and Hannah knew that if she did not act right then, the man would be lost to her forever. The action would be unladylike, but it was worth the cost, for it would win him to her.

"I believe I am feeling…dizzy," she said before summoning all her courage and closing her eyes, hoping beyond hope that he would catch her before she landed on the ground. Much to her pleasure, and her relief, he did.

As his arm went around her, her heart raced at how her body pressed against his. She did not know what had come over her, but the temptation was so great, she reached up and touched his arm. It was just as she had suspected, firm muscle resided beneath the cloth, and she thought her whole body would burn like a winter's fire.

"I just need a moment," she whispered, reveling in the fact her face was nuzzled into his chest.

"Should I get a doctor?" he asked.

"No," she said. "I believe I feel better now." She looked up at him. "Thank you for saving me," she whispered. It reminded her of a book she once read. The heroine had been saved from a band of highwaymen by the handsome hero. The woman was so overcome with love and gratitude, she whispered those same words as she fell into the hero's arms. It was then the hero kissed the heroine, and for a moment, she wondered if John would do the same.

"You are welcome," he replied in a shaky voice that left Hannah not only worried but a bit disappointed.

The door opened and Hannah moved away as Isabel walked outside.

"John, Laurence is searching for you," Isabel said. "He wants to introduce you to an old friend of his from his school days."

John patted Hannah on the hand. "Please, rest, and I hope you feel better soon.

"Thank you," Hannah mumbled, glad for the lack of lighting, for she imagined her cheeks had to be as red as a strawberry.

When John was gone, Isabel rounded on Hannah. "We must speak," she said, using that tone Hannah recognized as her voice of authority. Oh, she was in quite a pickle! Her sister grabbed her elbow and directed her to a place behind a bench. "What made you believe you could leave a party and be seen alone with a man?"

"It was just John…"

"I do not care if it was John or any other man! Few here know you, nor do they know he is a guest in our home. Perception is everything."

"I…was not feeling well and needed…"

"Fresh air?" Isabel asked. "And much to your eternal gratitude, somehow you convinced John to escort you lest you faint?"

Hannah nodded. "Yes." She had never been so embarrassed in all her life. Who was this woman she was becoming?

"When Mother told me you sneaked out of the house, I was mortified. Now you are sneaking away from a party! You cannot do such things. It is unladylike and will cause embarrassment not only for John but for yourself, as well."

"I know," Hannah said with a heavy sigh. "But I was concerned."

"Concerned? About what?"

Hannah swallowed. "John. I find I enjoy his company; however, there are other women who would like nothing more than to be in his company, but for reasons that are not proper. I am sorry, but I feigned illness in order to save him."

Isabel shook her head. "I do not understand. Save him from whom?"

"Other women," Hannah replied. "You see, there are some who would think him handsome…" She paused. Would Isabel truly understand? Did she herself truly understand? "I believe some of these women may have an interest in John for reasons that are…deceptive."

And I do not wish to see him with someone else, she added silently. Then she paused. What was she doing? This was not the person she truly was! How had she become this petty debutante? A woman reminiscent of Juliet?

However, Hannah could not stop the odd feelings that picked at her mind like a hen at the ground.

"Come with me," Isabel said, taking Hannah by the elbow and leading her to a nearby bench. "I must ask. Do you have feelings for John?"

Hannah sighed. "I am unsure," she replied. "It is all so confusing. I worry John will be taken by a woman who is completely wrong for him." She raised a hand to stop her sister from responding. "I realize it is unfounded and that he is not my responsibility; however, I cannot seem to help myself." Tears filled her eyes, but she blinked them back. She would cry for no man! "What is wrong with me? I am a woman of reason not a romantic fool!"

Isabel seemed to study Hannah. "I see what is happening here," she said. "I suspected something like this might occur, but I did not expect it to be so soon."

"What is that?" Hannah asked.

"I believe you have become enamored by John."

Hannah shook her head. "No! I refuse! I cannot, and will not, be interested in any man. I have my book to finish and…"

Isabel chuckled. "It happens when we least expect it. But remember this. You have yet to experience the season. Do not put all your eggs in one basket. Allow other men to ask you to dance and enjoy in conversation, but you must remain a lady at all times. No more feigning illnesses or attempting to be alone with a man. It would devastate Mother if she learned how you behaved tonight."

Hannah sighed. Her sister was right. "I am sorry," she said. "I understand and swear it will never happen again." Shame overwhelmed her, and she hoped her face was not blotchy from the tears she had failed to stop.

"I do not say this to be cruel," Isabel said as she dabbed Hannah's face with a kerchief. "Like Mother, I only want the best for you, and I will do anything I can to assure your life is as perfect as it can be."

Hannah embraced her sister. "I know. And I will do my best to act in the manner in which I was raised."

Isabel smiled. "Good. Now, what are we to do about John?"

"I honestly do not know what came over me. Now that I look back on the past couple of days, I find myself more embarrassed than ever. The best thing to do is to focus on my writing and keep my head about me." Then she giggled. "You know, I cannot take full responsibility for my actions this evening."

With wide eyes, Isabel said, "Oh? And why is that? Do you wish to place blame on me?"

"No, not you," Hannah said with a laugh. "It is Juliet. The years of listening to her stories have been a bad influence on me."

Isabel joined in her laughter. "One of her is quite enough, thank you," she said as she rose from the bench. "Come. Let us end this night with fun and speak no more on this matter."

As the night grew later, Hannah considered how she arrived with the sole goal of catching John's eye. Unfortunately, she struggled to keep her thoughts from the man. How she had gone from a deliberate intelligent woman to a lovesick fool, she did not know.

***

When John returned to the townhouse, the others retired for the night; however, John went to the drawing room to have a final measure of brandy. The night had been strange. Not necessarily abysmal, but rather odd. He had given Miss Tambling and Miss Wellington his best smiles and had thrilled in the blush on their cheeks. It was an act he had sworn off, and yet he had done it anyway, for it came so naturally, as easy as breathing.

It was the moment when Hannah appeared, that was when his night had begun to unravel into the confusion that consumed him now. Not because she had interrupted, however, but because he found her an enigma. How did one explain the type of woman Miss Hannah Lambert was?

The woman was a bluestocking, that much he had ascertained. Yet tonight she had acted the braggart, which he had not expected from her. Other women, those such as Miss Tambling, in fact, had those tendencies, but Hannah did not seem the type.

It was not only her behavior that was in question, but his, as well. He had escorted her outside—alone! She was not the typical privileged lady to be left alone in the company of a man; however, no other choice was to be had, not if she had taken ill.

And therein lay the next part of his confusion. When she told him she was unwell, it had somehow frightened him. Why would he become overly concerned for Hannah? Yet, when she fell into his arms, he had an overwhelming desire to protect and care for her that he could not explain.

With her in his arms, he felt strong and protective, and, he had to admit, he enjoyed the embrace to the point he did not wish to release her. In fact, he had dared to consider kissing the woman such was his immediate reaction to her. What had begun as a favor to his cousin to feign interest in the woman was becoming much more, and he no longer saw it as a game, which was what had him sitting alone in the drawing room drinking yet another brandy and unable to sleep.

By all accounts, he knew that women could not resist his smile, and therefore, he was confident he could choose any woman he desired. Hannah was far different from his typical conquest with her love of animals and books, and he found it difficult to not think of her as he did other women. In truth, he wanted to choose her, and that did not sit well with him. What had brought on this strange desire for a woman so unlike the others he had pursued in the past? A woman so unlike himself?

Perhaps he wanted to pretend interest to the point he had tricked his own mind. He considered this as he took another drink of his brandy, its liquid like fire as it soothed his throat. Now that he was driven by something beyond pleasing his cousin, should he continue this strange pursuit? As he imagined spending more time with Hannah, doubt crept into his mind.

He had done many things that, if she learned of them, she might just turn and run. Run as far from him as she could, just as he had run away from that problem he prayed would never find him. Yet, for whatever reason, he knew Hannah was kind; she would understand.

"I am glad you are awake."

John started and turned to see Laurence standing at the door.

His cousin shot him a wide grin. "You, my favorite cousin, have made me quite happy."

"Oh?" John asked as Laurence poured himself a drink. "What is it that I have done to merit such an esteemed title?"

Laurence laughed and walked over to refill John's glass. "My Isabel is happy, and that is all I care about."

"Well, that tells me little," John replied.

"You see, I told you how Isabel's mother wanted Hannah to attend the season, yet she did not want to?"

John nodded. "You did."

"It seems that Hannah has become a bit enamored with you. Isabel believes she will want to remain in London, and I have you to thank for that."

So, it was as John had suspected. "You are most welcome," he replied. "I did not mind." In fact, he wished to tell Laurence the truth, that he had come to enjoy the woman's company, as well, but he was unsure how to approach it without sounding a cad. His cousin had not asked him to woo the young lady, after all, but to make her more pliable for someone more appropriate for her.

Laurence chuckled. "I am glad you enjoyed the task. Now, your work is done. There is no need to continue with the charade."

"Well," John said, choosing his words carefully, "concerning that matter, I have realized that Hannah…" He paused. Could he risk the woman's heart if she came to learn of his past? The mere thought of her hurt or upset pained him. Yet, could he stop himself from seeing her?

Laurence gave him an expectant look. "Yes? What is it?"

John juggled his thoughts. No, he was not the best man for such a woman as Hannah. "I am glad to have made her happy," he replied with reluctance. "Now, with the season before us, I do hope she finds happiness."

"Look at you," Laurence said with a wide grin. "Always thinking of others before yourself."

John forced a smile, but he wished he would be honest for once in his life.

"So, tell me of this Miss Oakley," Laurence said. "You met her at the inn?"

"I did," John said. He remembered his initial thought of considering stealing a kiss from the woman, and he felt a sudden sense of guilt. He had never had such a reaction when he thought of winning a kiss! "We engaged in pleasantries, and now it appears her father is eager to do business with me."

Laurence shook his head. "I cannot believe your luck! Do not forget your cousin who invited you when you consider making a business deal with the man." He laughed and lifted his glass.

"I will not," John replied, lifting his glass, as well.

As Laurence chatted, John weighed his options. As much as he had grown to enjoy Hannah's company, he knew that he would not be the best match for her, nor she for him. They were simply too different from one another. Of course, she was unaware of that fact, for she only saw the man he presented to her. It would be best if he focused his energies on Lord Oakley and his business ventures rather than on a lovely bluestocking with beautiful blond hair and deep blue eyes.

Despite this decision, however, he could not stop his mind from turning to that particular woman and her being in his arms, and he realized that ridding himself of that memory would be much more difficult than he ever anticipated.

Chapter Ten

For the week following his decision to distance himself from Hannah, John came to the realization that he had made a wise choice, even if it was not necessarily the choice he wished to make. He continued to engage Hannah in conversation whenever he joined her and his cousins for one outing or another, but as soon as they returned home, he made whatever feeble excuse he could to leave whenever Hannah invited him to join her in the library or made other attempts to speak to him alone.

Unfortunately, all this did was confuse him more, for out of all of the women he had pursued, Hannah was the only whose feelings he cared if he hurt. That fact still tickled the edge of his mind as he walked down St. James Street.

It was late evening, and most of the shops had closed for the day. However, there were certain establishments still open, establishments that would provide a gentleman with a glass of brandy, gambling, and provide for other needs he might wish met. John had frequented such places often over the past four years, but now he was unsure if he wanted anything beyond a drink. In truth, he wanted to be near Hannah, but that was impossible, for he doubted he would be able to trust himself in her presence.

The endless cycle of frustration caused his shoulders to draw tight, and he came to a stop before a particular establishment which bore the name 'The Noble Gentleman'. To any passersby, the sign was meant to convey a sense of regard and esteem; however, the reality was far from respectable.

How often had I been 'far from respectable' myself by frequenting such a place? he wondered. More often than he cared to admit.

With a sigh, he opened the outside door, which opened to a small foyer where two men flanked a second door, their bulging muscles making it clear to anyone entering that foolishness was not tolerated. They offered no words as John walked past them, nor did John them.

As soon as he passed through the inside door, he was assaulted by the strong odor of smoke, the sounds of laughter or the shouts of anger, and the faint tune of a dulcimer somewhere unseen. Tables scattered throughout the room held groups of men playing cards or dicing. Women, also referred to as 'companions', smiled, laughed, and encouraged whichever man gave them his attention—and his coin.

John made his way to a long bar where a burly man quite older than he asked, "Whatcha havin'?"

"A brandy," John replied. He produced a coin and placed it on the bar before he turned to study the room. One of the men playing cards stood, raised a fist, and began shouting at another. Two chaps stalked over, grabbed the screaming fellow, and removed him from the building.

"Here ya go," the barkeep said.

John thanked him and took a sip of the brandy. He was always surprised at the quality of the drinks in this place; the club was not of the highest standard, although it was not of the lowest, either. Despite what took place there, it managed to stay open. He wondered how many palms were greased in order to keep it so.

Yet, was that not the manner of the London season? So many of the *ton* walked about with their noses in the air only to later scurry away in secret to partake in acts that were less than acceptable. It was hypocrisy at its best, and John was no better than any of them.

"The last time I saw such a handsome man, he told me I was beautiful."

John turned at the voice he recognized and chuckled. "Frances," he said with a smile. "It has been what? A year? And yet you look exactly the same." What he said was true. Her flowing red hair and blazing blue eyes caught the eye of many men, which in turn paid for the white gown and the sapphire necklace she wore.

"I shall take that as a compliment, my Lord," Frances replied. "Although, I do wonder if I am pretty enough to be bought a drink?" She gave him an easy smile, and he laughed.

"A wine for the lady, please," he called to the barkeep and then looked Frances up and down.

She blushed, and John felt a bit better. Yes, he had foregone never to do these actions again, but he had to admit that making a woman, even one such as Frances, blush was something that brought on a pleasant feeling.

When the glass of wine arrived, Frances took a sip. "Lovely," she said. "Much like you." She twirled a lock of her hair around a finger before taking another sip of her wine. "Every season you come here, drink and gamble, and yet you still have no woman on your arm."

"I may have a woman and simply have yet to tell you about her," he said.

A smile played on her lips as she took a step toward him. "I do not believe that," she said in a light tone. "You are a good man and would not be here if a woman caught your interest."

He chuckled. "You may be right," he said and raised an eyebrow at her. "Or perhaps I am a rogue who cares only for himself."

"Are you not a kissing bandit?" she asked with a feigned air of innocence.

"A kissing bandit?" John asked with a laugh. "And why would you believe that?"

She smiled. "How often have you offered me nothing more than a kiss when you could have had so much more?"

He chuckled. "I suppose I could be at that."

Frances set her glass on the bar and fingered his cravat. "Then do as you did last season and kiss me." She wore a coy smile. "Or have you forgotten how?"

John finished off the remainder of his brandy. Yes, he had kissed this woman in the past, and often she asked for more, as had many women before and after. However, it was the pursuit that always held his fancy, not the capture. Furthermore, Frances was one of the few friends he had, even if they shared in a kiss or two, and he had always enjoyed her company more than whatever else she had to offer.

Therefore, with confidence, he placed a hand on her cheek as he had done countless times before only to find that he could not bring himself to do it now.

He dropped his hand to his side. "I am afraid I cannot."

Frances raised a single eyebrow and leaned on the counter. "Whoever this woman is, you must go to her, for establishments such as these will be of little help to you."

"Who says there is a woman?" John asked defensively, although he had to admit that Hannah had captured him as easily as a fox could capture a hare. He was uncertain how he felt about that, for he was the one who did the pursuing on most occasions.

Frances chuckled as she retrieved her wine glass. "Never have you denied me a kiss," she said with that same sly smile she had worn so often before. "I have known many men, my Lord, and those who do not wish to share in a kiss have found a woman who has stolen their heart."

John considered her words. She was right, of course; he was not one to withhold a kiss. So, why was that the case now? He chuckled. "Perhaps next time I see you I will have a kiss for you."

She leaned over and touched his cheek. "If you ever need a friend, I am here. Now, leave and do not let me see you again."

John nodded and walked away, stopping near the entrance to the foyer. In times past he had entertained himself with women such as Frances in establishments such as these. Now, however, he realized those times were behind him. He was uncertain what lay ahead, but as he stepped out into the night, he knew he had to decipher it. And soon, for it was not in his nature to pass up a free kiss!

***

The wood crackled in the fireplace and the flames danced as Hannah took a sip of her wine. She had never been one for drinking spirits, unlike Juliet who seemed to have an endless supply on hand, but the wine relaxed her and gave her an excuse to sit in the parlor as she did now to wait for John to return.

Since her attempt to fall into his arms, the man had changed. Perhaps it was that inner change of which Sally had spoken and it needed more time to develop, but since that night at the party, John seemed to avoid her. When they went out, he engaged in conversation with her, yet he lacked the same interest he had possessed initially. In fact, when they visited the museum, the man had smiled only once during the entire outing. And she had missed that smile, for when he did so, her heart soared and her legs grew weak.

What a woman such as she would be doing having romantic notions for any man was beyond her. However, she could no longer deny the fact that she was attracted to him, and she enjoyed the warmth such feelings profited. Perhaps it was time for her to allow them to blossom, for many of the books she read said that few women could fight off such attraction.

One question still remained, however. Would she be able to balance her growing affection for John and maintain her love of writing? For her writing was her first true love, and she was unsure if she was ready to give it up just yet.

The sound of the front door opening made her sit up straight as a rush of excitement came through her. The last few nights when they had returned from one outing or another, John had rejected her invitation to join her for a drink. Therefore, she decided that she would already be waiting upon his return this evening. If he came to the library, he would have no excuse not to stay.

As expected,, the door opened, and John entered the room. "Laurence, I must ask your advice on something." He stopped when he saw her sitting in the room. "Oh, my apologies for disturbing you. I thought my cousin was here." He turned to leave, but Hannah called out to him.

"Please, stay," she said. "That is...I could use the company."

John seemed to study the open door, but much to her delight, he turned and made his way to the liquor cart. "Another glass of wine?" he asked.

Hannah nodded. "Please." She was thrilled he had taken notice of what she was drinking. It meant he took notice of *her*.

"I am surprised you are awake at this hour," he said as he poured the drinks.

"I found I could not sleep and decided to come here to read," Hannah said, which was partly true. "I assume your evening went well?"

"Well enough," he said, although he winced before he replied. He handed her the drink and took a seat in the chair opposite her.

She had hoped he would sit beside her. If she had not fallen into his arms as she had, making a complete fool of herself, she would not have chased him off. How confused he must be! This was not what she wanted for him.

What was she doing? She could not stop the guilt that grew inside. Had she already given up the woman she was for the first man in whom she had found an interest? It was so unlike her! Yet, was that not exactly what the heroines did in the books she read?

"I am pleased to hear," she replied. "A gentleman must be allowed time alone in order to partake in what he enjoys."

He raised his brows. "Is that so?"

"Oh, yes. In fact, when I am to marry one day, my husband will be able to do whatever he pleases with my blessing. As long as he is willing to allow me to do the same."

"I thought you were not concerned with marriage," he said with a small smile. "You told me as much."

Hannah's cheeks burned. "Well, that is true. I was merely speaking in theory."

He chuckled. "I see." He turned to look at the fireplace, appearing as if his mind were somewhere else. Had she done the right thing in asking him to stay? He had said the evening went 'well enough'. Did that mean it did not go well?

How selfish I am, she thought. "Is there something bothering you?" she asked. "If you need someone to confide in, I would be happy to listen. I promise I will keep whatever you share to myself."

"I appreciate you saying so," John replied. "That is what makes you a wonderful woman."

Hannah grasped her glass tightly to keep from beaming, but she was certain her blush had to have given away her feelings, for she could not seem to control the heat in her cheeks.

John leaned an elbow on the arm of the chair. "To be honest, I am well enough. It is just that I am burdened with a choice I must make."

"Oh?" Hannah said. "What sort of choice?"

"Business, of course," he replied and then sighed. "It is a business decision that I must make, and although the rewards may be great, I find myself a bit concerned if I accept. There is a chance the other party may be hurt in the process."

"I wish I knew more of business," Hannah said with a shake of her head, and she spoke the truth. If there was one thing she hated it was the manner in which men thought women too senseless to understand anything beyond embroidery or playing the pianoforte, something Hannah had been forced to learn but despised. "Regrettably, I know nothing about it. If you need advice on a book to read or something of a literary nature, I may be of help, however."

John smiled. "Your listening ear is most helpful," he said as he placed his glass on the table. "Well, I must be off to bed. Thank you again for lending your ear."

"Wait," Hannah said when he rose from the chair. "How might you hurt this associate?"

He looked down at his hands. "In the past, I made a bad decision that caused me to lose much and someone suffered in the process."

"And you feel badly about this?" Hannah asked as she studied the man before her. How often had she and her sisters disagreed on one thing or another? Conducting business could not be much different.

"I do."

"If it is a mistake," she said firmly, "and you mean not to make the same again, then you should move forward with confidence."

"And if I were to fail again?" he asked, his voice earnest. "Or if the person learns of my previous lapse and becomes angry that I had not divulged that information sooner? What do I do then?"

Why did he not simply tell her the details of this deal? It would make it much easier for her to give advice. Unfortunately, she could do nothing more than shrug. "Perhaps the person will understand."

He tilted his head and gave her a considering look. "I will think on your words," he said. "Thank you again for listening, and good evening to you." He bowed and left the room, leaving Hannah to stare after him.

Isabel would have the wisdom to advise him, she thought. However, despite his unwillingness to share in his problem, she could not help but notice the twinge of pain in his eyes. Perhaps there would be some way in which she could lend him aid. If only he would tell her what problem on which he was working! Men!

Chapter Eleven

The more time Hannah spent in London, the more she found the city a bright and vibrant place. In the two weeks she had been there, she had attended not one but two parties, a dinner with a distant relative of Laurence and a late tea with a friend of Isabel's. Besides the busy social calendar, she had purchased two new dresses that would be delivered in another week, a new pair of shoes, new gloves, and a variety of silk flowers to add to her hats. Although her initial reaction had been one of disdain and aversion, she found that she rather enjoyed her time here.

She would be the first to admit that the reason behind her enjoyment had more to do with the time she was spending with John than the outings themselves. They shared in similar interests, and he was ever so handsome. Yet, it was the manner in which he made her feel special that brought about this strange feeling of pleasure at every turn. He told her often that he admired her desire to write, which increased her belief that perhaps some men did not view women writers in the same way as most men did.

Although she had spent most of her time indulging in the interests of others, tonight was for her alone. She and Isabel were on their way to a secret meeting for writers; Isabel had spoken with certain people in order to gain an invitation. In her hands she clutched the ledger that hid her writing.

She watched the passing brick buildings with their ornate archways leading to the homes of the *ton*. Many would be preparing for one party or another hoping to find a suitable partner. She could have been one of those people, but luck had been on her side when fate placed John into her life. She had come to accept the fact that she was more than simply intrigued with him; not an easy feat when she had been so opposed to such a union for so long.

"You are quiet," Isabel said from the seat across from her. "Are you already thinking of the meeting tonight?"

The meeting. The reason for her agreement to come to London in the first place had now become secondary to why she wished to stay. John was the first. How strange that life could change so quickly.

"I am," Hannah replied. "You must tell Laurence how thankful I am for allowing this. He is very kind, even more than I had first thought."

"I will tell him," Isabel said. "He thinks much of you and Juliet; although, I do tend to disagree with him." She wore a tiny smile as she said this, and Hannah flicked her hand at her playfully. "I hope this meeting will help you with your book. Are you any further along in completing it?"

Hannah sighed. "No. We have been so busy, and, I am unsure how to explain it, but I am struggling to finish it."

"Certainly you have not lost interest?"

"Oh, most definitely not," Hannah replied. "I have grown to love the characters, yet now that the man is to propose to the woman, I find it difficult to write." There was more to it than she included in her explanation, but how could a woman who had never even considered love write such an idea into a story? Nothing she attempted felt right.

"I am unsure what to say, save this. Enjoy the meeting this evening, and perhaps the society will be able to lend you aid."

Hannah nodded. "That is my hope. It is why I seek their guidance. So many are far more experienced and have a greater knowledge than I."

Isabel laughed. "I would doubt that."

"Oh, but it is true." She leaned forward in the seat. "Albert was very..." Her words trailed off and she closed her mouth. Guilt overtook her as she recalled the kind man and his offer of marriage.

Perhaps she should write another letter giving him her answer.

"What is it?" Isabel moved to sit beside Hannah. "I can see it clearly on your face." She sat back and raised her brows. "Do you care for that man?"

"No, not in a romantic sense. You see, before we left for London, I was unsure if I needed him."

Isabel frowned. "Needed him? I am not sure I understand."

"What I mean is, although I did not want to marry him, I thought it best to leave that option open."

"Oh, Hannah," Isabel said with a sigh. "What did you tell him exactly?"

"That I was undecided and would give him my decision upon my return." She said the words in a near whisper, for she now understood how horrible she had been to the man. "I did not mean to give him false hope; honestly, I did not. And now I regret the manner in which I treated him."

"Then you must make it right," Isabel replied firmly. "Tonight, after dinner, you will write him a kind letter explaining that you wish to refuse his proposal. Make certain it is thoughtful; you do not want to hurt him further."

Hannah nodded. "I will. I promise."

Isabel placed a hand on Hannah's. "You are a good woman, and it will be a testament to your upbringing how you handle this situation." The carriage slowed, and Isabel glanced out the window. "Now, enjoy your evening. Lady Ellen has offered you her carriage when the meeting ends."

"I will," Hannah replied. She gave her sister a hug and then grabbed her book. "Thank you again for this."

Isabel smiled, and Hannah alighted from the carriage. The townhouse belonging to Lady Ellen Bismark had a bright red door and looming windows, and as she steadied her breathing, all thoughts of John and the London season dissipated from her thoughts. Now was the time to seek aid in fulfilling her dream.

With confident steps, she made her way to the door, which opened before she was able to knock. A butler, who was quite young for such a position, stood at attention.

"Miss Lambert," the man said with a bow. "Lady Ellen is expecting you. Please follow me."

Hannah stepped into the house. It was smaller than she expected, but it might have been due to the deep red walls that peeked from between so many paintings, it was as if they were fighting for space. Along the walls sat numerous tables, each with some sort of sculpture or figurine, and between each table stood a potted tree. Hannah felt as if she were walking through a dense forest, a well-decorated forest, as she followed the butler to a set of double doors, each with a wreath hanging from it.

With heart racing, she waited as the man opened the doors. How many members would be in attendance? Had any of them published before? Would they be able to help her with completing her novel? Did she have the nerve to even speak?

"Miss Lambert," the butler announced when he opened the door.

The room differed from the foyer only because the walls were white rather than red. Five women, two in clothing that was all black, sat in several club chairs and a settee, each with a glass of wine in her hand. By no means ancient, most had more gray in their hair than any other color.

"Ah, here she is," a woman said as she rose from her chair. She was the youngest of the group, perhaps only a few years older than Hannah, with pretty blond hair and blue eyes. "Hannah, we have been expecting you. I am Ellen; we do not use titles in our little group. We find it much too restrictive."

"Thank you for having me," Hannah replied.

Ellen walked over to a corner, the skirts of her red dress flowing around her ankles, to where several bottles of spirits were displayed. "A glass of wine, my dear?" she asked, although she was already pouring.

"Yes, please," Hannah replied.

"This is your first season, is it not?" Ellen asked.

"It is. I was ill last year and therefore unable to attend."

Ellen gave her a small smile. "A mystery illness?" she asked with a wink. "It seems to inflict many select women in their first season."

Hannah could not help but laugh. The woman made her feel comfortable, and she had a suspicion the two would become good friends.

"Now, ladies," Ellen said, "I would like to introduce the newest member of our society. Hannah."

The ladies gave polite smiles, and Hannah felt awkward standing as they seemed to appraise her.

"This is Diana. She has not written a word in, what is it, dear? Four years?"

The woman named Diana, her hair gray with touches of brown, nodded. "I believe that is so. However, I wonder why you must remind me at every turn." She spoke in a teasing manner, and Hannah could see the camaraderie the two women shared

When the remainder of the introductions were made—Dorthea, Matilda and Frederica were very polite and had a whimsy about them that matched that of Ellen—Hannah was finally offered a chair. When Ellen returned to hers—a club chair covered in the deepest red Hannah had ever seen—her skirts seemed to disappear into the fabric. Hannah had to purse her lips to keep from laughing.

After a few more minutes of polite conversation, Ellen raised her glass and called the meeting to order. "We have important matters to discuss this evening, and I feel we are safe speaking of them in the company of our newest member."

Hannah could barely contain her excitement. "Yes, I shall tell no one of the matters of which are discussed here. You have my word." This did surprise her; women meeting to discuss the craft of writing would not have been widely accepted, and she would do nothing to undermine its existence.

"And there we are, ladies," Ellen said with a wide smile. "She is to be trusted."

Hannah took a sip of her wine. Although she did not know these women, she decided already she liked them.

"With that being said," Ellen continued, "we must discuss Lord Hudson."

The other women nodded, but Hannah paused. Did this Lord Hudson own a publishing business? Perhaps he had a connection that allowed the women to gain an audience with other authors.

Ellen leaned forward as she lowered her voice and said, "He was spotted on St. James Street, and the establishment he entered was questionable indeed."

The women gasped in unison.

Hannah was confused. "Do you mean a publisher's office?" she asked.

Several of the women laughed, and Ellen replied, "No, my dear. St. James Street is where men spend the majority of their time, and there exist some men's clubs where gambling and prostitution reign. Let us just say that Lord Hudson went into a house not inhabited by nuns."

Hannah's eyes went wide as the realization of what this woman meant, and Ellen continued her story. Although her reason for attending the meeting had nothing to do with such matters, she found herself intrigued by the stories. All women enjoyed sharing in the latest news, and Hannah had to be patient, for she suspected the discussion would eventually turn to their writing. Therefore, as she sipped at her wine, she listened with interest.

***

John regretted few things in life, and telling Laurence he had no interest in any sort of relationship with Hannah had proven to be one of the greatest. He should have spoken up and told the man the woman had captured his interest, and that these new feelings inside him were overwhelming. However, Hannah deserved better than he, and therefore, John kept his thoughts to himself.

This evening, Lord Oakley had invited him over for dinner, a lovely broiled salmon and stewed spinach, and they had shared in pleasant conversation with Miss Oakley in attendance. Now, however, they sat in the drawing room, a bright room filled with golds, yellows and browns, sipping brandy and discussing business, and John was glad Miss Oakley had indicated she had matters to deal with elsewhere. Throughout the meal, the Viscount's daughter had sent him several smiles with which John was all too familiar, and John was well aware that her father had noticed.

The fact of the matter was, after Hannah, he found Miss Oakley so much like other women, she may as well have been plain. However, he doubted Lord Oakley would appreciate John's thoughts on his daughter.

"This is the finest brandy in all of London, would you not agree?" Lord Oakley asked.

"It has an interesting flavor," John replied. "May I ask where you procured it?"

Lord Oakley laughed as he stood before the fireplace, the roaring fire behind him giving him an evil aura. "Now, why would I tell you that?" the older man asked. "In order for you to serve it at a party? I think not." The man laughed again and went to a chair covered in yellow and brown stripes. "I must ask you, Stanford, why have you not secured a bride?"

The question caught John off-guard. This man was blunt, to be sure. "The last few seasons, I have not had the pleasure of meeting the right woman," John said, and an image of Hannah popped into his head. "That is until…"

"My Catherine," the Viscount replied for him. "Do not think I did not notice your shared smiles at the dinner table. For the last two seasons, I thought she would find a suitable husband; however, now that she has met you, I am beginning to believe this season will finally be her last."

John swallowed hard. If he spoke the truth now, what would happen to the business deal? Yet, how could he allow this man to believe he was interested in his daughter? And how did he keep finding himself in these situations? "I do not think…"

"No, you are right," Lord Oakley said with a wave of his hand. "Such matters should be discussed at a later date. You are here for business and I suspect that is where your mind is."

"You have read my thoughts," John replied, relief washing over him. "You mentioned seeking a partner for some businesses you have. What types of matters were you considering?" The man had a vast empire of wine, and John was well aware of the money the man gleaned from his investments. If John could have even the smallest portion of the business, he would be a wealthy man indeed.

"Each year, the parks and streets become more crowded. Men seeking women and women seeking shops. On Portland Street, I am in the process of securing new properties, which include a jeweler's and a millinery."

"I am afraid I have little experience in those types of businesses," John said, feeling deflated. "I doubt I would make a wise partner."

"The truth of the matter is, I do not need a partner to run them, for I have the proper staff in place already for that. Rather, I am in need of an overseer of sorts. You see, if we were to do this together, you overseeing these new customs would allow me to pursue other business matters elsewhere."

"Elsewhere?"

"Indeed," the man said. "Too many years I have come to London, and I grow weary of it. I would like to spend the rest of my days outside of the city. Many areas outside of London are growing exponentially, and I want to be a part of that."

"I agree. Since I was a boy, I have seen villages grow to the extent they are nearly cities."

"And they will continue to do so," the Viscount said. "Therefore, my question is this. Do you plan on staying in London for the foreseeable future?"

"I do," John replied. "To be honest, I came this season with plans to remain here."

Lord Oakley slapped his knee. "That is wonderful. My Catherine wishes to remain, as well, and is never remiss to mention it. It would be wise to consider courting her, for my hand is in many profitable enterprises."

John stifled a sigh. "I will need time to consider it, but I would hope to conduct business with you regardless of my decision of courting your daughter."

The Viscount tapped a finger to his lips. "Admirable. I respect your reply, for in truth, it was a test."

"A test?" John asked.

"Indeed," the man said with a laugh. "It was the very fact you did not say yes immediately that is a testament of an acute businessman, one who does not make quick decisions but rather thinks things through beforehand." He refilled John's glass although it was not yet empty.

"I appreciate you believing so," John said.

The older man placed the decanter on a nearby table. "Now that we have gotten that out of the way, I do want you to consider speaking to my daughter again. She will make a wonderful bride."

"I do not mean to be rude," John said carefully. The last thing he wanted to do was offend this man, "but I must…"

"Father?"

John turned to find Miss Oakley at the door, and he jumped to his feet.

"My apologies for interrupting, but I am worried for Lucy."

Lord Oakley frowned. "Your lady's maid?" he asked. "What is wrong with her?"

"She has a pain in her stomach," Miss Oakley replied. "Will you come check on her?"

"I suppose I can," the Viscount said. "I will return shortly."

John nodded. This would give him the opportunity to leave without incident. Unfortunately, Miss Oakley smiled at him as she had in the times prior; however, this time it had a slyness to it that he had not noticed before. He shook his head. Perhaps it was simply his imagination.

"Have your discussions with Father gone well?" Miss Oakley asked as she came to stand before him.

"They have," John replied.

She moved in closer to him, and he had to fight the urge to take a step back. "I am glad we are alone."

"Are you?"

"Oh, yes," she said breathily. "That is what I have been wanting since your arrival, and the reason Lucy is pretending to be ill. Now my father is busy with her, and I am here with you."

John was at a loss for words. He had encountered many women such as Miss Oakley, and he had enjoyed their company. This woman, however, reminded him too much of another, one whose relationship had not ended so well.

"You see," she cooed, "I am a collector of sorts."

"A collector?" He went to take a drink of his brandy, but she took the glass from his hand and took a sip. She grimaced. "Father has poor taste. The bottles in my bedroom are far better." She set the glass aside. "As to my collection…"

"I believe we have…"

She placed a hand on his chest. "I must first collect payment."

He gaped at her. "Miss Oakley, this is most inappropriate."

She smiled as she snaked a finger between the buttons of his waistcoat. "I have seen many men such as you," she whispered. "Men who believe their smiles and words can woo a woman and in turn win their heart. However, I am no fool. In fact, I know what you seek, for it is what I seek, as well."

She leaned in and touched her lips to his, and when she moved away, she held a five pound note in her fingers. "You see, I collect kisses, and I thank you for the payment." She slid the note into the front of her dress, her eyes sparkling as if daring him to go after it. "Tell Father you have no interest in me for I have none in you." She then winked, gave a mock curtsy, and left the room, leaving John to gape after her.

What had just happened? In a way, he wanted to laugh, for if he told anyone about his interaction with the daughter of the Viscount, he would not be believed. And he could not blame them, for he would not have believed it if he had not experienced it himself.

The truth of the matter was he had been bested at his own game!

So, why did he feel shame? Had he not done nearly the same to dozens of women? However, as thoughts of Hannah entered his mind, he realized the foundation of his guilt; if she were to learn of this kiss, whatever relationship they had developed, as limited as it was, would disintegrate.

"She is well, now," Lord Oakley said when he returned. "Women are prone to make matters worse than they are. You have yet to endure the wails of a woman in childbirth." He shook his head as if the memory was unfathomable.

"Yes, well, if you will forgive me, I must be on my way. I have matters at home to attend to."

"Yes, I must complete some work of my own. Shall we meet again?"

"Yes, I believe we should," John said, although business was the last thing on his mind at the moment. In fact, all he cared for was seeing Hannah and asking permission to court her. He would have to take a chance, and if she learned of his past, he was confident she would forgive him. After his encounter with Lady Catherine, what he wanted became abundantly clear, and being without Hannah was a punishment he could no longer endure.

Once outside, he wiped his mouth in disgust on the sleeve of his coat, the thought of what had transpired making his stomach churn. He took a deep breath and stepped into his waiting carriage, ready to tell Hannah what he felt for her.

Chapter Twelve

As each minute passed, Hannah began to realize that the writing society was less about writing and more a gossip club. In the beginning, the talk had been interesting, but as they continued to discuss all sorts of sordid matters—gentleman in houses of ill-repute and gambling halls, women who carried children from men who were not their husbands and the like—she became more disheartened. She felt horrible for the actions of many and prayed they were not true, for how could two people swear a life together only to consort with a servant?

"Her father is quite upset, of course," Matilda croaked, her black dress giving her already pale skin a sickly look to it. "By all rights, he should be after all the money he spent on her dresses." The other women nodded, and Ellen smiled at Hannah.

Her eyes dropped to the book in Hannah's hands, and as if recognizing her discomfiture, said, "Ladies, I believe our newest member may be here to seek our aid with her writing. Therefore, before we are able to bring this meeting to a close, we should listen and offer whatever advice we are able."

Relieved, Hannah smiled. All was not lost after all! She took one last sip of her wine, realizing she had consumed more then was customary for her, for she felt a bit giddy. "It has been my dream for a very long time to become a published author."

"As is with many women," Frederica said, her wrinkled features reminding Hannah of a prune, "you will soon learn that dreams are best left as dreams and nothing more."

Not caring for such advice, Hannah ignored the woman and continued. "Currently, the man will ask the woman for her hand, but although the characters love one another, I feel as if an important piece is missing."

Dorthea sighed. "You are young, and I understand the problem you are facing, for I came to the same predicament in my story."

"You did?" Hannah asked in surprise.

"Indeed. You see, in these types of stories, the man swears his loyalty to the heroine and promises her all her dreams will come true, but the truth is, no such men exist. Therefore, it makes writing about him practically impossible."

"I find that difficult to believe," Hannah replied firmly. "Surely these novels have some bases of truth?" She looked at each of the women for reassurance in her statement but did not find it. "But what of your writing? Surely you have used some of your own life experiences to create your stories." The women looked at one another, and Hannah was in shock. "You mean, you have all given up on your writing because you have lost your belief in it? What is a writing society where writing is not the topic of discussion?"

Matilda looked down at her hands. "We do speak of it from time to time, and some of us still put words to parchment. However, we have come to know that finding anyone willing to publish anything but poetry by a woman is near impossible. Also, if one did find a publisher willing to secure her work, would her husband agree? I tell you, it is unlikely."

"I thought the right man would do such a thing," Hannah said with annoyance. This group was far different than the one she had attended in Albert's cottage. However, most who attended those meetings were younger, as was she, and therefore saw the world much differently from these women.

"The hour grows late," Ellen said, and the ladies began to rise. "We shall meet again next week."

Hannah remained seated and forced a smile as the women bid their farewells and left one by one. When only she and Ellen remained, they walked out to a carriage that awaited out front.

"I suspect our meeting was not to your liking," Ellen said.

Should she be honest and risk offending the woman? Had she not been kind enough to allow Hannah to attend? "It was pleasant and I enjoyed myself," she said. However, the lie did not sit well with her. "I did not expect the advice that was given, if I were to be honest.

"The others have a way of saying what they think regardless of how it may be received. Although what they said seemed cruel, it was the truth."

"That I should give up on my dream?" Hannah asked in shock. "Since I was a child, I have wanted to write stories, and I am so close. I cannot turn back now."

"May I give you a bit of advice?" Ellen asked kindly.

Hannah nodded. "Please."

"I, too, was once like you," the woman said sadly. "I dreamed of writing a novel that would take the world by storm. Then I met my husband, who sadly passed nearly two years ago."

"My condolences," Hannah said.

"Thank you." Ellen smoothed her skirts, as if what she said made her uncomfortable. "Although Patrick did not support me in writing, he did not stop me. It was my vow that, after my children were grown and married, I would take it up once again. However, I was not blessed with children before his death, and my days remained busy with other things. Now, if I am honest, the passion I once had left with Patrick's passing."

"I believe I understand," Hannah replied. How her heart hurt for this woman, but she hoped she, herself, would not be forced to have such an outcome in her life.

"Do you wish to marry and have children one day?"

If it had been a month earlier, Hannah would have given an adamant no. Now, however, she was not as certain. "I believe so," she replied. "I have found myself interested in a man..." She might not have notions of marrying any time soon, but the possibility of marrying John was intriguing.

"Then your time will be spent with your family. As it should be. My advice is to finish your book before you are wed, for you will have no time once that occurs."

"What if he supports me?" Hannah asked. "Surely it will be fine to do so if that is the case?"

Ellen chuckled and patted Hannah's hand. "Of course, it would be. However, the point is this. You cannot have two dreams that interfere with one another. Finish your book and then move on to a life as other ladies do."

"Is that why Dorthea advised as she did?" Hannah asked. "That my struggle with my novel is not based on enough fact? That once wed, a woman must give up on her dreams? Is that why I struggle?"

"You struggle because you are innocent, and that is a beautiful thing. Regardless of what you have heard tonight, if you seek to finish and publish your book, then do so. I wish the best for you."

"Thank you," Hannah said. "It is my dream, and I will not stop until it is fulfilled. That much I can promise you."

"Then we will drink to your success," Ellen said with a warm smile. "You are welcome to return to any of the meetings, although I believe you have learned what little you can from us."

Hannah nodded. "I will think on it. Thank you."

The driver opened the door, and Hannah moved toward the carriage, but Ellen grabbed her arm.

"The season can be difficult to navigate, especially the first time. I believe we are friends, and I suspect we will become even more so. You never have to send a card, so please come by my house if you need someone with whom to speak or if you are simply in need of companionship."

Hannah placed her hand on top of that of Ellen. "I will, thank you." She stepped into the carriage in much better spirits. Hannah found Ellen very likable and she was certain they would meet again, and sooner rather than later.

During her journey to the townhouse, she thought of what she wanted from life. She *would* finish her novel regardless, but she also could not stop thinking of John. Would he, as he had said, allow her to pursue her dreams? Was he as interested in her as she was in him?

Or was she that innocent young girl Ellen mentioned this evening? She could only answer these questions if she spoke to John.

Once home, Hannah was pleased to see Isabel and Laurence approaching in the foyer.

"How was your evening?" Isabel asked.

"It was not what I expected, but I did enjoy myself," Hannah replied. "I admit I learned much. Thank you again for allowing me to attend." She glanced toward the drawing room. She wanted to speak to John and tell him of the night's events. "Is John occupied? It seems he has all but disappeared as of late."

"He went to dine at the home of Lord Oakley," Laurence replied. He reached into his pocket a produced a card. "This came for you earlier."

Hannah whispered her thanks and took the card, her heart sinking. She had forgotten John had meant to go to the house of Lady Oakley and her father, and she found the idea of him being with the woman in any capacity made her sad. In fact, it tore at her heart, and she worried the woman had won him over while she, Hannah, played the silly girl.

"Lord Cecil Cooper wishes to call over," Hannah said after she read the card. "Do I know him?"

"I believe you two met at the party Hugh gave," Isabel replied. "Do you recall the man speaking of museums?"

Hannah nodded, remembering vaguely a bore of a man with red hair and a long nose.

"Will you accept?"

It was just the thing that would keep her mother and Isabel happy, but she had no interest in making a decision at the moment. What she wished to do was speak to John, to learn if he had any interest in Miss Oakley, or if his interests lay elsewhere.

To her delight, the front door opened and John entered.

"Are we hosting a party in the foyer?" he asked, his eyes bright and his breath reeking of alcohol. To make matters worse, a long blond hair clung to the shoulder of his coat.

So, I suppose I have my answer already, Hannah thought, her stomach doing flips as she attempted to keep down her evening meal.

"We were just discussing Hannah's evening," Laurence said with a laugh. "Did your meeting go well?"

"Yes," John replied. "I have a good chance of doing business with Lord Oakley here in London. A jeweler's, of all things."

Just the thought of John spending his days in such a place made Hannah want to weep. She imagined him adorning Miss Oakley with the jewels he had on hand, of him slipping a gold ring on her finger.

When he had spoken of business a few nights earlier, Hannah had not understood then that he spoke of Miss Oakley's father.

Why had she been distraught over his happiness? She was not his mother, nor his keeper. In all reality, she should have been relieved; had she not been concerned with the path she had nearly gone down?

What bothered her most was the realization that she had pushed him into the arms of another woman with her flippant behavior. Juliet might be able to act in such a headstrong manner, but it was not becoming of Hannah. She had to stick to her books, for that was where her strength lay.

"As to your earlier question," Hannah interjected, doing her best to keep her emotions under control, "I believe I shall send Lord Cooper a reply first thing in the morning. It would be an honor to spend time with such a respectable man. Will you help me choose the right dress? I wish to plan now, if you are available."

"I am," Isabel said with a wide smile. She gave Laurence a quick kiss on the cheek. "I will speak with you later."

As they walked up the stairs, Hannah glanced over her shoulder and felt a sense of confusion wash over her, for the smile John had been wearing when he entered was gone, and a frown had now taken its place.

***

John sat brooding in the library, a book in his lap, of which he had yet to read a word. It had been five days since he had returned to find Hannah speaking of accepting a card from another man. The thought of the sender of that card having an interest in her made him both angry and sad, his frustration directed more at himself than anyone else.

How could he have allowed himself to have feelings for the woman? Then he had mussed it all with the wild belief that he was not good enough for her. Now he had driven her right into the arms of another man, and he had no one to blame but himself.

His choice of the library had been twofold. It was a quiet place in which to think, but his true desire was to be in the room in case she chose to bring her Lord Cooper there. So far, however, the two had closeted themselves—and Isabel—in the drawing room.

The door opened, and John closed the book but was disappointed when Laurence entered the room.

"I secured tickets for The Royal Theater this Friday evening in Covent Garden," Laurence said. "And, before you ask, I have a ticket for you, as well."

John smiled as Laurence took the seat opposite him. "That is wonderful," he replied. "Thank you for your generosity. I look forward to attending."

Laurence waved a hand of dismissal. "Think nothing of it. We are family, and I..." He paused and frowned. "You seem different. Is everything all right?"

John set the book aside. There was no sense in keeping secret his burden. "I believe I may have made a horrible, and costly, mistake."

"Oh?" Laurence asked as he leaned forward. "And what mistake would that be?"

"You see," John said, hoping he would not sound as foolish as he felt, "it has to do with Hannah."

Laurence sat back, a surprised look on his face. "Hannah? What has the girl done now?"

"Forgive me. She has done nothing wrong. I am struggling to get the words right."

Laurence chuckled. "Sometimes it is best to simply say them."

"Very well," John said. "The fact of the matter is, I have come to find her company more agreeable than I would have thought. What began as a favor to you and Isabel has become something more." He glanced down to find his hands clenched so tightly, his knuckles were white. "When I returned from my business meeting with Lord Oakley, I was more certain than ever that Hannah is a lady I would like to court."

To John's surprise, Laurence laughed. "Why, that is wonderful!" he said. "Yet, with such good news, why are you so glum?"

"She is in the other room entertaining Lord Cooper," John said with a sigh. "I am afraid I may have missed my opportunity and another man has beat me to it. I do not blame her, for I waited much too long to approach her. Yet, now that I have found my courage to do so, it is too late."

What he had hoped was to receive wise council but was taken aback when the man merely nodded. The room was eerily quiet for some time, and John shifted in his seat. However, as the minutes ticked by, he found he could wait no longer. "If Lady Lambert or Isabel feel me unworthy of calling on Hannah in an official capacity, then I suppose I would understand."

Laurence shook his head. "No, I am sure her mother would approve, and I believe Isabel already does. What does concern me, however, is whether or not your feelings for her are true."

"How can you say such a thing?" John asked. "You dare question my motives?"

Laurence raised a hand. "Now, now," he said. "I do not doubt your integrity. However, I do wonder if by my hand forcing the two of you together has brought about possible false feelings."

"I can assure you it did not. You see, I have told Hannah I was interested in books and poetry and a host of other things when I was not. Granted, we have many subjects in which we do not share an interest; however, somehow I cannot stop thinking about her. It is as if she has taken possession of me."

"It sounds much like when Isabel and I first married," Laurence said with a sigh. "There were circumstances, many of which do not need repeating, nor do they matter, for there was a spark between us." He walked over and placed a hand on John's shoulder. "It was my determination to win Isabel's heart that won in the end. If you feel this strongly for Hannah, which it seems you do, then tell her."

"And if I were to ask her and she rejects me? What then?"

"Do you care for her?"

John nodded. "I do."

"Then you will want her to be happy no matter her reply." He squeezed John's shoulder. "I will leave you to your thoughts, but remember this. Sometimes one must give up what he believes he wants if he is to get what he truly wishes."

When Laurence was gone, John stood and walked over to a window, which looked out over a small garden. A movement caught his eyes, and he watched as Hannah and Lord Cooper walked together along the path, Isabel following behind them. What he expected was a joyous or happy expression, but what he saw instead was sadness. Perhaps it was not too late after all!

Hurrying to a small writing desk, he took out a piece of parchment and found a quill. He had no idea how this plan would work, but if he did not make the attempt, she would be lost to him forever.

Chapter Thirteen

In preparation for Lord Cooper's arrival, Hannah had selected a white dress with a lace pattern along the hem of the skirts as well as the sleeves. With the matching gloves adorned with lace, she felt beautiful, and Isabel had told her as much.

As she sat in the drawing room, Lord Cooper sitting across from her and Isabel at her side, Hannah could not stop her mind from drifting to John. When he had returned home that evening five days ago with that blond hair on his coat, her flustered heart had forced her to blurt out the acceptance of Lord Cooper's request to call. Perhaps allowing the man to go to the arms of Miss Oakley had been the wise choice at the time, but now as Lord Cooper continued to speak, she realized what a mistake that had been.

"It was then when I came to the conclusion," Lord Cooper was saying, his arrogance prevalent, "that the servants in my household, although loyal, are a simple lot. It is quite confounding that they manage to survive in life at all."

Hannah offered the man a smile in an attempt to show interest in what he had to say, but it was not an easy task. Lord Cooper was perhaps thirty years of age with red hair and features that she would not have considered unpleasant, if it were not for his nose getting in the way. She wondered why he had never married, but now that she had endured his incessant complaining, she began to suspect the reasons why. He spoke only of himself, what he possessed, and had not a good word to say about any of it. Not once did he ask anything of Hannah.

"Nevertheless, they serve me well, and I have selected a few to travel with me to London for the season. In the past, I have been much too occupied with other matters than to take time for myself or to search for a potential bride. Yet, this season has bestowed upon me a gift—the chance to pursue what I want." The grin the man wore made Hannah wish to excuse herself and run away. Then, much to her surprise, he asked her a question. "How are you finding the season thus far?"

"I am enjoying it," she replied, glad at the opportunity to speak for the first time. "The parties have been lovely, and the atmosphere..."

"Such a waste of money," he interrupted with a dismissive wave of his hand. "It is why I host my parties toward the end of the season, when everyone has had their fill of wine and food. One must always be careful of their expenditures."

Hannah looked to Isabel for help, and like before, the woman came to her rescue. "Lord Cooper, I am curious to know. In what activities do you partake when your busy schedule leaves little time for socializing?"

"A most excellent question, Your Grace," he replied. "I am honored to answer it."

Hannah tried to suppress her frown. Since Isabel had become a duchess, the manner in which the *ton* spoke to her had changed dramatically. If Isabel said the sky was blue, the *ton* would applaud her and marvel at how acute her observations were.

"Like most gentlemen," the man replied, "I prefer to hunt than to attend parties. However, I do enjoy a good book. One must be well read to get ahead in this world."

For the first time, Hannah smiled. Perhaps a part of the man was human after all. "Which novels have you read?" she asked.

Lord Cooper drew back as if she had spit poison and burned the man with her words. "Novels?" he said with a sneer. "I do not read such rubbish, for they only make the mind lazy. I only read books concerning true subjects, but I am particularly fond of books on business. Have you read The *Wealth of Nations* by Adam Smith? No, of course you would not. Few women find such intellect intriguing."

As the man droned on about what he considered the best book ever written, Hannah found her thoughts turning once again to John and his love of books. How she wished he was here instead of this man! But no, he would be thinking of Miss Oakley rather than her if he were here.

"The day is lovely," Isabel said. "Would you like to take a stroll through the garden? The flowers are gone for the season, but the air will do us all a bit of good."

"That is the most excellent of ideas," Lord Cooper replied. "Truly, I had secretly hoped to be able to view them."

Hannah considered laughing, but she decided against it. The manner in which he fawned over Isabel was outrageous, even more so than others of the peerage. Casting a glance at her sister, she gave her a small smile, which was returned with a wink. She would have to find a way to thank the woman later.

The day was indeed fine. The sun shining down on them eased the light chill that hung in the air, but anything was better than the confines of the house in the company of the pompous man at her side.

As they walked, Lord Cooper continued his tirade—something about the "filthy chimney sweeps" and how they apparently pilfered some of his silver the last time they had been in his house. She doubted the poor dirty children were the cause of his missing items; if they began stealing, no one would invite them into their homes.

At one point, she glanced up to see John staring out the window to the library. He wore a sad expression that surprised her, and she wondered if there was anything she could do to help. But he turned away from the window and disappeared.

Lord Cooper was complimenting Isabel on a fountain, gushing as heartily as the water that flowed from the jug held by a statue of a woman.

Finally, the moment came when the man went to take his leave, and they walked him to the foyer. "I must be on my way," he said as they headed back to the house. "I hope to send another card and perhaps call over again, if that would be acceptable?"

What Hannah wished to do was decline now, for she would prefer to stare at the walls than to spend another moment in his company.

However, she had made a promise to Isabel.

When Hannah did not respond, Isabel said, "When your schedule allows, do send another card. I am certain Hannah's reply will be as swift as it was before."

"Most excellent, Your Grace," he said, beaming. "Thank you for the tour of your gardens, and for your company, Miss Hannah." He turned to Isabel. "And please inform His Grace how much I enjoyed his home, for I have never seen any finer."

"I will be sure to do that," Isabel replied. "Weber will see you out."

Lord Cooper smiled and walked to the door where the butler waited for him to walk through. Once the door was closed, Isabel let out a sigh. "I have been in the company of some of the driest men in my time, but Lord Cooper is the worst. What a bore!"

Hannah gasped. "Isabel! You should not say such things."

"Oh, do not pretend you do not feel the same way," Isabel said in a whisper. She glanced around her. "You must promise me one thing, however." Hannah nodded. "He is a friend of Laurence, so if he asks, tell him you found the man interesting. I do not want to hurt him by saying unkind words about his friends."

Hannah giggled. "I will do that. However, what do we do if he asks to call over again?"

Before Isabel could respond, John came walking toward them. "Hannah? May I speak to you for a moment?"

Hannah nodded. She glanced down at the letter in his hand. Perhaps Miss Oakley had written to him and he wished to share his joy for its contents.

"I must speak to Laurence," Isabel said before walking away, leaving Hannah and John alone.

"May we go to the garden?" John asked. "I want to share something with you, but I do not want others to overhear."

"I understand," Hannah said. Indeed, this must be about Miss Oakley. Pain stung her heart, and she knew tonight she would weep for what was lost.

Once outside, she followed him to a crossing in the path, far enough away from the house to not be overheard.

"I must tell you about myself, and you..." He shifted on his feet, and Hannah braced herself for the pain that was to come. "I must admit that I find myself at a loss for words," he continued with a weak chuckle.

"I have learned that truth is best spoken from the heart," Hannah said. "That is what Forbes, our butler, told me once."

"He sounds like a wise man."

"He is," Hannah replied. The man was stalling, and she was not helping by allowing him to do so. "Please, say what you need to say."

John held out the letter to her. "For you."

With a trembling hand, she took it from him. "I am unsure if I should read this."

"I would be honored if you did."

Hannah nodded and opened the letter.

My Dearest Hannah,

When I went to the home of Lord Oakley, although we spent our time discussing business, I found I could not stop thinking of you. Forgive me for putting my thoughts to paper, but I did so in hope to appeal to you.

When you accepted Lord Cooper's invitation, I felt a sadness come over me, for I believed that another man might win you over and have the joy of listening to you speak and be in your company. I realize now that I may be too late, but if it is your desire, I would consider myself the luckiest of men if you would allow me to court you.

Sincerely,
John Stanford

She stared at him for a moment, unable to form words, but then she managed to say, "I thought...Miss Oakley..."

"No," he said with a shake of his head. "I have no desire to be around her, and truth be told, I doubt I will see her again unless I do business with her father." He took a step toward her, and Hannah thought she would faint from the nearness of him. "I cannot imagine

114

being in the company of any other woman but you. I am not the man you believe I am, nor is my past one of which I am proud. However, I believe that is behind me and…"

"Yes," Hannah said, her throat dry. "I accept your offer of courtship." Then she surprised herself by throwing her arms around the man. She was even more surprised when his arms encircled her waist, and she found she never wanted to let him go.

However, the moment came, and she released him. "Your past. You mentioned it has bothered you."

John nodded. "I can assure you my foolish ways are behind me. In fact…"

Hannah placed a finger to his lips to halt his words. "It does not matter," she whispered. "The past shall remain behind you…and us. We will speak of it no more."

He smiled down at her, and she found herself returning his smile. "I believe we are best served sharing our good news with your sister and my cousin."

"Yes," Hannah said. "I believe you are right."

With joyous hearts, she took his arm and returned to the house. Hannah had experienced something about which she had only read and written, and like her novel, she knew in her heart the ending would be happy.

***

Candlelight flickered, creating shadows across the wall as Hannah paced her bedroom. How dreary the day had begun, but how wonderful it had ended! Who would have thought that she, Hannah Lambert, lover of books, would have ever been courted by a gentleman and be happy about it? Not only did it please her, her mother would be proud. The only thing missing was Juliet here to share in the good news.

She stopped her pacing and widened her eyes. Courting was a serious matter! The typical road from such an arrangement oftentimes led to marriage. If John were to propose marriage, would she accept? It was not that she could not imagine being married to the man, but she was unsure if she was ready for such a step. And what about her novel?

A knock came to the door, and Hannah smiled as Isabel entered. She could not have been happier to see her.

"For a woman who is courting, you seem more concerned than pleased. Or am I wrong in my assumption?"

"I am pleased, but I find it all a bit unsettling. What if he asks me to marry him?"

Isabel let out a laugh. "I imagine it will be some time before he asks for your hand. From what I gathered earlier, it was difficult enough for the man to ask you to court."

"You were spying on me?"

"I was merely keeping an eye on the two of you," Isabel replied with a small smile. "I saw the eagerness in his face to speak to you, and you were without a chaperon. Let us just say it was my way of chaperoning without interrupting." She tilted her head. "Come, let us sit." They made their way to the settee. "Is something else bothering you?"

Hannah sighed. "I do not believe he would lie to me, but I rather have some concerns." She smoothed her skirts absently. "What of him and Miss Oakley?"

Isabel raised her brows. "Miss Oakley? Why on Earth are you worried about that woman?"

"The night he returned from dinner with Lord Oakley, he had a strand of hair on his coat, and the color matched that of Miss Oakley."

"I see," Isabel said. "Ask yourself one question. Why would John ask to court you if he was interested in another woman? As soon as word got out, what would he gain by maintaining a secret relationship with Miss Oakley?"

Hannah pursed her lips. "You make a valid point. I did not consider that." There was the shame of his past that he had mentioned, but that was not for her to share. Granted, it was still a concern, but she had to push that into the back of her mind. If he wished to inform her, he would. Otherwise, it was John's secret to keep.

"The truth of the matter is," Isabel continued as she took Hannah's hand in hers, "there must be trust in order for any relationship to be successful. Do you trust John with all your heart?"

Hannah did not have to take time to think of her response. "I do. The strange thing is that I believe I have garnered a deep affection for him, but I am unsure. I have read about love and even written about it in some form or another, but this is the first I have experienced it for myself."

"I imagine you will find out for certain soon enough," Isabel said.

Hannah giggled. "Not that I did not want to, but I thought it would be with Juliet you would be having this conversation, not I."

"Why would you believe that?"

"Because I had sworn off the season, suitors, courting...anything that might lead to love." She shook her head in wonderment. "Now I find myself enjoying those things I once despised."

"You never despised the idea of love," Isabel admonished. "You simply did not believe it was right for you. Look at your writing. Do your characters not fall in love?"

"Yes, they do," Hannah said with a laugh. "That does not mean I had plans of such a life. If I had written about pirates, it does not mean I wish to be a pirate."

"No, of course not," Isabel said with a light chuckle. "You know, there was a time when I thought that love was not meant to be; that it only ended in heartbreak."

The words shocked Hannah. Had Isabel not loved her first husband, Arthur? Perhaps it was because he died she spoke as she did. She wished to ask, but Isabel kept her life close to her breast. If she wished to share her story, she would, but not a moment before.

Isabel waved her hand as if the brush away a draft of melancholy. "Be that as it may, we are here in London for the season, and the world lay before you. Enjoy yourself." She rose and turned toward the door. "Oh, and do not forget that John will be leaving for his family home in the morning."

Hannah nodded. John had claimed during dinner that, now that they were courting, his staying in the same house as Hannah would be inappropriate. She was sad he would be alone there, but his reasoning was sound.

"What was that?" Isabel asked.

Hannah did not realize she had mumbled. "Oh, nothing," she replied as she took the candle in hand. Another task awaited her, and she followed Isabel to the door.

"Where are you going?" Isabel asked suspiciously.

"I must write a few letters," Hannah replied. "One to mother and one to Forbes to share the good news, and one to Albert to decline his proposal. I have been so caught up in recent events, I had nearly forgotten to write them."

Isabel smiled. "Do not stay up too late. We will see them sent off tomorrow." She pulled Hannah in for a hug. "Good night."

"Good night," Hannah replied.

Once in the library, Hannah lit a few candles and then sat at the writing desk. Besides informing her mother of her recent courtship, she would write to thank the woman for pressing her into attending the season. In her letter to Forbes, she would thank the man for his wise advice and to inform him that she missed his company. The letter to Arthur would be the most difficult, for she did not wish to hurt him, but it had to be done. She could no longer keep him waiting.

She dipped the nib of the quill in the ink and began to write. It was an hour later when Hannah yawned and returned the quill to its place for the final time that evening. Collecting her letters, she placed them in the desk drawer, hoping she would not forget to send them in the morning.

Chapter Fourteen

Although she had spoken with John every day since he had left the townhouse, Hannah thought he never looked more handsome than he did now as he stood beside the carriage. He wore a deep blue coat and a crisp white shirt that did little to conceal the wide chest. With his strong arms and bright smile, Hannah would have readily agreed if the man wished to whisk her away to a faraway land and marry her as soon as they arrived.

"Hannah," he said as he took her hand and kissed her knuckles, "you look beautiful."

Hannah smiled and looked down at her gown. Light blue muslin with white stripes, she had fallen in love with its woven bodice and flowing skirts as soon as she had seen it in the catalog. However, the manner in which he looked at her made her love it that much more, and she worried her cheeks were hot enough to ignite a fire.

They were on their way to the Royal Theater with Laurence and Isabel, and Hannah suspected it would be a night she would never forget. She had never been to the opera, and that in itself would have been unforgettable, but to do so with John was another thing entirely.

She drew her shawl in tighter to ward off the cold of the winter evening and glanced at John. "Is your coat new?" she asked as an excuse for staring at the man. "I do not recall seeing it before."

"Indeed, it is," he replied as he straightened lapels that did not need straightening. "I was able to collect it just this morning."

When their eyes met, Hannah could not stop the smile from spreading across her lips. She may not have a deep understanding of love, but she could not deny the spark that they possessed.

"Since my cousin has been so gracious in securing tickets for tonight, I have something for us all." He reached into his coat. "In three weeks' time, we will go to Astley's Circus."

"The circus?" Hannah gasped. "So, Juliet was telling the truth!" Juliet had spoken of a circus in London with animals and other forms of entertainment, including a man who could juggle fire sticks. Hannah had dismissed it at the time as one of her sister's outlandish tales.

"Oh, yes," Laurence said. "Astley's Circus does exist." He turned to Isabel. "You have heard of it, have you not, my dear?"

"I had not," Isabel replied. "Although, it does sound exciting. Thank you for such a wonderful gesture."

"It is the least I can do," John said as he returned the tickets to his inner pocket. "After all you and Laurence have done for me." When he said this, he had turned to Hannah, and she caught the meaning behind the words.

What he said was true, for it was Laurence who allowed Hannah to join them for the season, and it was Laurence who, in turn, had invited John to join them. The more she thought about it, Hannah came to realize how wonderful Laurence was.

"There is no kinder gentleman, nor one as noble, as you," Hannah added, looking at Laurence. "I, too, thank you for allowing me to join you and Isabel for the season."

Laurence chuckled. "Think nothing of it," he said. "But I insist you flatter me no more."

Hannah smiled, and her heart went out to the man. Although Isabel never spoke of it to her, Hannah knew the man's leg pained him from time to time. However, Laurence was the type of gentleman who did not make an issue of it. She doubted she knew anyone as brave as he.

The conversation moved on to the play and what they expected in the experience, and Hannah could not stop her mind from driving to the possibilities of the future. As Isabel said, John would more than likely wait to propose marriage, but she suspected she knew her answer if he did.

***

"The Royal Theater," Laurence said as the four stood outside the carriage on Haymarket Street.

Hannah looked on with awe at the massive white building and its four large columns as men and women dressed in their best finery made their way up the steps to stand beneath the large portico. The chatter of those around them, combined with their laughter, added to the magic of the evening. However, when Hannah spied two large statues, she gasped and pulled on John's coat, not caring if she appeared a child gaining the attention of her mother when she saw a kitten.

"Look!" she whispered. "Tragedy and Comedy. I have only read about them, but to see them in person? What an adventure!"

John nodded. "It makes me happy that you are happy."

Hannah sighed in awe. How beautiful it was to share such wonders with a man such as he, but to have him understand the significance behind it made it that much more magical.

"Your Grace," a man in dark livery said with a bow. "I am Harold and will be your steward this evening. It is an honor to have you as our guest."

Laurence acknowledged the man with a dip of his head. "I am pleased to be here."

"If you will follow me, please," the steward said.

Another man opened a door, and the party walked into a vestibule. To their left was a grand staircase wide enough for a dozen men standing shoulder to shoulder to ascend. They followed Harold up the carpeted steps, which led to a large landing with so much red fabric covering the furniture and floor, Lady Ellen would have been impressed.

Through another door, they walked down a short hallway lined with curtained openings, and they stopped at a box that contained four seats that looked out over the theater. Beneath them, the seats were filling quickly, and they faced a wide stage flanked by deep purple velvet curtains that matched those behind them. The backdrop consisted of a painted blue sky with rolling green hills, and the front of a small cottage sat before it. A grand arch connected two tall columns placed on either side of the stage, each displaying the Royal Crest in gold. On either side of them were enclosed boxes like the one in which they sat as well as others on the opposite side of the theater.

"Isabel," Hannah said when she looked upward, "look at the ceiling!" Intricate patterns that resembled a spider's web laced the ceiling that was so high, it seemed to reach up to Heaven itself.

"It is wonderful," Isabel said, "but we must sit."

Hannah nodded in embarrassment as Laurence and John stood waiting patiently for them to take their seats between them. As Hannah sat, John took the seat to her left and Isabel to her right, leaving the furthest right seat for Laurence. Hannah never thought she would attend such a production, and now that she was here, she was nearly in tears.

"These designs," John said in a loud whisper as he ran his hand along the banister, "the craftsmanship is commendable."

Indeed, the woodwork was impressive with its rose, thistle and shamrock carvings in deep gold embossed into the walls of the box.

"Much money has been invested in the theater," Laurence replied. "I never realized how intensive the sum required was until now. It was certainly well spent."

A hush came over the crowd as a man walked onto the stage, and Hannah felt a rush of excitement as the gas lights lowered.

"Although much has changed since the fire that attempted to take away our theater," the man said, "there is much that has remained the same."

A sudden scuffle brought a collective gasp as a man was dragged away by two others as he shouted obscenities that made Hannah's cheeks burn.

"Vagabonds who try to sneak in," Laurence explained in a low whisper. "Apparently, it happens often, sadly."

"Speaking of matters that remain the same," the announcer said with a light chuckle that made the audience laugh, including Hannah.

She glanced over at John, who seemed to be as enthralled as she. Now they would have yet another topic of discussion to share.

"Tonight, I promise, will be a magical night. One that you will never forget…"

As Hannah listened, she knew the man's words were true, for the night was already magical, and it would only increase as the evening continued.

***

The play had entered its fifth, and final, act some time ago and was sadly drawing to a close. As the actor on stage spoke his lines and the woman looked on, Hannah imagined it was she and John instead. Her heart clenched and tears welled in her eyes as the man spoke.

"For neither the sun rising nor setting has shown such beauty as thee," he said.

The woman took a step toward him, a bouquet of flowers clutched in her hands. "For the love you have shown me shall light a path. A path from which we will never waver."

"That not even the darkness is able to impede," Hannah whispered. She had read this play so often, she knew all the lines by heart.

Applause erupted, and everyone stood, Hannah included, tears streaming down her cheek. John offered her a kerchief, which she took with gratitude. As the applause continued to rumble through the room, she leaned closer to John to be heard. "That was beautiful; do you not agree?"

"Indeed," he replied. "Far better than I could have hoped. I am surprised that I found it so engaging." Hannah thought the comment odd, and her expression must have shown her thoughts, for he added, "I am afraid I have been worn out all day, which had me concerned I would not find the production as captivating as it was."

She smiled. "Yes, fatigue can be quite a burden. I am pleased you were able to enjoy it." She turned to Isabel, who also had tears in her eyes. "I believe I am understanding love more," she whispered as the shuffling of the audience rose around them. "It is that bond two share when they have overcome any obstacle that might stand in their way."

Isabel nodded. "That it is." She turned to look at Laurence, and Hannah did not miss the adoring look she gave her husband. "And yet, it is so much more."

Hannah followed the group back down the hallway behind the boxed seats and out into the vestibule. The announcer had promised a night of magic and wonder, and he could not have been more forthcoming with his pledge. However, it was not only the play that had brought about such things; it was the joy of watching it with John at her side that made it as wonderful as it was.

Chapter Fifteen

John walked into the sitting room of his home and gazed out the window. Many thoughts possessed his mind this day, but Hannah was at the forefront of them all. They had attended the play together ten days earlier, and although a gentleman would never admit such a thing, the performance had him nearly in tears. He had never given serious consideration to the notion of love, not until he had met Hannah.

In the beginning, he had thought her a boring wallflower, one who secretly hoped to one day become a spinster. Not only had the woman shown to be much more than a simple wallflower, she had taught him to appreciate the arts. Despite what he had told her, he had never had a desire to read or attend the theater. In reality, visiting pubs and stealing kisses had been more his style.

Now, however, it was as if he had matured in some way. The thought made him chuckle. He may think himself a man, but his actions were more that of a schoolboy, especially with the manner in which he decided to come to London in the first place. He had run away like a child, and he could not quiet the troubles that nudged at the back of his mind. Perhaps it was foolish to worry about what had taken place in the past, but, then again, one must assume every situation and prepare for it.

A carriage pulled up in front of the house, and John smiled, for he knew to whom it would take him—the woman for whom he had feelings, strong feelings, in fact. He was not certain if what he felt was love, per se, but each time he was apart from Hannah, the deeper his longing for her grew.

He walked to the front door where his butler stood waiting, John's coat and hat in hand.

"Thank you, Chambers," John said as the man helped him into the coat.

"May I get you anything else, my Lord?" the butler asked after handing John his hat.

"No, I believe I have everything I need," John replied as he buttoned his coat. "I shall return this evening."

"Very good, my Lord," Chambers replied with a bow before opening the door.

John's feet seemed to glide down the steps and out to the waiting carriage, a glorious afternoon sun glowing in the sky. When the door to the carriage opened, John was surprised to find Hannah waiting, as beautiful as a lady could be in her green dress and hair pinned up with two long curls framing her face.

"Hannah," he said with a smile as he kissed her hand. "How wonderful you came to collect me."

In the past, Hannah's blushes fed his ego, but now her crimson cheeks warmed his heart. Across from her sat Laurence and Isabel, Laurence dashing in a green frockcoat and Isabel handsome in her bronze gown.

"I feel quite important having everyone come to collect me," John said with a grin. "Are we not dining at your house this evening?"

Hannah appeared beside herself with excitement. "Oh, we are," she said with a wide smile. "Laurence has said he has a surprise for Isabel and me."

John raised an eyebrow. "Is that so?"

Laurence chuckled. "Perhaps."

"This is all so mysterious," John said with a laugh. "Should I not be let in on this little secret?"

"And how is it you believe I should tell you when the ladies are present?" Laurence asked.

John leaned back in the seat. "Will I find this surprise as fulfilling as they?"

Laurence gave him a stiff glare. "We will not discuss it any longer," he said firmly.

Everyone went quiet, and John shifted in his seat. The carriage trumbled along, and Laurence said, "Lady Brunswick was to host a party in nine days. Unfortunately, the woman met with an untimely death. It seems she was thrown from the back of her horse two days ago."

"Is that the surprise?" John asked, and then bit his tongue when the women gasped. "My apologies. I suppose that was a bit uncouth of me."

"I would say so," Isabel admonished.

Laurence sighed. "I knew little of the woman." He looked at John. "She was a widow, I believe, but her friend Lord Richard Minn mentioned you knew her. Is that true?"

John felt Hannah's gaze on him, and he shifted in his seat once more. "I did," he replied, suddenly nervous. "I met the woman two seasons ago and attended her party last year. I remember she was a kind woman, somewhat older than you, Laurence, but I remember little else." Guilt plagued him, for he had not spoken the complete truth, but it was one of the many incidences about which he preferred Hannah never learn.

"Are you all right?" Hannah asked with clear concern. "Are you running a fever?"

"A fever?" he asked dumbly.

"You have sweat on your brow, so I was worried…"

He pulled a kerchief from his coat pocket. "Oh, not at all," he replied with a nervous laugh. "It is a bit close in here is all."

"Would you like me to open a window?"

He shook his head. "That will not be necessary. We will be at the house soon."

"Speaking of returning to the house," Isabel said, giving Laurence a pointed look. "What of this surprise you mentioned? You cannot expect me to believe that John was our surprise." She giggled. "No offense," she said to John.

John laughed. "None taken. I cannot imagine myself being a surprise for anyone." He glanced at Hannah and was pleased to see her cheeks flush again.

"You must be patient," Laurence replied cryptically. "You will learn soon enough. We are here."

Hannah glanced out the window. "But we have only returned home again," she said, clearly confused.

Laurence laughed. "Indeed, we have. Come now. Your surprise awaits."

They allowed the women to alight first, and John stopped Laurence. "What is this surprise?"

Before Laurence could answer, two squeals erupted from inside the house.

"Nathaniel!" both women cried in unison.

John followed Laurence inside and found both women smothering a boy of perhaps thirteen with kisses and tight embraces. "Who is this?" John whispered.

"That, Cousin, is the newest Baron Lambert, Isabel and Hannah's brother, Nathaniel."

The boy had the same blond hair and blue eyes as his sisters, but that was where the semblance ended. Perhaps he took after his father more than his mother, as his sisters did.

Hannah pulled away, holding the boy's arms out to his side. "How is it our little brother is growing up so quickly?" she asked.

He gave her a horrified look. "I do not know," he replied. "I suspect I shall grow for at least another five years."

As Nathaniel fought off his sisters' affections, John could not help but laugh as the boy wiped his mouth on his sleeve. "Enough, already!"

Hannah turned to John. "Nathaniel, I would like you to meet Lord John Stanford."

"It is a pleasure, my Lord," Nathaniel replied, giving John a stiff bow.

"And mine as well, young sir," John replied. "Please, call me John."

The boy smiled, and then Isabel drew him back to her with a bombardment of questions.

Laurence leaned in and whispered, "Come with me a moment. We can steal away while the siblings get reacquainted."

John followed him down the hall to the library, where he took a seat opposite his cousin. Gone was the smile Laurence had worn upon arriving at the townhouse, and John felt uncomfortable under the man's steady gaze.

"I received a letter from your mother."

John groaned. He should not have been surprised, but he had hoped to avoid any discussion of his true reasons for leaving Cornwall.

"She said that you had traveled to Wales to do business for six months. Yet, when you arrived at my door, I was told a different story."

"I...had a disagreement with Mother," John said. It was a partial truth, but a truth, nonetheless. "I am sorry for lying to you."

Laurence sighed. "Disagreements happen in families," he said. "However, you must swear to me that you will write the woman and tell her where you are. I am afraid I do not understand, however. Why would you tell her you were going to Wales of all places?"

"I realize I should not have lied to her, but I promise to write to her first thing in the morning. And as to why I chose Wales? Well, it seemed the perfect place to go into hiding, and she would never have believed I had gone to Scotland. She knows all too well I do not enjoy the cold."

"See that you do write. You are far too good of a man to be so dishonest, especially to members of your family. Please, never lie to me again. I can be trusted in any matter; you should know that."

"I will not lie to you again," John promised. Then a thought came to mind. "Since I can trust you, I need advice in a particular matter."

"We have a few minutes." He chuckled. "Although, I believe Nathaniel will be relieved when we rescue him from his sisters."

John laughed, but then took a deep breath. "Hannah's love for the arts, for books, theater and wildlife?"

"Yes? What of it?"

"In order to win her over, I lied to her about having the same interests. However, now I find myself enjoying them as much as she.

My question is this. Do I tell her that these interests are new to me, or do I simply enjoy them and not admit that I had lied in the beginning?"

Laurence nodded as he sat back in his chair. "This is partly my fault," he said. "Perhaps you can be honest and say you exaggerated your love of reading and such things. Then you may tell her the truth, that you find enjoyment in those activities more than you did before. Hannah will understand."

"Do you believe so?"

"I do," Laurence replied firmly.

Relief washed over John as he rose from his chair. "Thank you for your council in this," he said, shaking Laurence's hand. "I appreciate it."

"Think nothing of it." Then he paused. "Lord Minn mentioned that last season a rumor circulated concerning Lady Brunswick and yourself. Do you know of this rumor?"

"It depends," John replied, attempting to hide his apprehension. "What was the rumor?"

"Apparently, you kissed her. In the drawing room at a party she gave last year."

John knew that a month ago, the old him would have lied, but he had changed and refused to do so any longer. "It was in the library, actually. It was a foolish act on my part kissing the woman."

Laurence was silent for a moment, and then he asked, "And what do you think of what you did?"

That was an easy question to answer. "I am ashamed."

Laurence smiled and clapped him on the back. "That information is something I would not share," he said. "Do not allow the action to cause you shame. Things like that happen when we are young; well, to some of us. I must admit it never happened to me, but that is neither here nor there. As long as they do not happen again, the past is the past."

"Never again," John replied. "No woman will draw my eye, for I now only see Hannah."

It was a relief that he could confide in Laurence. Granted, Lady Brunswick had not been the first, and there were many after, but those days were gone. And he meant to see to it that it never happened again.

***

Hannah was ecstatic at seeing her brother and had to give him one more kiss. The poor boy frowned and wiped his cheek, causing both Hannah and Isabel to laugh.

"Do not worry," Isabel said. "We are finished...for now."

"I love you both," Nathaniel said, "but I cannot endure any more kisses. But if you have a sweet, I will take one of those."

He wore such an innocent smile that Hannah could do nothing more than sigh. "I will get you as many sweets as you wish," she replied. "But I must know. How is it you have come to see us?"

"His Grace...Laurence wrote to me, and I had a free day today, so we organized a visit."

Hannah could not believe how well-spoken her brother had become. It occurred to her that he truly was no longer the little boy she had adored but was slowly becoming a man. A man who would one day take over the running of Scarlett Hall.

"We are glad you were able to come," Isabel said. "Is there anything you wish to do while you are here?"

"No," he replied. Then a sad look came to his features. "I do wish Mother were here. And Juliet. Then I could be with all of my family."

Hannah had to admit that she missed their mother, as well. In fact, he had hoped the woman would visit soon.

Then a bolt of fear hit her. The letters! She had not sent them, and it had been over two weeks since she had written them!

"I will return in a moment," she said. "And do not worry; I will return with your sweets."

Nathaniel gave her a smile and then followed Isabel to the drawing room. How she adored him!

She made her way to the library and heard voices coming from within. So, this was where Laurence and John had gotten off to! She turned to leave, but when she heard John's voice, she froze in place.

"It was in the library, actually. It was a foolish act on my part kissing the woman."

To keep from crying out, Hannah had to cover her mouth as she hurried past the door and to the kitchen. Tears brimmed her eyes as she held the bowl of sweets close to her. Had John met someone else? Or was he speaking of Miss Oakley? Her stomach knotted as she tried to calm herself, but she was much too overwhelmed to do so. She did not know how long she stood there, but when she heard footsteps, she turned to find John walking toward her.

"Hannah?" he asked, his voice filled with concern. "Are you all right? You look as if you have been crying."

Try as she might, she could not stop a tear from escaping her eye, and he hurried over and took the bowl from her.

"What is wrong?"

"Do you truly care for me?" she whispered, finding looking at the man difficult. "Is there another woman you care for more? Someone far prettier than I?"

He placed a finger under her chin and forced her to look up at him. "There is no woman more beautiful than you," he said. "I swear to you that is the truth."

She gazed up at him and so desperately wanted to believe him. "I overheard you speaking with Laurence. You said you kissed another woman."

He sighed.

So, it was true. Now he was going to end their courtship.

"I will not lie to you," he said, his voice quiet. "I did kiss a woman at a party last season. It was foolish, and I cannot place blame on drink, for the actions were my own."

Hannah swallowed. "I see. And did you care for this woman?"

He chuckled. "No. In fact, I hardly knew her..." His voice trailed off. "Hannah, I swear that I see now that my actions that night were that of a fool. If you must know, it was Lady Brunswick, the woman Laurence mentioned in the carriage earlier. However, I swear to you that no woman in this world compares to you."

She nodded and wiped her eyes. Although his words upset her, what had happened was in the past, and the woman was now dead, as sad as that was.

"I must confess something more," John said.

"Go on, although I must admit that I am afraid." Her heart beat against her chest, and she wondered if it would break through her ribcage. Yet, when John took her hand in his, a peace came over her.

"When I first met you, I found your intelligence and beauty overwhelming. I am afraid I told falsehoods, however. The truth is I do not read for pleasure, nor do I enjoy outings such as the theater. Or I should say I did not, for I thought it would be a bore."

He had lied all this time? She had felt a connection with him, but now she realized the man she thought he was did not exist. How foolish of her to believe a man could be interested in the same things as she.

"But as we spent more time together, as I experienced life as you see it, I found that I have come to genuinely enjoy those things. In fact, I cherish what we do together."

Hannah was uncertain what to say. She had come to have a great affection for a man she thought she knew. How could he expect her to accept that?

"Please," he begged, "just one more thing. I have never had an interest in a woman as I have for you. I must admit that I have come to admire you greatly."

"You care for me that much?" she asked, her breath catching in her throat.

He nodded, and when he smiled, it warmed her heart. "I have been such a fool," he said. "But that is in the past. I stand here before you admitting as much. If you can look beyond the mistakes I made before and look into my heart, you will see it only beats for you."

For all the stories she had read, all the tales she had heard, and all the words she had written, none could have prepared her for this moment. For the first time in her life, she understood what it all meant. John had been honest as he spoke of his past and confessed his lies, and although what he had said hurt, he spoke with humbleness and sincerity. She had no other choice.

"I forgive you," she said with a smile. "And if you do not like to read, just tell me so. I will not force you to do something you do not enjoy."

His smile broadened. "I purchased a copy of *Hamlet* and am now reading it. I want to be able to discuss authors who are real and not those who write about pudding."

This made them both laugh, and without thought, Hannah threw her arms around him. He pulled her in closer, and she found his hold comforting.

She brought her lips close to his ear and whispered, "I must admit that I have feelings for you, as well. Thank you for telling me what was on your heart."

When the embrace broke, she smiled as he reached up to wipe away her tears. "You are a wonderful woman. Thank you for understanding."

As they made their way back to the drawing room, the bowl of sweets in her hand, Hannah knew she did not simply care for this man, for it was something much stronger. Love was the most beautiful of all things one could have and would make one do anything for the other. It would allow them to forgive, to move past any hurt, and even heal broken hearts. There was nothing Hannah would not do for the man for whom she had come to care.

Chapter Sixteen

He had come to the realization that he would do anything for Hannah. The love he had developed for her knew no bounds. He was unsure at what precise moment it had occurred, but it could have been any number of moments. Perhaps it was when he saw her for the first time, for he had thought her intriguing. Or when she shared secrets concerning her life, for she was intelligent. Or maybe it had been when she wore a particular dress that made her even more beautiful than he already thought her to be. Whatever the case might have been, it was clear that they shared in a destiny together.

So many times, he had worried that she would see through his ruse, that she would learn that he was not the person he was pretending to be. However, she had not, for she was an innocent and therefore never questioned the masquerade, which only made his affection for her that much greater.

He moved silently down the hallway that he knew how to traverse by heart and opened the door to the library. When it creaked, he paused to listen for anyone who would come to investigate, but the house remained as quiet as ever. Once inside, he inched the door closed until he heard the tiny click and stopped to listen again. Nothing.

Removing his coat, he placed it across the bottom of the door. Now he would be able to light a candle, for tonight he had a specific item in mind—the ledger in which she kept her writings.

He moved across the room to one of the bookcases, the light of the single candle giving enough light to see the spines of the books, if he brought it close and squinted. His finger touched each tome, but none were the one for which he searched. As he glanced down the long rows, a particular book overhung the shelf, and he growled in annoyance. He was meticulous if he was anything, and books were not meant to be unaligned! If they were, it only meant disorder, and he did not enjoy disorder in any form. However, when he attempted to push it back, something impeded its movement.

Strange, he thought, and he pulled out the book and reached into the space behind it, his fingers brushing another smaller book. Curious, he pulled it out and saw it was a small journal bound in dark brown leather. Taking the book to the nearby writing desk, he set down the candle and opened the book.

It was a journal! How fortunate! The beginning of the writing was boring, and he almost returned it to its hidden place. However, his curiosity made him turn the page, and he was delighted he had taken a chance, for what he read made his heart race with excitement. He now had everything he would need to complete his final task, and he had someone to thank!

Clutching the journal in his hands, he snuffed the candle and donned his coat now that it was safe that no light would be seen beneath the door. Sure footsteps made their way through Scarlett Hall, a home he had always envied and that one day would be his.

Outside the room belonging to Eleanor, he paused. Hearing no movement, he pushed the door open. Although he had entered the woman's room many times under the cover of night, the excitement and fear still returned, for if the woman woke, how would he explain his presence in her private chambers?

However, she never woke, and he took his time to walk over to her vanity table and ran his fingers across the long expanse of polished wood. Perfumes, brushes, and other lady's necessities were neatly organized, unlike the bookshelf in the library. How he had never noticed the misaligned book before, he did not know, but he was glad to have seen it this night.

He moved to the bed and smiled down at the sleeping woman, her breathing steady and rhythmic. "I always knew you were not perfect," he whispered. "And now I have the proof, for I know your secret." His fingers ached from how tightly he clutched the book, and the excitement was almost too much to bear. "Thank you for allowing me to learn of it."

He leaned in and brushed his lips to Eleanor's forehead. She scrunched her brow, and his heart froze. He could not allow her to wake and see him leaning over her! However, she let out a sigh, rolled to her side, and faced the opposite wall.

With relief, he released his breath as he stood and made his way back to the hallway. Before he closed the door, he looked back at the indistinguishable mound on the bed. "Your secret is safe with me," he whispered. "As long as you obey and give me my heart's desire."

He closed the door with a soft click. His heart desired not only Hannah, but the home he had always coveted. The journal he now held would give him both, and for that he would always be forever grateful to Lady Eleanor Lambert.

***

Eleanor read the letter once again. It had arrived three days earlier, and she found her heart warm further each time she read it. It was wonderful to have Hannah enter into a courtship, and with a man for whom she cared and who was worthy of her hand. Truth be told, she could not have asked for more—he was a marquess!—and she had Isabel to thank. Once again, her eldest daughter had saved their family; this time by leading Hannah to love.

She placed the letter on the desk. When she had learned that this man Albert had proposed marriage—a sheep farmer of all things!—she had become angry, and fear had claimed her soul. What man of his station would believe he could make claims on a daughter of Scarlett Hall? The idea was absurd at best! Hannah was intelligent when it came to books and other such academics, but she did not fully comprehend of that which men were capable.

According to the letter, this Lord John Stanford was everything Eleanor would have dreamed of for her daughter. Now that Hannah was safe from harm, Eleanor felt a weight lift from her shoulders. One more daughter seen to.

The door opened and Forbes entered. "My Lady," he said with a bow, "Lady Ann will be arriving as planned to be chaperon to Miss Juliet. Will there be anything else? Some tea perhaps?"

Eleanor smiled. "No, thank you." She lifted the letter from the desk. "I had thought the worst for Hannah, but it appears she is well taken care of, for which I am well pleased."

Forbes walked over to her. "I must admit the news brought me joy, as well." He shook his head. "Although I care for all of your children, I must admit that I have felt a special bond with Miss Hannah over the past year."

Eleanor was not surprised. In her neglect for her daughter, the girl had gone to Forbes in order to have someone in which to confide. Although she felt guilty that it had happened, she could not change the past. Furthermore, what harm could there be in her daughter confiding in their butler? Was he not oftentimes more an extended family member than a servant?

"I know you do," she said, "and I am aware she has sought you out for guidance. I am certain she has always met with wise counsel."

Forbes chuckled. "I am not certain about the wisdom of my counsel, but you are kind all the same."

"Hannah would not waste words writing a letter to someone for whom she did not care or respect."

"I am honored to be held in such high esteem," the butler murmured with a bow. "Ah, before I forget, I have scheduled time to collect your dress two days from today."

"Excellent," Eleanor replied. "With Lady Anne coming to watch over Juliet, our trip to London will be without worry." She sighed. "It has been some time since I have been back to London. I must admit I am looking forward to it."

"As you should be, my Lady," Forbes said. "Miss Hannah is in love, and Miss Isabel—I mean, Her Grace—is married. Your children are growing and starting their own families."

"Indeed," Eleanor replied. She walked over to the window. "Gone are the days when I would look out and see them playing. I can still picture Juliet and Isabel arguing and Hannah sitting under the tree with a book on her lap, Nathaniel beside her listening to her read."

"Do not despair, my Lady," Forbes said.

Eleanor started; she had not heard him approach and had not expected him to be standing right beside her.

"Although things are changing," he continued, "they must happen in order to usher in a new age."

Eleanor sighed. "What you say is correct," she said. "Thank you for reminding me."

They stood in silence for a moment, and then she turned to him. However, he was no longer there. As usual, he had left without a sound, leaving her alone with her thoughts.

The truth was she had done everything she could to insure her children were happy. Two daughters were where they should be—or near enough so. Now she had two more children to look after—Juliet and Nathaniel.

Her eyes fell to the tree under which Hannah had spent a majority of her young life. The words Forbes spoke could not have been truer; a new age had come for them all, but especially for Hannah. Love had come to the girl's heart, and soon would follow talk of marriage. And in her heart, Eleanor knew Scarlett Hall would once again be filled with sounds of laughter.

Chapter Seventeen

Since Hannah's realization that she did indeed love John, she had spent the past two weeks fretting over the ideal gift for him. Now, she stood in Hatchard's on Piccadilly in search of the perfect book. The man had expressed a genuine interest in literature, and she could not help the warmth in her heart as they shared in that interest. Not only had they discussed the latest book he was reading, but he also showed an enthusiasm for the novel she was writing. The latter pleased her more than the former by far, and she could not believe her luck in finding such a man.

However, that was not her only source for excitement. Isabel had promised to accompany her to inquire about how one went about publishing a book, and Hannah could barely contain herself whenever she thought about that meeting, which, she had to admit, was quite often. How perfect her life had turned out! She had a gentleman for whom she had an affection, and she would see her dream of publishing realized. Indeed, she had to be one of the luckiest women in the whole of England.

Hatchard's was a lovely bookstore that had opened nine years earlier, but Hannah could not have been more pleased at the selection. The walls were lined with bookshelves filled with every book ever printed—or so Hannah thought. Perhaps that was an overestimation, but she imagined it had to be close, for there were so many. Choosing the right book was going to be a challenge, to be sure!

She perused several shelves before a table caught her eye. A stack of books bound in red cloth had gold embossed on the front cover; a journal! What a perfect gift! John could write his thoughts, his poetry, whatever he chose in such a book.

She chose one and moved past an old man in a dark tattered coat. He held a book to his nose, inhaled deeply, and then sighed. She found the actions strange, and she could not help but give him a curious look, although she knew it was rude.

"It was printed in Cornwall," the man said with a smile. He sniffed it again. "Yes, I have no doubt; the ocean has a peculiar smell there."

Hannah's eyes went wide. "You can tell where a book was printed simply by its odor?" she asked. Before the man could reply, she lifted the journal to her nose and inhaled. "I smell…nothing. Perhaps the shop in which it was bound?" She sniffed it again. "Have you ever been to Dover? I do get a sense of the place."

The old man eyed her for a moment, and then he began to laugh. "It works every time," he said with a shake of his head. "Forgive me. The truth is, I looked at the first page; this is how I knew where it was published."

Hannah walked away feeling foolish. She could not believe how silly she had been. Smelling a book to see where it had been printed, indeed! For a woman who viewed the world through the lens of logic, she certainly had fallen for a silly notion quite easily.

She paid for her book and left the store. Isabel and John had gone to another shop, and she was anxious to be away from Hatchard's after that debacle, so she stopped a man. "Excuse me. Do you know where MacMillan's is by chance?"

The man gave her a bow. "Yes, Miss. If you were to walk down the street that way," he pointed behind him. "Come to the next street, take a right, and walk to the end. Then you take a right, and it's about halfway down aways."

Hannah attempted to picture the directions in her mind and smiled. "So, it is behind this building but one street over?"

The man nodded. "Right you are. There's an alley just down that way," he pointed in the direction in which he had been headed, "but I'd not recommend it. It's not all that safe for a lady like you to walk alone."

Hannah thanked the man. *How silly*, she thought. *To think I cannot take care of myself.* She clicked her tongue. She had been fooled once today, she was not about to allow it to happen again. The man's smile told her he would get a good chuckle at seeing her walk all the way around when a faster route was available.

She glanced up at the sky. Dark storm clouds had moved in and thunder rumbled in the distance, which meant most people had rushed to nearby shops in order to be out of the coming rain, leaving the footpath nearly empty. Another reason not to take the long way around.

She walked to the alleyway and stopped to squint into the shadows within. The path before her was long and winded around to disappear from sight. She glanced in the directions the man had given her. Perhaps she should take the longer route after all.

Thunder rumbled again. No, she was no longer a child but rather a strong woman, and so, with shaky legs that belied her strength, she entered the alley. Her footsteps were quick, and not ten paces in, she turned to look over her shoulder. There stood a man with his hat low over his brow, the shadows concealing his features and giving him a menacing look.

Fear overtook her, and she began to run. She had to reach the safety of the other side of the alley! However, before she reached it, she cried out as her foot caught in a hole, sending her crashing to the ground.

"Hannah?" the man who now stood looming over her asked. "It is you! Are you all right?"

Hannah looked up and her eyes went wide. "Connor?" she asked in a shocked tone as she stared up at Isabel's former brother-in-law.

Connor Barnet reached out a hand. "Here, let me help you."

She accepted his aid and stood on wobbly legs, and he placed his hands on her waist. "Whoa there," he said. When she righted herself fully, he added, "There now. I cannot believe my good fortune in seeing you."

She smiled and tested her ankle, relieved that she had not injured herself. "Thank you," she said. "I thought you were a thief or a murderer."

This brought about a bout of loud laughter. "I am many things, but most certainly not either of those." His eyes seemed to study her, and she found his gaze disconcerting. "I am glad to see you, for I have inquired about you."

"Have you?" Hannah asked, and she realized he had yet to remove his hands from her waist. She wished to tell him to remove them, although she was uncertain why it caused her such distress.

"I have," he said. Why did he sound angry now? But no, it could not have been, for he returned to the earnest tone she had known him for in the past. "When I saw you at the party at Applewood Estates last month, I wanted to tell you that I thought you the most beautiful woman there. Many may see you as plain, but I assure you, I do not."

"Connor," Hannah gasped as she attempted to push the fear from her voice. The storm clouds gathered above them, and the alley darkened further. "I must ask you…"

"I am almost finished telling you what I must," he demanded. Then his voice softened once again. "You have captivated me unlike any woman has before. In truth, I have gone to Scarlett Hall several times to ask your mother's permission to court you. However, each time I arrived, I could not follow through with my request. You see, I chose to come to you personally because I knew what your answer would be."

Hannah could not stop the pounding in her heart at the intense gaze of the man looking down at her, and when he brought his hands to her arms, the fear only intensified. "You appear frightened," he said, frowning. "I am not here to hurt you; I only wish to tell you my desire for you."

"I cannot," she whispered as tears filled her eyes. "Another man is courting me."

His hands dropped to his sides and he took a step back. "This cannot be," he said as he shook his head. "I thought…" He looked away for a moment, glaring down at the ground. When he rounded on her, his jaw was set and his face was red. He grabbed her elbow, sending a pain up her arm. "Who is this other man!" he demanded.

Hannah pulled away from the man and began to run, frightened beyond measure.

"Hannah, wait! I am sorry! I did not mean to frighten you. Listen to me, please. I meant no harm!"

Her legs moved faster than they ever had, and this time she did not turn to look behind her. When she reached the other end of the alley, she collided with a couple who was walking past.

"Are you all right?" the man asked.

Hannah pushed away just as someone said, "Hannah? What happened?"

Relief washed over her as Isabel hurried up to her, and Hannah threw her arms around her sister and wept.

"Have you been hurt?" Isabel asked. "What were you doing in that alley?"

"I am all right," Hannah said as she accepted a kerchief from her sister. Then something occurred to her. If she were to tell Isabel the truth of what happened, not only would it cause problems between Isabel and Laurence, her sister would be forced to endure the shame of her former brother-in-law accosting her sister.

She glanced toward the alley; Connor was nowhere in sight. Perhaps he would leave her be now that he knew her current availability. Nothing would be gained, and all too much lost, if she told the truth.

Therefore, she lied.

"I came down the alley and a large dog chased after me." She looked down at her mussed skirts. "I fell in the process, but thankfully, I was able to get back up and get away before he attacked."

Isabel sighed and brushed at Hannah's skirts. "You must get that cleaned," she said. "I am afraid it may stain." Then she smiled. "But I am glad you are safe. Come. John is waiting for us."

Hannah nodded but glanced toward the alley once more, glad to see that it remained empty. Connor had been livid when she told him about John. It was as if the man would not take no for an answer. However, it did not matter what he felt for her, for her heart was with John, and there, she would remain safe.

***

144

Hannah followed Isabel and John to a shop with a sign that indicated it was "Martin and Sons Publishing", and she whispered a thrill of excitement that made her grin. After all the years of dreaming, she would finally seek a publisher for her novel! Despite her excitement, however, a thread of fear made her stop at the door, unable to move. What if she made a fool of herself, and in turn of John and Isabel?

Her sister seemed to sense this and offered Hannah a warm smile. "You have the right to inquire," she whispered. "No matter the reply, you may ask."

Hannah took a deep breath. Her sister was right; what harm could simply inquiring do?

When John opened the door for her, she could not help but feel a sense of safety. All the fear she had felt in the alleyway had disappeared, and she knew it was because of this man. "I am honored to be here for this occasion," he whispered as he leaned in toward her. "I wish you the best of luck."

"Thank you," Hannah replied. With a confident step, she entered the building. The inside was much smaller than she had anticipated. Two bookshelves on the walls to either side of her gave the already small space a cramped feeling with books not only lining the shelves but also stacked on top and piled in front of them on the floor.

In the back of the room behind a counter sat a man with curly gray hair, a book propped open as he leaned against the counter. Isabel nodded, and Hannah approached the man, her heart wishing to escape her chest.

Without looking up, the man said, "I'm sorry. We're not seeking any employees, and it's doubtful I'll be needing any help anytime soon."

"I am not here in search of employment," Hannah said, surprised that her voice was not wavering. "I am here to inquire about publishing a book."

The man looked up and sighed. Then he glanced at John. "Can the gentleman not speak for himself?"

"It is I who am inquiring," Hannah said, keeping her vexation at bay—barely.

The man rubbed his temples and closed his book with a snap.

"I do not mean to interrupt your work," she continued, although what she could have been interrupting, she did not know. "I can make an appointment if you would prefer."

A curtain over a door behind the man moved, and a woman entered, a teacup in her hand. She set the cup on the counter. "Oh, hello," she said with a bright smile. "What a lovely hat."

"Thank you," Hannah replied. She had changed out the trimmings that morning to match her lavender dress.

The old man reached for the teacup, and Hannah had to stifle a laugh when the woman smacked his hand. "Phineas, no one wants to hear you slurp your tea." She turned and smiled at Hannah. "Now, how may we help you?"

The moment had finally come, and it took all of the courage Hannah could muster to speak. "I am currently penning a novel."

The man groaned, but when the woman shot him a glare he quieted once again.

"Please, continue," the woman said.

Hannah could not help but smile. "Thank you. You see, since I was a child, I have had a love of reading, and that led to a love for writing. What I am writing now is a romantic novel," -another groan followed by another glare- "that I would like to see published one day."

Old Phineas snorted. "We don't publish books for women; there simply is no market..."

"Enough, you," the woman snapped. "Pay him no mind. What is your name?"

"Hannah. Hannah Lambert."

The woman smiled. "I'm Albina Bragg, and this old coot is my husband, Phineas." She leaned on the counter. "The truth of the matter is few bookmakers will publish books by women, but we do." She shot the man a glare that dared him to speak against her. "Despite what most men believe, many women have seen great success in their published works. Take Mary Pilkington, for example. Her *Delia* received a marvelous reception, as did Fanny Burley's *Camilla*. I'm a proponent of women doing more than scribbling a few words of poetry or writing children's books. If your book shows any bit of promise, we're certainly willing to consider it."

Phineas snorted, picked up his teacup, and made his way through the curtain from which Albina had entered. His wife rolled her eyes but then smiled again.

"You say you're in the process of writing this novel?"

Hannah nodded. "I am." She did not wish to mention how she had been struggling as of late. "It is nearly complete, however."

"I want to be honest with you," Albina said. "I can't make any promises that Phineas will agree to publish your book. I can cause a ruckus, but ultimately, the decision is his."

"I understand," Hannah replied.

"When you have completed it, bring it around and see me. You can count on me taking the time to read it."

"I appreciate your time," Hannah said. "I have never been happier in all my life."

"Then by all means, leave now!" the woman said dramatically. "The sooner you get back to your work, the sooner you will return."

Hannah thanked the woman again, and she led John and Isabel outside.

As luck would have it, the storm clouds had passed, and the sun shone brightly. Was there any better sign of the wonderful days that were ahead?

Chapter Eighteen

Thus far, the season had surpassed any expectation Hannah could have ever considered. She had made new acquaintances, Lady Ellen for example, and found she enjoyed attending parties more than she believed she would. And in her pursuit of her dream of seeing her novel published, she had found a possibility of seeing that completed.

However, despite those wondrous new findings, one shone brighter than all the others, something she never would have thought possible—she had found love. Her feet no longer touched the ground, and John's smile spoke far more than the quill could write on parchment.

It was that adoration that now guided her hand as she continued her book. Each line was carefully crafted, and the characters—two people she had adored before—were now closer to her heart. For now, she understood what it meant to fall in love and therefore knew how her hero and heroine would react.

When she completed her novel, she would share it with Lady Ellen and the other women of the writing society as a way to show them that love did exist, not only on the page but in the world around them.

Stifling a yawn, Hannah returned the quill to its holder and wiped at her fingertips with a kerchief. That was the one downfall to writing to which she would never become accustomed—ink-stained fingers. However, it was well worth being forced to wear gloves at all times if it meant completing her manuscript.

The door opened and Isabel entered. "We will be leaving for the circus soon. You do not want to keep John waiting."

Hannah smiled and rose from the chair. "I would like to ask you something," she said as she walked over to stand before her sister. "However, I ask that you keep it in confidence."

"Yes, of course."

"When a woman comes to love a man, is it appropriate for her to express such feelings, or is it expected she wait until he expresses how he feels for her first?"

Isabel gave her a smile. "You would not be speaking of John, would you?" Hannah nodded. "As I thought. It is my counsel that you speak it when the moment is right."

Hannah frowned. "How will I know when the moment is right?"

"Trust me," her sister replied, "you will know."

Hannah sighed. "I hope so."

"You will," Isabel said as she patted Hannah on the arm. "Now, we must wait until later to continue this conversation. Laurence will grow frustrated with us if we are not in the carriage ready to go soon."

Hannah donned her gloves, gave herself one more glance in the mirror, and followed Isabel from the room where Laurence and John stood waiting.

"I think tonight will be wonderful," John said as he offered Hannah his arm. "I have been twice before and have not been disappointed yet."

"I look forward to it," Hannah replied as she placed her hand on his forearm. "And I agree; it will be wonderful." *For tonight will be the night I tell you of my love for you*, she thought. She just hoped he would reply with the same.

***

Hannah had never experienced such a spectacle in all her life. Astley's Circus was held in an amphitheater with open and boxed seating that wrapped around in a half moon allowing all a clear view of the performances that took place in the large circle of dirt below them.

The standing area was full of people from all walks of life—ladies in beautiful dresses stood beside young men in clothes filled with patches. Unlike the theater and its polite whispers, the air was filled with raucous laughter and shouts of excitement.

John had secured them seating in one of the enclosed boxes, and the show would begin shortly. Although she looked forward to the show ahead of them, Hannah found the excitement of informing John of her love for him excited her all the more. She was unsure when she would express her feelings for him, but the idea of saying such things while a performer conducted his act seemed inappropriate. Nor could she tell him during the carriage ride home with Isabel and Laurence listening.

At one point, she considered writing it, but the idea was much too impersonal for such an important admission. Regardless, she was so caught up in her thoughts that the sudden applause of the crowd startled her and she began to shake.

"Are you all right?" John asked as he leaned in close to her.

"Yes," she replied, feeling her cheeks burn. "I am fine."

She turned her attention to the performance area where a man in a bright red jacket entered the circle carrying a cane behind three dogs walking side by side. The man held up the cane, and the dogs sat in unison. Then he tapped the cane on the ground twice, and the dogs reared up on their hind legs, and to Hannah's surprise, they walked upright across the ring before they jumped over the cane the man had stretched out before him. Hannah could not help but join in the heavy applause at each trick performed.

"This is marvelous!" she said. When she turned toward John, she was pleased to see he wore a smile, as well. "I never expected to see such feats!"

"It will only get better," John said. "This is only the beginning."

Was he speaking of more than the performances happening before them? Could he have been speaking of their future together? For the first time, Hannah considered that, if he were to ask her to marry him, she would accept without thought.

Returning her attention to the circle, she was impressed as another man joined the dog trainer. He performed several feats on the back of a horse, and soon, jugglers were tossing swords and fire sticks in the air, making the audience gasp in fear they would cause themselves harm.

Hannah laughed so loudly, she thought her voice would carry over the laughter of the crowd as a host of clowns joined. However, just when she thought the acts could not get any better, eight men entered all dressed in white shirts and banging at large drums. Every performer moved in sync to the beat they created and stopped as one when the drummers struck a final beat.

For a moment, the room was left in silence, but then the crowd roared in approval, and Hannah was as enthusiastic as everyone.

"I know this is not the theater you desire," John shouted near her ear in order to be heard, "but it is something I wanted to share with you. I hope it has met your approval."

"It has been far better," she replied, "for it has exceeded my expectations. I must admit that I cherish anything you share with me."

To her surprise, his cheeks reddened, and that now familiar warmth entered her body. Yes, it was about time she shared her true feelings for him.

And it will be soon if I have anything to do with it, she thought as the second act began and a host of knights waving green flags depicting a dragon rode out into the circle.

***

The third and final act was underway, and Hannah leaned forward as a carriage rode around the vast sea of performers. Now it was the knights who juggled and the clowns who sat on horseback. Even the dogs marched alongside the men in uniform. Although it was not Shakespeare, Hannah had never enjoyed herself as much as she did at this moment.

Then, to her disappointment, the show came to an end, the last act a man who walked across a rope, jumped off, and landed on a horse without so much as a totter. Saluting the crowd, one by one the performers marched away behind the large curtain. The applause was thunderous, and Hannah found herself standing and clapping her hands just as wildly as everyone else. As the applause came to an end and laughs and talking replacing it, Hannah let out a sigh.

"I do wish to return sometime," she said. "If the season only consisted of the circus, I would want to return every year for that alone."

Laurence laughed as he and Isabel faced them. "I certainly plan on returning," he said, "as does Isabel."

Her sister nodded in agreement. "Most definitely."

Laurence offered Isabel his arm. "Shall we discuss this back at the house with a few drinks?"

The group gave their approval, and with John at her side, the four made their way out of the booth and joined the others who moved down a long, yet narrow, hallway.

"The dogs," John said. "Each time I see them perform, I want nothing more than to purchase such animals. Or maybe I may teach them myself."

"That would be fun," Hannah said. "And if you needed help, I would offer my services."

He smiled. "I would like that."

At the bottom of the stairs, a man in one of the performer's red coats stood pointing toward one of the side doors. "Forgiveness," he was saying, "but there's been a small fire and the back alley is blocked. Please continue into the main area and you may exit from there."

"A fire?" Hannah gasped. "Let us hope it has been extinguished!"

The line of people slowed at the door that led to the main hall.

"There are too many people in here," Laurence said, turning to face them. "Take care as we make our way through. Stay close together and follow me so we are not separated."

Hannah nodded, and John leaned in. "Do not leave my side," he said.

"I will not," she replied as her hand tightened on his arm.

They moved forward in the line, and soon they stepped through the door into the main hall, Laurence and Isabel in front of them. Apparently, no one wished to leave, for it was as if everyone who had been in attendance stood laughing and shouting to one another, many with bottles in their hands.

Hannah widened her eyes when a man in a ragged suit lifted a bottle to his lips and drank as one left in the desert for too many days. When a woman in a faded dress kissed his cheek, onlookers roared with approval. With each step taken, Hannah's worry increased as the crowd grew denser, and soon she felt as if she were suffocating.

Just as she came close to giving into the panic, an arm wrapped around her waist, and she turned to see John smiling at her. She allowed him to propel her through the throng of people, and she felt much safer.

At one point, a small part of the crowd near them broke free, and a woman dressed in a fine blue dress shrieked. A man with missing teeth and a gray beard had removed his shirt and was flexing his arm muscles.

"Someone tell Stanley that George the Handsome wants to join the circus!" he shouted to the delight of the onlookers.

Not all were impressed, however, as a man in a well-tailored coat rushed over and punched the old man in the jaw, sending him backwards into the crowd. "How dare you act like an animal in the presence of ladies!" he yelled.

Several more screams resounded as the assembly pressed forward, and when a man easily double the size of most men backed into her and sent her crashing to the ground, she cried out in fright that she would be trampled by the now panicked crowd. However, by some miracle, she managed to stand, but John was no longer beside her.

Several groups of men began fighting, creating more panic as gentlemen held their wives in an effort to lead them outside. Fear enveloped Hannah, and tears welled in her eyes as she desperately searched for John.

"Hello, beautiful."

Hannah looked on in horror as a man took a swig from a bottle and then gave her a toothless grin. No one took notice, and any who did either turned his nose up at her or ignored her completely as they attempted to reach the exit.

Fearing she would die, Hannah pushed forward; however, the room was much too crowded and too many people were in a panic to escape. She could no longer hold back the tears as bodies pushed at her. Would she ever see John again? Why had she not told the man how deeply she cared for him? That she in fact loved him? What if she had wasted her last opportunity to share what she truly felt?

Her heart jumped into her throat when a man fell to the ground beside her. She wanted to help him, but she could do nothing as he disappeared under the feet of those around them.

Breathing was becoming difficult as bodies pressed against her. She was scared and, even worse, alone. Yet, as all hope began to leave her, she heard her name.

"Hannah!"

She turned to see John fighting his way through the mob.

"John!" she shouted back. She reached out for him, but he was too far away. When a man tried to push John out of the way, Hannah screamed, but John elbowed his way past.

"Hannah!" he cried again, and Hannah tried her best to reach him, but she was jostled back once again. With an outstretched hand, her gloved fingertips touched his as tears flowed down her face, and they ebbed away from each other once again like two pieces of driftwood flowing on ocean waves.

As if by a miracle, John broke through the final line of people and wrapped his arms around her.

She wept into his chest, unable to believe he had found her.

"Shh," he whispered into her ear. "You are safe now. I was so scared for you."

"As was I," she replied. "But I am safe as long as I am with you."

"Listen," John shouted just a woman slapped a man near them, "We must move to the side against a wall or we'll be separated again. We will be safer there. Now, do not let go."

"Never!" she shouted back.

He nodded and began to push through the crowd toward the closest wall. Hannah held onto this coat and kept as close as she could so as not to be separated from him again, and when they reached the wall, they worked their way to an empty spot below a set of stairs.

Before she could blink, John wrapped his arms around her waist and pulled her toward him. Just as quickly, he turned her to her back was against the wall, and he pressed his body against hers providing a cover of protection as the angry crowd moved past them.

"You will never be hurt," he said as he gazed down at her, his arms placed against the wall on either side of her as if bracing himself against the mob that pressed from behind.

The noise around them seemed to fade, and it was as if they were the only two in the room.

"I must tell you something," he said and then grunted when a body pushed him toward her. "If we are to die tonight, in this crowd, you must know that I love you."

A tear of joy came to Hannah's eye. "And if these grounds are to be our final resting place," she said, her voice trembling, "know that I love you, too."

It had been earlier that night that Hannah had asked Isabel when one should confess love to another. Although Astley's Circus was the last place Hannah could have imagined professing such words, she said them regardless, and the love in her heart doubled. And as they whispered the word love again, Hannah considered her upbringing for just a brief moment. One must always be a lady and sustain from acts that could ruin her reputation, or so she had been told often from a young age, and she had done her best to adhere to such standards.

Yet, as the crowd around them continued to panic, Hannah felt a calmness come over her. If she was to die, she had one more last thing to do. Perhaps John had thought the same, perhaps their hearts had spoken one to the other, for their lips met, and like their love for one another, became one. It was the most beautiful thing Hannah had ever experienced, and no words could have captured her thoughts. For within that kiss, her heart fluttered, her breath became short, and happiness like none she had ever experienced passed through her body like a burning sensation.

As the kiss broke, John continued to protect her. And although the people around them continued their violence, she had never felt safer in all her life.

Chapter Nineteen

Hannah was uncertain how long she remained in John's arms. It could have been in the space of a breath or as long as an hour; however, it did not matter. She wished to remain there her entire life. His scent was titillating, and fully masculine, and she could not get enough.

John glanced over his shoulder. "I believe it to be safe now," he said. "Are you ready?"

She nodded, but inside she was screaming, *No! I wish to remain here forever!* However, what would she do under his protection, standing against a wall at the amphitheater?

When John moved away, Hannah could not help but gasp at what she saw. Women with torn dresses and disheveled coiffures. Men with sleeves missing and blood-covered shirts. More than one person lay on the ground as others attended to them. Several people limped through the door, while others hung their head as if in shame for their actions this evening.

When John took her elbow, she relished in his touch as they walked toward the door. He looked from side to side as if ready to stop anyone who would attempt to hurt her. He reminded her of Edmund, a hero from one of her favorite stories, but even that man was unworthy of standing in John's shadow.

They reached the door without incident—the waiting room had cleared significantly while Hannah had been under John's protection—and they made their way to the foyer. As soon as they were through the doors, the smell of smoke assailed her, and she turned to see the building directly to their right lying in ruins. Although it was no longer in flames, smoke continued to billow into the sky. Bystanders stood across the street and stared at the building while those who had been in the amphitheater stood in small circles to recount their stories.

"Your sister and Laurence," John said as he stared at the burnt building. "Let us pray they have already reached the carriage as I asked."

Hannah could do nothing more than nod, she was so filled with worry. If anything happened to her sister, Hannah would be destroyed.

John never released her arm as they made their way away from the smoke to where a line of carriages waited. She sighed with relief when Isabel came running toward them.

"Hannah!" Isabel cried. When she reached them, she pulled Hannah into a tight embrace. "Oh, you are safe! I was terrified...the mob...I thought you were hurt."

"Everyone pushing separated me," Hannah explained, realizing she was another recounting her story. "I thought I would die, but then John saved me."

"Thank you," Isabel said to John and then surprised Hannah by throwing her arms around him, as well. Isabel embracing someone outside of her family was a rarity. "I am so glad you both are safe."

"And Laurence?" John asked.

Isabel turned, and Hannah followed her gaze to where a man leaned against a wall, his hand gripping his leg. "While protecting me, a large group of six people fell, one of them against his leg. He is in pain, but he refused to rest in the carriage until you were both found safe."

Hannah's heart went out to the man as they walked over to him. Laurence straightened, the ever-valiant man, but his eyes widened as Hannah hugged him. "Thank you for caring for my sister. You are the kindest and bravest of men."

Laurence turned several shades of red. "Thank you for saying so," he said. Then he spoke to everyone. "Let us be thankful we are all safe. We may leave with only a few bruises, but others I imagine received broken bones. I have not heard of anyone dying, however, so that is gratifying."

Hannah shivered at the thought as Isabel slipped her arm through Laurence's. The manner in which the two smiled at one another brought a smile to Hannah's face, for it was the smile of those in love, one about which she had once wondered but now understood.

"I believe we should return home," John said. "I for one need a drink."

Everyone laughed and made their way to the carriage, and although Hannah pretended not to notice, she watched as Isabel helped Laurence up the step. Her sister was a woman of strength and heart, and her love for the man knew no bounds. Then Hannah looked at John and realized that she felt much the same for him as Isabel did for Laurence.

***

The clock had long since struck midnight, and Hannah, having washed up and changed into a dress that did not have a ripped skirt or the smell of smoke, sat in the drawing room with a glass of wine as she listened to Laurence recount his version of the events of that evening.

"When we reached the bottom of the stairs, I told Isabel that the room was far too crowded and that someone would be hurt if they fell. When I heard the woman cry out, I knew trouble was at hand."

Hannah nodded. His story was much what she and John had experienced, only Laurence and Isabel had been able to reach the exit much more quickly despite his leg injury.

"How long do you believe you waited for us to exit?" John asked. Hannah wondered the same.

"I would say a half hour at most," Laurence replied. "I wanted to go back in and search for you, but Isabel said it would be fruitless. The mob was much too large and unruly, and any attempt to push back against them might have left me trampled beneath their feet."

Hannah was uncertain, but she thought he sounded as if he were disappointed rather than relieved he had not returned.

Isabel must have heard his disappointment. "My husband speaks as if he failed. However, as always, his heart was right."

"Isabel was correct in her assumption," John said. "The danger did worsen with each passing minute. I am thankful you two made it to safety when you did, for any one of us could have lost our life at every turn."

The crackling of wood in the fireplace was the only sound for a few moments, each person in his or her thoughts.

"What of you?" Laurence asked, his voice making Hannah start. "What happened?"

Hannah's cheeks burned and she swore Isabel gave her a knowing nod. Yet, how could the woman know she and John kissed?

John was quick to reply. "When the fire began, Hannah and I were separated in the crowd. I attempted to find her, but the surge of people was like an ocean wave driving me further away." He turned to look at her. "I knew I needed to find Hannah, and I made an oath to myself that I would. Finally, as I fought against the crowd, I saw her." He had yet to take his eyes off Hannah. "Lady or not, she would not succumb to the disorder of the mob around us. And although I was able to force my way through, I found her standing in courage."

Hannah smiled and wished to reach out and take his hand. "He is kind, but in truth, it was his bravery that saved me," she said. "For he shielded me as those around us fought one another in order to escape."

"It appears that bravery and nobility run through your family," Isabel said. "And I am glad you were there for her." She turned to Hannah. "And speaking of family. Do not forget Mother is to arrive Tuesday."

"I have not forgotten," Hannah said. "I am excited, for I have much I wish to tell her." Her book was near completion, which was one of the pieces of news she wished to share. That and her love for John. "And John has agreed to join us for dinner on Wednesday."

John gave her a warm smile. "I look forward to meeting the woman who raised such admirable women."

"Oh!" Isabel said with a gasp. "I forgot to mention that we will be hosting a party on Friday."

"A party?" Hannah asked. "Yes, you did forget to mention this!"

Isabel shook her head. "Somehow I had thought it was next month until Laurence reminded me just last week. Mother also mentioned in her letter that she was excited to attend, as well."

"She will be with us that long?" Hannah asked in surprise. "And what of Juliet?"

"She is to remain with a chaperon," Isabel replied. "Mother will be staying with us for a week."

When first Hannah and then Isabel yawned, Laurence stood. "I believe I am ready to retire for the night." He turned to Isabel. "My dear?"

Isabel stood. "Yes, I am hardly able to keep my eyes open." She leaned in to kiss Hannah. "I will see you in the morning."

"Yes, I must be off to bed, as well," Hannah replied. "So much happened tonight, but I still have yet to feel the effects. How strange." Then, as if a bucket of water had been poured over her head, the recollections of what had transpired that night came over her, and she trembled at the thought of what would have happened if John had not been come to her rescue.

"It is over now," John said as he looked down at her. "You are safe."

"Yes, I am," Hannah replied. "Because of your bravery. Thank you again for protecting me."

John smiled. "It was my honor." He sighed. "Although I do not want to, I must leave. You and Isabel have a busy weekend, but I will see you on Wednesday."

That was another five nights away, and Hannah wondered how she would survive without seeing him for that long. "Until then," she whispered. She desperately wanted him to grab her, to press his lips to hers. Instead, he gave her a slight nod of his head and then turned to leave.

Hannah sighed and walked over to Isabel.

"Do my eyes deceive me?" her sister asked, a sly smile playing at the corner of her lips. "Or am I witnessing a woman in love?"

Hannah giggled. "They do not. I admit that I am in love, and he has said as much to me."

Isabel hugged her. "When was this shared?"

"While we waited for the crowd to disperse at the theater," Hannah replied with a laugh. The memories of John shielding her with his body brought heat to her face—and a tingling to her skin.

She was glad her sister did not ask if anything else had been shared, for Hannah doubted Isabel would be excited to learn that John had kissed her—and in public.

After saying their good nights, Hannah went to her room and donned her night dress. Under the heavy blankets, she thought of the awe of the circus and the daring of a handsome gentleman who had saved her from imminent danger. And, as she closed her eyes, Hannah realized how wrong so many women were. For the stories of love in romantic novels were indeed based on true events.

Chapter Twenty

The weekend had been filled with shopping and relaxation, but now Hannah was filled with excitement as she stood outside the townhouse and a footman set the steps beneath the door of the carriage. Her mother had arrived, much later than they had expected, and Hannah could not wait to share with her the events that had transpired since her last letter.

With a quick glance at the driver's seat, Hannah was pleased to see Forbes climb down from the perch as agile as a man half his age. As her mother stepped out of the carriage, Hannah could not help but smile. She owed this woman so much! If it had not been for her mother's insistence in attending the season, Hannah's novel would not have been nearly complete and Hannah would not have found love.

"Mother," Hannah cried as she hurried over and threw her arms around the woman. "I am so glad you are here."

"I can see that," her mother teased. "I am glad to be here, as well. I apologize for arriving so late." The light glow of dusk told them how late it was.

"As long as you have arrived safely," Hannah replied. "And Forbes," she embraced the man, "I am happy to see you."

"As am I, Miss Hannah," the man replied.

Hannah took a step back and studied the man. For years, she had been able to share secrets with him, and although many of the *ton* would have frowned upon the closeness they shared, Hannah did not care.

"There is so much I must tell you."

"I look forward to that," he said. "I am afraid, however, it must wait. It seems everyone is ready to go inside."

"Forbes has only just arrived," Isabel said with a bit of admonishment, "and there will be plenty of time to talk later."

"He does not mind," Hannah replied defensively and was pleased when she saw Forbes nod in agreement.

They entered the house, and Forbes helped the footman with the bags while Hannah followed Isabel and her mother into the drawing room. Hannah sat beside her mother while Isabel took a seat in one of the wing back chairs across from them.

"And how was your journey?" Isabel asked.

"It was well enough," their mother replied. "Although I am finding my old age makes journeys less comfortable then they once were."

Hannah shook her head. Their mother was not yet two and forty and thus far from old.

"Fortunately," the woman continued, "the weather was pleasant and the roads smooth."

"Laurence asked me to give his apologies for not being here upon your arrival," Isabel said. "He and John—John Stanford is his cousin, if you remember? Anyway, he and John are meeting a man concerning business this evening and will be unable to join us for dinner."

"I suppose both men are attempting to secure a future for the women in their lives?" their mother replied with a smile. Hannah thought her cheeks would burn down the house. "Therefore, there is no apology needed, not after all your husband has done for us."

Hannah had no idea what Laurence could have possibly done, besides marrying Isabel, but she dismissed it.

Her mother turned to Hannah. "And you? Have you finished your book?"

"No," Hannah replied. "However, I believe I will have it finished in the next month or two." She shared what the publisher—or rather the wife of the publisher—had said.

"It will not be an easy path," her mother said. "There are many things the publisher must consider. However, I do not doubt your book will shine amongst the others they receive."

Hannah beamed with pride. "Thank you," she said and then paused. "I wanted to ask…"

The door opened and Forbes entered carrying a silver tray with a tea set.

"Forbes," Isabel exclaimed. "you have just arrived. Why not take some time to rest? We have a butler in attendance here."

Forbes smiled as he set the tray on the table. "I have not served the three of you at once in some time," he said. "I could not help but ask young Chambers for the honor of doing this for you."

None of the women could argue such a point, and Forbes poured their tea before bowing and leaving the room.

Their mother smiled over her teacup. "So often Forbes has gone above and beyond his duties as butler," she said. "We have been lucky to have him in our home."

Hannah nodded, and she took a sip of her tea as her mind returned to Scarlett Hall. Then she started. "Mother, how horrible of me! How is Juliet?"

Her mother's eyes drew tight with worry for a moment. "Her foot is healing. She refuses to use a convalescence chair and insists on using crutches of all things to move around, but she has been able to do so quite well. Annabel is staying with us in order to help with Juliet."

Hannah glanced at Isabel, who gave a slight shake to her head. So, something was amiss. For all the wonderful news her mother had for them, the woman was hiding something.

"Hopefully she behaves," Isabel said. "She is getting far too old to be playing her silly games."

The conversation continued, moving from one subject to another. Hannah wanted to discuss John, but one did not simply bring up a topic of discussion in the middle of discussing the purchase of a dress. When the talk turned once again to Lawrence, Hannah became hopeful she would be able to bring up John.

Then her mother surprised her by outright asking, "Is there anything you wish to tell me about John?"

Pleased to finally have the opportunity to share her wonderful news, Hannah replied, "The fact of the matter is, we are in love, and I believe he will ask me to marry him."

Her mother's response could not have been more pleased. "That is wonderful!" she said as she hugged Hannah. "I was so worried! But to hear this makes me happier than you can ever realize. So, tell me how this all came about."

Hannah shared the various outings they had experienced, what had happened at the circus, and their confession of love for one another. She did not mention the kiss they shared, but she doubted rather highly either woman would be as excited for that particular event as she.

"Now I find myself wanting to be near him at every possible moment," Hannah said at the end of her tale.

Her mother reached over and took her hand. "That is what it is like to be in love," she said. "I truly am happy for you." Then she turned to Isabel. "I am happy for you both. My dream was for my children to marry for love and for no other reason." She sighed. "I hope you do not mind if I lie down for a while. I am exhausted and need to rest."

Isabel covered a yawn. "As do I."

Hannah looked up and was surprised to see the sun well past its zenith. She, too, felt drained, as if explaining her life to her mother had taken all her willpower. However, she did not want to go to bed just yet.

"I believe I will read for a while before retiring," she said.

"Well, be sure to rest if you need it," her mother counseled.

Hannah smiled. "I promise I will."

When the two left, Hannah sat thinking about the plans for the following day. John was to arrive for dinner in order to become better acquainted with her mother. Her thoughts turned to him asking for her hand in marriage. She had no doubt it would happen, the only question was when.

Smiling, she rose and poured herself a glass of wine. She returned to her seat on the couch and sipped at the liquid as images of what life married to John would be life played in her head.

***

Hannah awoke with a start and her eyes settled on the dying embers inside the fireplace. When she glanced at the clock on the mantle, her eyes went wide, instantly snapping her out of her drowsiness. It was past one in the morning! Her cheeks heated as she recalled the dream she was having. She must have nodded off thinking of John, for in her dream, she and John stood beneath a tree in the middle of a field, their lips locked in a passionate kiss. She could almost feel his lips pressed against hers, and the thought brought a smile to her face.

Rising from the couch, she stretched and then made her way to the door. She needed to get to bed; sleeping on the couch was not the best idea. When she opened the door, she nearly screamed when she walked into the tall, imposing figure of her butler.

"Forbes!" she gasped, her heart racing. "You startled me."

"My apologies, Miss Hannah," he said with a bow. "I came to see if you had retired for the night."

"I am afraid I fell asleep," she replied. Then she frowned as she took a step backwards into the room. Forbes followed her in. "How did you know I was here?"

The man smiled. "I came in an hour ago and thought I would let you rest a bit longer. You appeared to be sleeping so soundly, I could not bring myself to disturb you."

Hannah was relieved he had not, for what she had been dreaming would have embarrassed her far greater than she cared to admit. Yet, that was silly; he could not have known of what she had been dreaming!

"Thank you," she replied. The man had always been so caring, so kind. "Before I go to bed, I wanted to share something with you."

"I would be honored," the man replied. He turned to close the door. "I do not know the servants in this house; we do not need any curious ears."

"No, we do not," Hannah replied. She took a seat on the couch and patted the place beside her. "Please, sit with me."

The butler nodded and did as she bade.

"The news of which I wrote in my letter to you?" Hannah said. "It is my hope and suspicion that he will ask for my hand. I believe him to be the worthiest of suitors."

"It appears to be so," Forbes replied.

"He is brave, strong, and kind. His heart is gentle, and I believe that he is what I need in my life."

"If you are confident in your decision," Forbes said, "then I wish you all the best."

Hannah frowned. The man did not seem as happy as she thought he would be. "Do you have something you wish to share?" she asked. "Please, your opinion is important to me."

Forbes shrugged. "I am but a mere butler," he replied. "Certainly, you can receive better counsel from others."

Hannah sighed. "Please."

The older man chuckled. "Very well, if your heart is telling you this man is the one for you, then I am happy for you." His smile faded slightly. "You are certain he is the one for you? You have no doubts he cares only for you and no one else?"

"I have no doubt," she replied, although his words bothered her. She had not doubted John's sincerity in the past, but now she could not help but wonder.

"I have spoken out of turn," Forbes said as if hearing her concerns. "My apologies."

"No, you are right to ascertain that I am making the right decision."

He smiled. "It is only because I care and do not wish to see you hurt."

"Thank you," Hannah said and then gave the man an embrace. "I have always cherished speaking with you. You are a true friend, and I wish for you to speak to John at the party, even for a moment. I believe you will like him."

"I am sure I will," Forbes replied. Then he added, "I have a present for you." He reached into his coat pocket and produced a small ornate wooden box with a rose carved into its lid. "This is for you."

Hannah could not help but feel overwhelmed with gratitude. "You are too kind," she said. She took the box from him and opened it, her eyes widening as she removed a hair pin, one of her favorites overlaid with jewels. Now, however, it had a blue butterfly with two green gemstones for eyes and gold webbing for wings that had been added to it. She smiled. "It is beautiful! Is this mine?"

He nodded. "I found it in the library under a seat cushion not long after you left for the season. It must have fallen at some point."

Hannah frowned. She did not recall even losing it, but she pushed the thought away.

"I must admit," Forbes continued, "I found I missed you all the more when I came across it, and when you wrote about Lord Stanford, I knew you needed something special."

Tears welled up in Hannah's eyes. "You remember how much I adore butterflies," she said, touched by his gift. "You knew that and put it into my favorite pin. I will wear this at the party on Friday." It truly was a beautiful addition, and Hannah was overcome with emotion. "I have missed you, as well, and I do not know how to thank you for such kindness."

"Perhaps I can be the first to see it on you," he replied. "Might I have that honor?"

Hannah nodded and placed the pin in her hair. "What do you think?"

"It is just as I suspected," he replied with a smile. "There is no comparison. Miss Hannah will be the most beautiful woman in all of London."

A tear escaped Hannah's eye, and she hugged him once more. "Thank you for everything," she whispered. "You will always have a special place in my heart."

It was at that moment that Hannah realized she had never seen the man smile wider than he did just then.

"As will you in mine, Miss Hannah."

Chapter Twenty-One

John placed the quill back in its holder and sighed. What a relief it was to finish the last letter, this one to his mother explaining that he was in London and not in Wales as he had led her to believe. The others were to various women from whom he had stolen kisses and then left them to wonder if he would return. In those letters, he apologized for his childish behavior and had asked their forgiveness for his forwardness.

The old John relished in his previous deed; however, the new was disgusted with the acts in which he had partaken. His hope was that the letters would bring peace to those women he had wronged and therefore bring peace to himself. A peace that had come through meeting Hannah, the woman he loved.

He grinned as he opened one of the tiny drawers in the writing desk and removed a small box. Inside it held a ring. Hannah had captured his heart and mind, and his plan was to propose to her. He was not certain if doing so tonight after dinner would be the best time; he would speak to Laurence about the matter.

His carriage would be ready in just a few minutes, and he would then be off to spend a wonderful evening with not only Hannah, but her mother as well. He had spoken only briefly to Lady Eleanor, and he looked forward to engaging in conversation with her in hopes he would meet her approval. However, he knew deep inside that, even if she did not, the approval of Hannah was all he needed.

The door opened and Chambers entered the room. The butler gave a deep bow. "Your carriage is ready, my Lord. Is there anything I must attend to in your absence?"

"No," John replied but then looked at the letters on the desk. "Yes. I will need these letters posted tomorrow."

"I shall see it done, my Lord," Chambers replied with another bow.

"Good. Then I suppose that is all," John said. He went out to the entry and allowed Chambers to help him with his coat.

"Do take care," the butler said as he handed John his hat. "The weather has turned a bitter cold."

"I will," John said and then sighed. "Tonight is important to me, for the mother of the woman I care for will be joining us for dinner."

"I have no doubt she will be most impressed by you," Chambers replied.

A loud knock on the door made them both turn. John frowned. He was not expecting anyone. However, perhaps it was the driver. That, of course, made little sense, and John waited for Chambers to open the door, curious as to who would come calling without sending word beforehand.

His curiosity turned to dread when he saw who waited on the other side of that door.

"Mary," John whispered. His heart raced as the very woman from whom he was running stood beside her mother on the stoop of his London home.

"Lord Stanford," Lady Harding said in her haughty tone John would have recognized anywhere, "I know such arrival without invitation is unorthodox, but considering the circumstances of your disappearance, I thought it was warranted."

John sighed. "Perhaps we can arrange a time..."

"I believe it is imperative we speak now," the woman said, the soft wrinkles at the corner of her mouth deepening with her frown. "Unless you prefer I tell all of London of my daughter's heartbreak?"

Fear coursed through John, for he knew that such talk would not only ruin his name but also destroy what he had developed with Hannah. With an important dinner in less than an hour, he truly felt at odds as to what to do. He glanced at Mary, who looked at the ground, giving now indication as to her thoughts.

He would invite them in, clear the air, and still have enough time to arrive at Laurence's townhouse, albeit late more than likely. However, he had no choice.

Therefore, he forced a smile and moved aside. "Please, come in. We should speak at once."

The two women entered, and John leaned in to whisper to Chambers. "Tell the driver to wait. I should not be long, but I must take care of this matter."

The butler nodded and collected the ladies' cloaks before giving a bow and leaving John to lead them to the drawing room.

"I am glad you have come," John said as he offered them a seat on the couch.

"Are you?" Lady Harding asked, a sly smile at the corner of her mouth. "I would have thought that, by escaping to London, you were attempting to avoid my Mary. You are aware you left her brokenhearted, are you not?"

Guilt stabbed at John, and he gave a nod. Like the others, he had not meant to hurt her. However, with her blue eyes and hair the color of wheat, he had wooed the woman until he received what he wanted. A kiss.

"I understand," he said. He stood and pulled the bell chord. "I will have tea sent up immediately. I imagine you are chilled."

The idea of tea seemed to please Lady Harding, for she smiled. "Indeed," she replied with a light shiver.

For the first time since their arrival, Mary looked up at him. There was no doubt the woman was handsome, and John felt horrible for what he had done to her and the way he had left things between them. Her eyes seemed distant and sad, and it pained him to know he was the cause of that sadness.

"I take it your journey from Cornwall went well?"

"Yes," Lady Harding replied. "The roads are far better than when I was young."

John nodded, although his stomach continued to knot. "The weather is cold, is it not?"

The conversation felt stilted, as if both he and Lady Harding were just becoming acquainted. John looked at Mary. "And what about you, Miss Harding? How are you faring?"

Mary smoothed her skirts, and John wished she would speak; he needed some sort of indication as to what she was thinking.

Then she surprised him by responding, "We had snowfall in Cornwall. I believe you would have enjoyed it."

Lady Harding gave a heavy sigh. "Enough talk of weather," she said, her steady gaze moving to John. "I journeyed here not to speak of snow but something far more important." Dread filled John as the woman leaned forward. "I must know. Are you a gentleman of your word? Do you still intend to marry my daughter?"

***

Concern had tickled Hannah's mind when, ten minutes after dinner was to begin, John had not yet arrived. However, traffic could have held him up, or so she thought, and she waited with her family.

When John had not arrived an hour after the appointed time and Laurence announced they would begin without him, her worry increased monumentally. Throughout the entire meal, Hannah picked at her food, her appetite depleted as she wondered where John was. Every noise, every carriage that trumbled by, had her straining to listen for the knock that would announce his arrival.

Now, at ten at night, Hannah sat in the drawing room near tears. Had something happened to him? What if he was in an accident or he was taken ill? He was a man who was never late. In fact, he tended to be early to any event. This was no ordinary event; this night was important to Hannah, and John was well aware of that fact, for they had spoken often over the course of the days since learning of her mother's visit.

Her mind drifted to her conversation with Forbes and whether she had any doubts about the man. Yet, although Miss Oakley came to mind, she quickly pushed the woman aside. He had remained a gentleman with that particular woman as much as any since she and he had begun courting, so it would not be another woman. No, something terrible had happened, and nothing she did eased that thought.

"Hannah," her mother said from beside her, "His Grace asked you a question." Although Laurence had repeatedly asked her mother to address him by his Christian name, she refused. Her mother had said on many occasions that she had too much respect for him to address him in any other manner.

"My apologies," Hannah said, turning her attention to her brother-in-law. "I did not hear you."

"I was asking about the party. Is there anything you or Isabel need beforehand?"

"No, thank you," she replied. "We have been to every shop in London; I doubt there is anything left to purchase." This brought on a bout of laughter, and Hannah had to force herself to join in.

Isabel set her wine glass on the table. "I really must speak to you concerning your gown," she said. Hannah went to argue but she caught a look in Isabel's eyes that caused her to nod in agreement instead. Isabel turned to their mother. "Must you leave Sunday? You will be tired and I believe your journey can wait another day."

"Yes, I must," her mother said with a sigh. "I really should not have left Juliet and would feel better if I returned to her as soon as possible." She turned to Hannah and patted her hand. "I am glad I came, however."

Hannah smiled. "As am I." Now if she could just get John to arrive, everything would be perfect.

Her mother stood. "I believe I will retire for the night. I am afraid the hour has grown much too late for me. Good evening."

Hannah kissed her mother's cheek and bade her a good night as Isabel and Laurence walked to the door, their heads close together. Hannah could not hear what they said, but Isabel kissed her husband's cheek before he followed their mother out of the room.

Once Hannah and Isabel were alone, Isabel closed the door.

"Do you wish to speak to me about my dress?" Hannah asked, although she had a feeling before Isabel spoke that her sister had another topic of discussion planned.

"No, of course not," Isabel replied. "That was simply an excuse. I wish to speak to you about John."

With her heart in her throat, Hannah nodded. Did Isabel have news? "I believe he may be in danger, yet no one seems to be worried but I," Hannah said doing nothing to hide her frustration.

Isabel reached out and took Hannah's hand. "It is lovely that you care for him, and I understand your worry. The truth is, he may have gotten caught up in a business meeting with no means for escape. How many times did Father do the same? Men can speak of trivial things for hours, and if money plays a part in their game, more reason for them to remain."

"I know what you say is correct," Hannah said with a heavy sigh. "However, something does not feel right. Do you not have times when you feel the same for Laurence?"

"I do," Isabel replied thoughtfully.

"Then I must ask a favor. We must go to his home. I cannot wait here until tomorrow; I must know he is safe. If he is in a meeting elsewhere, his butler will know."

Isabel glanced at the clock. "I do not believe..." She looked up at Hannah and sighed. "Oh, very well. You are right, and I must admit, I am worried myself."

"Are you?"

"Indeed. Laurence dismissed the notion that John may be in trouble, but this night was important to you. There is no reason he would have missed it, even for a business meeting. Not without sending word."

Hannah threw her arms around her sister. "That is what I thought! Thank you!"

Isabel pulled away and placed her hands on Hannah's shoulders. "We made an oath, do you remember?"

"Of course." How could Hannah forget? The three sisters and their cousin Annabel had stood in a circle as they held hands and swore to always be there for one another, and Hannah had no reason to believe it not to be true.

"An oath made is no good unless it is kept. I will inform Laurence of our plans and see the carriage readied."

Hannah could not help but sigh with relief as Isabel left the room. They would be at John's house soon, and she could learn what had caused him to miss the dinner, and, more importantly, allow her to ascertain that he was safe.

Chapter Twenty-Two

What John had hoped would be less than an hour turned into three, and he was growing more and more frustrated with his callers. They refused to agree to any terms, and as Lady Harding continued her rant, John sneaked a glance at Mary. What trouble he had caused these women!

John recalled what had brought on the issue they currently discussed. He had called on the younger Harding, the second in a week. They had gone out to the garden for a stroll, in the company of a chaperon, of course; however, when John hurried Mary into a corner, leaving behind said chaperon, he had pounced. Well, perhaps pounced was not the correct word, although it was the word Lady Harding had used on more than one occasion since then. Regardless, he had the opportunity to be alone with Mary, and therefore, he turned to shower her with compliments for her beauty and intelligence — mostly her beauty — and they had shared in a kiss.

Unfortunately for him, Lady Harding had also chosen to take a stroll in the gardens, and she just so happened to turn the corner and catch them with their lips pressed together. He could still hear her cry of anger, as well as feel the panic that had welled up inside him, and he found himself unable to stop the tumble of words that followed. Of how his intentions had been pure. Of how he had meant to ask for Mary's hand in marriage.

The woman had gone from angry to joyous at his words, and the two had stood on the stoop of the house, waving as he rode away.

What they had not expected, apparently, was to learn that he had gone away with no intentions of ever returning to Cornwall.

Lady Harding cleared her throat, breaking John from his thoughts. "My apologies," she said, "but I believe I left my reticule in our carriage. Would your butler accompany me to retrieve it?"

"Of course." John replied. He pulled the bell chord. "My man can retrieve it for you, if you would rather."

"No, I must see to it myself."

John nodded, and when Chambers arrived, he explained the assignment. When the woman and the butler were gone, he turned to Mary.

"I am sorry for all this," she said. "My mother refuses to listen. She continuously demands we marry." She sighed. "I am unsure what you wish, but I must be truthful with you."

"Please," John said, surprised. "I will do the same."

"Although I thought our kiss to be pleasant," the woman said as she looked down at her hands, "I must admit that I have no feelings for you." She looked up at him, tears rimming her eyes. "You see, I am in love with another, Lord Laskey by name. We met at a party last month, and I admit we have grown quite close in the recent weeks. Please, I do not mean to upset you."

John stared at her in amazement. And joy! "You are?" The woman nodded. "That is fantastic! You see, I have found a woman myself, and I must admit that I have fallen head over heels for her." He paused and walked over to the writing desk. When he returned, he handed Mary the letter he had written to her.

"What is this?" she asked.

"An apology," he replied. "I had meant to post it to you tomorrow, but now that you are here... Read it later; it explains the man I was and the man I have become."

Mary nodded and slipped the letter into her pocket. "What are we to do about this matter? She will not listen to me and has taken complete control over my life these past months."

John thought for a moment. There was only one thing he could do. The woman was possessive of Mary—she had always been thus as far as he knew—and would insist she remain near her even after her daughter was married. Perhaps he could use that to their favor.

"When your mother returns, whatever I say, agree with me. No matter what, you must agree."

Mary scrunched her brow but nodded, nonetheless. "I will."

John returned to his seat just as Lady Harding returned, and he rose as if he had been sitting there all along. Once the woman was seated once again, he said, "You have expressed your desire that I marry your daughter, and I have come to the realization that I must accept."

Mary had a panicked look on her face, but she said nothing, much to John's relief.

Lady Harding gave a derisive sniff. "I am glad you have come to your senses," she said. "We shall begin the planning for a grand wedding at once. My sister Martha will be in attendance, as will my cousin William and his family."

"That is what I wished to discuss with you," John said. "You see, my finances as of late are not what one might consider 'stable'. Unfortunately, I cannot afford a large wedding. However, that will change once we return from India."

"India?" Lady Harding asked with eyes wide. "What is in India?"

"I have been in London to make arrangements to do business there with Lord Laskey. Do you know him?"

"I do," Lady Harding said as she glanced at her daughter. "Mary has spoken to the man in the past."

John suppressed a smile. "You see, he is a man of wealth, far greater than I." Lady Harding's eyes widened, and John could see the greed in them. As he suspected; her concern had little to do with the daughter's virtue and more to do with the money the mother hoped to garner. "You see, I will be in his employ, and with Mary as my bride, we shall raise our children in India." He turned to Mary and flashed her a smile. "What do you think of this plan? Do you accept this arrangement?"

"To go to India and possibly never return?" Mary asked. "It is a wonderful idea..."

Lady Harding jumped from her seat. "My daughter will not be married to a man who is nearly bankrupt!" She was close to shouting.

"Nor one who wishes to whisk her away from her family. Come, my dear, we have no reason to remain."

"But, Mother," Mary said as she rose from her seat, "what am I to do in Cornwall?"

She could be in the theater, John thought with a silent laugh.

"You will return Lord Laskey's card, that is what you will do," her mother snapped. "He is by far a more suitable prospect for you." Chambers helped the women into their cloaks, even as Lady Harding continued to rant. "You will marry a gentleman such as Lord Laskey, and certainly not a rogue!"

John feigned offence but then sighed. "Perhaps that would be for the best. Lord Laskey is known for great wealth. If I take on the majority of his foreign accounts, and with the bulk of his businesses near Cornwall, he would never have a need to leave for India."

"And that is what is needed," her mother replied with a firm nod. "Taking my daughter across the world, indeed! Good evening to you, Lord Stanford."

John gave her a deep bow. "And good evening to you, Lady Harding."

She turned to her daughter. "Come, dear. We have a long journey tomorrow."

Mary sobbed into her gloves, but when she looked up at John, her eyes twinkled with mirth and she wore a secretive smile. "Thank you," she whispered.

John smiled and closed the door behind the two women. Running away had been a huge mistake, he realized, but he had finally faced his demons. *Or rather that one demon,* he thought with a laugh. No, that was cruel.

The sound of voices outside made him peek through the curtains of the front window, and he groaned when he saw Hannah and Isabel speaking to Lady Harding and Mary. He opened the door just as Hannah stepped onto the stoop, and he could see the tears on her cheeks even before she reached the door.

***

The breeze blew at a gentle, but steady, pace, causing Hannah to shiver as she and Isabel emerged from the carriage. Several of the homes on the street had light glowing in the windows, including John's, which brought her a rush of hope that he was safe. She pulled her shawl in tighter just as two women exited the house. One of the women was close to Hannah's age and the other was much older. Her mother perhaps? Regardless, the woman wore a scowl that matched the blackness of her dress.

"That man is a rogue!" the older woman said. "Have no doubt that he will steal your virtue, make promises of marriage, and then run like the bankrupt coward he is!" She turned to the younger woman beside her, who stood with her head low. "Come, Mary, let us leave this dreadful place!"

Confusion and fear returned as Hannah watched the young woman being led off. Could it be true? Was John a rogue who had taken advantage of that poor woman with the promise of marriage only to run away?

She turned to Isabel, attempting to stave off the fear that swirled inside her. "I must speak to him."

Isabel glanced up at the house. "Perhaps we should return later."

"No," Hannah replied firmly. "I must speak to him now."

The look Isabel wore told Hannah what she already feared to be true; that the women who left had spoken the truth concerning John. However, Hannah had to find out for herself. Unfortunately, she could not stop the tears from flowing. She had spent the last three hours fretting over his safety, and this last had been the point of breaking.

The door opened and John stood there, as handsome as ever. "Hannah, I am sorry for missing dinner this evening. Unfortunately, I had an unexpected guest, and I did not anticipate they would remain for as long as they did."

"Who was she?" Hannah demanded, trying to maintain her composure and knowing she was failing miserably.

John shifted from one foot to another. "An old friend."

Hannah recalled the conversation between her and Forbes. Did she have any doubts? Now she certainly did.

"Her name?"

"Miss Harding. Mary."

"I will ask you this only once," she said, struggling to keep her voice calm, "and I do not wish to hear lies. Were you to marry her?"

John closed his eyes. "It was a misunderstanding," he replied. "I can assure you that Mary left here tonight happy and is returning to the man she loves. Which, I might add, is not me."

Hannah shook her head. What lies this man spouted! What she had seen was not a content woman but a woman who hung her head in shame and hurt, both far from happy.

"Her mother spoke of her virtue..." She was unable to finish the thought. The mere thought of what could have been crushed her.

"I will not lie," John said. "We shared in a kiss. It was only once, and her mother caught us. It was in fear that I promised to marry the woman. However, I immediately came to London to get away from them."

"You told me you wanted a fresh start," Hannah snapped. "That was a lie." He went to reply, but she continued. "Then I find your love of books and nature was a lie. Last year you kissed a widow. When do the lies end?"

John hung his head, but Hannah was not finished, not yet. She had one more question to ask.

"The night you returned from dinner with Miss Oakley?" she asked, afraid to know the truth. "I noticed there was a strand of blond hair on your coat. Did you..." She swallowed hard. Did she want to know the truth? Yes, she did. "Did you kiss her, as well?" Her heart raced, and she willed him to tell her that he had not. That her fears were unjustified, yet, as soon as he sighed, she knew the truth. Her heart broke into a thousand pieces.

"The truth is, she kissed me," he replied.

Hannah shook her head in wonderment. Did this man ever stop lying?

"I swear!" he said. "It was she who kissed me! I had meant to leave, and she gave me a kiss, which I did not want. And when she did, I immediately regretted that it happened."

Hannah clenched her fist. The man had no honor. Did he honestly expect her to believe that a woman such as Miss Oakley had been the instigator of a kiss? And that he had not enjoyed it? She fought back the hysterical laughter that bubbled up inside her. "I do not believe you," she replied. "You are a liar and a rogue. Everything about you is a lie, and I wish to never see you again."

She turned to leave, but he caught her arm. "Wait!" he said. She looked down at his hand and he released her, but she did not move. "I admit that, until the day I met you, I was what you say. My actions were not that of a gentleman. However, I swear to you on everything dear to me that I am a changed man. *You* changed me, and I have put those ways behind me."

Hannah studied the man she had grown to love, her heart clenching. "Goodbye, John." As the words left her lips, she knew they were meant as a final farewell. No longer would they share in laughter or attend parties, and even worse, share in the laughter they once had. For Hannah had experienced love, and now, as she hurried away as the man she loved called to her, she vowed to never love again.

Once inside the carriage, Isabel embraced her. "What is it? What did he say?"

Attempting to compose herself, Hannah leaned back in the seat. "It is true," she said, surprised at how even her voice sounded. "He was meant to marry that woman. And Miss Oakley? He kissed her, as well. He has kissed many women, tricking them as he did me..." Her words trailed off as the night of the circus entered her mind. "He told me he loved me and kissed me, too."

"Oh, Hannah," Isabel said. "I am so sorry."

The carriage jostled forward, and Hannah felt numb.

"If I would have even had the slightest idea he was like this," Isabel said, "I would never have allowed him near you."

"This is not your fault," Hannah assured her sister. "It is mine."

Isabel gasped. "Do not say such a thing!"

"Why not?" Hannah demanded. "It is only the truth. From the moment I saw him, I went against everything I believed. I allowed him to enter my heart, and now it is broken." She sniffed. "I knew this would be the outcome of love."

Isabel took Hannah's hand in hers. "There was a time after Arthur when I thought the same as you. It was the darkest time of my life. Then I met Laurence, and I can tell you that love is possible after you have been hurt. It may not be with John, but perhaps one day with another man. However, you should never swear it off completely."

Hannah recalled first seeing John. The way his smile had captivated her, how his words warmed her. She had been naive, much like Lady Ellen from the writing society had said. The notion of love and dreams were true, but Hannah had thought herself wiser than other women when in reality she was not.

She had strayed from her original dream, and now she made a vow she would always keep. "There is nothing for me here in London," she said. "I will never fall in love, nor will I complete my book. Stories are nothing more than fiction, and although stories end in happiness at times, reality ends in heartbreak, and the pain is worse than anything I have ever experienced in my life. I will never put myself in that position again."

Isabel drew her into her, and Hannah wept as the carriage continued its journey through the streets of London. Her purpose tonight had been to find the man she loved, but now she wanted nothing more than to never see him again.

Chapter Twenty-Three

The wine helped soothe the trembling brought on by her sadness and anger, but it did little to ease the pain in her heart. Hannah sat in the drawing room before a roaring fire, and she stared at the dancing flames without seeing them. Isabel had gone to bed twenty minutes earlier leaving Hannah alone with her thoughts. Thoughts of the happy expectations she had held for her life. Thoughts of John asking for her hand in marriage. Of them dancing together at parties. Of them dining together with her mother. Of her completing her book.

However, the opportunity for such events happening had passed. She would return home with her mother next week and never return to London, or leave Scarlett Hall ever again, for coming to London had been a mistake. She had been right all along; love had no place in her life. All she had was her writing, and that would have to do.

The door opened, and her mother entered the room, a book in her hand. She walked over and poured herself a glass of wine before joining Hannah on the couch.

"Isabel informed me of this evening's events," her mother said as she glanced at the fire. "I am sorry for your heartbreak."

"It was foolish for me to come here," Hannah said with a sigh. "The season is not the place one goes to fulfill one's dreams, but rather one of hurt. It is where dreams end and the truth reveals itself."

"And what truth is that?"

"That love does not exist. Men seek their own carnal pleasure and will say anything in order to assuage it."

"His Grace is not that way," her mother said. "Nor is…"

A sudden burst of anger had Hannah jump from her seat. "Do you not see what you have done to me?" she shouted, unable to keep the hateful words from tumbling from her lips, her ire was so great.

"And what have I done?" her mother asked, her face full of sorrow.

However, Hannah would not allow the woman to play her games. "You promised that the season would be one of happiness for me! I wanted to remain at Scarlett Hall because I knew that something such as this would happen. I wish I had never come!" She knew she was acting like a child, but she could not help herself. If a tantrum was what it took to release her hurt, then as a child she would behave! Otherwise, she would explode if she kept her feelings bottled inside.

"Until tonight, you were pleased you came," her mother said. Hannah wondered how she could remain calm in the face of her daughter's anger. "You spoke of your love for John, your dream of completing and publishing your novel. Do you no longer want either of those things?"

Hannah gave a mocking laugh. "How could I write about something that does not exist?" she demanded.

"Tell me what happened," her mother said. "Concerning John."

Hannah sighed and sat beside her mother. "It began when I first met him…"

She poured out her heart, explaining how she had been intrigued by him, how he had used her love of reading to get to her, lying in the process, and ending with their first kiss at the circus. She felt a sense of relief when she finished.

"And tonight, learning what I had about Miss Harding and Miss Oakley, well, I knew he could never love me. He has lied to so many women, how can I possibly trust that he is not lying to me?

Her mother sighed. "I understand the heartache you are enduring. In time, you will heal from it, I promise. I do not expect you to meet another man anytime soon, but in time you will learn from this. Furthermore, the season is long and far from over. Why give up now?"

Hannah shook her head. "I will return with you to Scarlett Hall and never leave again."

"I see," her mother said before taking a sip of her wine. "And your dream of publishing? Are you willing to leave that here in London, as well? And what of John? Do you wish to never see him again?"

The latter question made her pause as a familiar longing flashed inside her. However, she pushed it aside. "May I return?" she demanded.

Her mother placed her glass on the table. "I want to give you something." She thrust the book she had brought with her into Hannah's hands.

"What is this?"

"An unfinished dream," her mother said as tears filled her eyes. "A young woman once wrote a story and never finished it."

"You wrote a novel?" Hannah asked in shock as she opened the book. It had no title, but she flipped through the pages of fine penmanship until she reached the end. "Why did you not complete it?"

Her mother winced as if in pain and took Hannah's hand. "My reasons do not matter. What does matter is, like you, I have always loved books. You may not believe this, but I also had a dream of publishing a book."

Hannah gasped. "I never knew! Mother, that is wonderful!"

Her mother gazed at the fireplace. "It was a beautiful dream, I admit, but such aspirations were considered that of a wallflower." She chuckled. "Perhaps I could have been considered a wallflower back in my younger years."

Her mother, a wallflower? Hannah could not imagine her mother ever being thought of in such a manner. "I do not believe it," she whispered. "Not you."

Her mother smiled as a single tear rolled down her cheek. "Oh, but it is true," she said. "However, that is not the point. You see, when we put our words to paper, they are more than words that echo our heart. They are our dreams, our love, our passion transferred to the page."

Hannah nodded. "I have thought of it in the same way," she said, still unable to believe her mother had once felt as she.

"If you decide not to seek having your novel published, I will not force you to do so. However, you must finish your book. Do not give up on your dreams, for you will regret them forever." The words were spoken with such pain, Hannah thought her heart would burst.

She sighed. "How can I write a story about love when I cannot experience such in life? A couple who is happy and in love? It does not exist, or at least it does not exist for me."

"But it does. However, it is not easily attained. Will you at least think about completing it? Do what I never did and fulfill your dream."

Hannah sat staring down at the book in her hands. If this was what her mother wanted for her, she would agree. "I will," she replied.

When she attempted to return the book to her mother, the woman pushed it back. "No, you keep it. My gift to you."

Hannah held the book against her breast. "Thank you," she said. "I will cherish it." They were silent for a moment, and she flipped through the pages once more. "Concerning your return journey? May I join you next week if I decide to do so?"

Her mother stood. "Forbes and I will be leaving Tuesday morning. You decide what you believe is best for you. But I ask one thing that you must do."

"Yes, of course."

"You spoke of John running away from his problems?"

Hannah nodded.

"As you have now seen, the past will catch up to you. If you believe leaving London will solve your heartache, then you may join us. However, do not do it simply to run away from your problems. But the decision is yours."

Without another word, her mother left the room, and Hannah sat staring at the book. Perhaps her mother was right. Running away had not served John well, and it would do her no better."

***

Rogue. That was the word that had defined John a good portion of his life. A man who sought his own pleasures without regard for what impact such actions would have on the women he pursued. A man who led any woman to believe his intentions were more than the simple kiss he received in return.

Love. That word described quite well his feelings for Miss Hannah Lambert. Never in his life would he had thought he would fall in love, and yet, here he was. And how much he wanted to watch that love grow!

Unfortunately, his actions from the past had finally caught up with him. If he were the only affected party, he could endure the consequences. However, the woman he loved had felt the repercussion of his mistakes, and that had been more than he could manage, for it had crushed his heart as much as it had hers.

When Hannah had said goodbye, he knew she intended it to be forever; that she wished to never see him again. That alone caused his heart to ache all the more. How he wished he would have told her the truth from the beginning. She was a kind, understanding woman, and surely she would have seen that he had changed from the rogue he once was. Now, however, it was too late.

The last few days since his world had come crashing down had crept by, each moment sluggish, and each time he thought of her was more agonizing than the time before. He had attempted to write letters, and each attempt failed to express the words he wished to share. None said enough, expressed enough, of his regret for what he had done.

The party at the home of his cousin was to be held the following evening. John had looked forward to attending, to be in Hannah's presence the entire night. Now, he knew he would not be welcome. If he could have just a few moments with her, all would be well. If she had the opportunity to see what was truly in his heart, perhaps she would forgive him.

Sighing, he swept the paper off the desk, upturning the inkwell in the process. He paid it no heed. What good came with crying over spilled ink? He gave a weak chuckled at his mind's attempt at humor; he was not in the mood for jokes.

The sound of raised voices had him turn toward the door. Who could be calling today? He was not expecting any guests, and he prayed that Mary and her mother had not returned.

As he rose from his chair, Chambers entered with a hasty bow. "His Grace…"

He was unable to finish the announcement as Laurence swept past the poor butler, his face red and scowling. The man was irate, indeed! Never had he seen his cousin so angry. John barely took notice of Chambers bowing and leaving the room. Somehow, he envied the butler.

Caution, that was what John needed to take at the moment. "If you would allow me to explain…"

Laurence reached out and grabbed John by the lapels and slammed him against the wall, forcing all his breath from John's body. "You have broken that poor girl's heart!" he shouted, his breath hot on John's face. "I spoke of your honor, of your integrity, and Isabel believed me! You have shamed me beyond belief, beyond anything I could have ever fathomed!"

John struggled to regain his breath, but he managed to sputter, "I-I know! I am sorry! Please, let me explain!" Laurence narrowed his eyes. Was he readying himself to strike John? "Please! I beg of you! Just give me a moment and I will tell you everything."

"You are family," Laurence said in a low, seething tone, "therefore, I will listen. However, know this. You are never welcome at my home again! Is that clear?"

John nodded, and Laurence released him. He took a deep breath in an attempt to regain his composure. "Until the day I met Hannah, I was not a gentleman. In fact, I was a horrible excuse for a human being. I spent many hours in the company of women in a manner that I should not. I came to London to escape. You see, I had promised Lady Harding that I would marry her daughter."

Laurence's scowl deepened. "That is not a promise given lightly."

"Yes, you are right," John replied. "However, I was frantic and spoke out of turn." He explained what had happened on that fateful day, which turned into a full-fledged confession of his life before meeting Hannah.

"Mary told me she has no interest in me, that, in fact, she has her sights on another man. Therefore, I sent her mother on a trail that would lead her to him. Mary will be happy, her mother will be pleased, and I will be free to return to Hannah. I swear on everything I have that I love her. Do you not see? The woman has changed me for the better!"

Laurence walked over to one of the wing backed chairs and placed his hands on the back. "Isabel changed me," he said in a voice so low, John had to strain to hear. "I was a much different man than I am now." He turned to face John. "What do you propose to do?"

"I wish only to speak to Hannah once more. To bare my soul to her. If, after she learns the entire truth, she wishes to never see me again, I cannot lie, it will crush me. However, I swear upon my title of Marquess that I will never bother her, or anyone else, again. Regardless of her answer, I am finished with my old ways."

"Do you truly mean this?"

"I do," John replied as he drew himself up to his full height and jutted his chin. "I swear that if she rejects my apology, I will leave for the remainder of the season so there is no chance she is hurt further by seeing me again."

Laurence seemed to study him for a moment. "You do love her," he said. "I can see no lie."

"That is because I do love her," John said. He reached into his coat pocket. "It is why I wished to ask for her hand in marriage. That is, until..." He could not get himself to speak of the atrocity of what had happened one more time.

Laurence reached out and placed his hand on John's shoulder, but this time it was not done in anger. "I apologize for my conduct," he said. "You can understand my anger concerning Hannah."

"Trust me; I understand," John replied with a chuckle. "I would have done the same."

"We are still family. At the worst of times, we must stand together. Therefore, this is what I propose you do."

"Yes, anything," John said eagerly. And it was the truth; he would do anything if it gave him the opportunity to speak to Hannah.

"Tomorrow evening, arrive late to the party. By that time, Hannah will be immersed in the goings-on. We will arrange for you to speak to her in private." He pointed a finger at John. "You must swear to me you will be honest and tell her everything."

"You have my word."

Laurence squeezed his shoulder. "Very well, then. I shall see you tomorrow evening."

John nodded, and as Laurence walked to the door, John called out to his cousin once more. "Thank you," he said. "For believing in me when it seems no one else will."

Laurence smiled. "Let us hope Hannah believes you, as well."

A moment later, he was gone, and John returned to his desk, his thoughts on the party. This was his one and only chance to tell Hannah that he truly loved her. If she denied him, if she rejected him, he feared what life would be like without her.

Chapter Twenty-Four

The party had begun well over an hour earlier, and Hannah remained long enough to greet the guests before stealing away to her room. She tried her best effort to enjoy the festivities, but she could not fend off the loneliness she endured without John. Now, as she sat at the edge of her bed in the glow of the single candle, she allowed the memory of her last encounter with him to enter her mind.

The truth of the matter was, she had been unfair to John. Her heart had been broken, just as it was now, and her anger and hurt made her ignore his apology. Furthermore, when she had confronted him concerning Lady Oakley, he very well could have lied; however, rather than doing so, he had told the truth, even if it caused her pain. Or at least some variation of the truth, for what kind of woman would kiss a man of her own accord?

She sat up. Had it not been she who had initiated the kiss at the circus? Could it have been true that Miss Oakley had done the same? Even if it was true, however, that did not excuse what he had done to Miss Mary Harding. How could he promise marriage and then simply run off? So many questions! What she needed was to speak to him, now that the wound was not as fresh, in order to learn what exactly had transpired. Where it would go from there, she was uncertain, but it was a start.

The fact was, as much as her heart hurt, and although she had sworn off love—this time for good!—she had to admit that she still loved him. Would that love make her foolish enough to love him again? Her mind raced in confusion as a light tap came to the door and Isabel entered.

"Do you wish to remain here all night and leave me to care for our guests alone?" Isabel teased. She sat beside Hannah. "What are you doing here?"

"Thinking," Hannah replied.

Isabel laughed. "Thinking? Thinking of what?"

Hannah sighed. "Of John and what we had. I do not know what to do concerning him."

"Do you wish to see him again?"

"If only to learn the truth," Hannah replied with a nod. "I cannot help but wonder if he is truly repentant of his deeds. That perhaps he has changed. I am unsure what to do."

"Allow me to tell you a secret," Isabel said. "Laurence went to speak to him yesterday, and he believes John is remorseful. He says he believes John's actions in the past were not that of a gentleman, but that he is sincere in his repentance."

Hannah could not help but smile as a glimmer of hope returned. "I hope that is true."

"He will be in attendance tonight. Laurence told him that, if you are willing to listen, he may explain what happened. Is that what you want?"

Hannah thought of her dreams. There was a great risk of being hurt once again, but she needed this one last opportunity to hear what he had to say. "Yes, I am willing to listen."

"Good," Isabel said as she patted Hannah's hand. "I shall see you in a moment downstairs."

Hannah nodded, and when her sister left the room, she went to the mirror and smiled at her reflection. She had worn a new blue gown made of velvet with silver threading and white lace. Then her eyes fell on the new butterfly clip, and she added it to the elegant coiffure Sally had done for her. The sapphires twinkled in the light of the candle, and she smiled all the more. Tonight, she would speak to John and perhaps take another chance at love.

With the candle in hand, she made her way down the stairs, the sounds of talk and laughter floating from the ballroom down the hall on the ground floor. At the bottom step, she snuffed out the candle and placed it on a table. If her conversation with John did not go as planned, she would return to her room despite the gaiety of the party going on elsewhere.

When she turned, she gasped as she collided with Forbes.

"Forgive me, Miss Hannah," he said as he placed his hands on her arms. "I did not hurt you, did I?"

"No," she said with a small laugh as she brought her hand to her breast. "I did not hear you approach."

His hands left her arms. "Your mother informed me that I will not be needed this evening; therefore, I am on my way to pour myself a small drink and then retire for the night. Is there anything I may get you before I go?"

She shook her head. "No, I believe I have all I need." She placed her hands on her skirts. "Do you like my gown?" she asked with a wide grin. Then she leaned forward. "Do you see? It matches my new pin!"

"It is as beautiful as you, Miss Hannah," Forbes said. "It is not a dress nor hairpin that makes it so, but rather what is in one's heart."

Hannah sighed at his words. "Thank you."

He bowed and walked away, and she turned toward the ballroom. With each step, the sounds from within grew louder, and Hannah wondered if John had already arrived. Isabel had not said if he was here or not, only that he had said he would be here. She paused at the door and peered inside.

The room was magnificent, almost as grand as the ballroom at Scarlett Hall. It had brighter white walls and a massive chandelier with dozens of candles in gold holders. Dozens of women in the latest fashions spoke with men in the finest clothing, and her heart warmed when she saw Laurence speaking with another man. He had been a wonderful addition to the Lambert family, even if the truth was that Isabel was an addition to his. Regardless, he was a kind and generous man, and he made her sister very happy.

Her gaze fell on that sister and their mother, who stood speaking together and appeared happier than either of them had been in a long time. They did not remain together long, for Isabel, the ever-attentive hostess, was soon off to chat with other guests.

Then fear gripped her when her eyes fell on a figure beside a table that held a variety of foods. There, standing alone, was Connor Barnet, and images of him accosting her in the alley popped into her mind of their own accord. She was finding breathing difficult, and now she wished she had told Isabel what the man had done. The manner in which he had held her, trapping her like a hound trapping a fox. The memories terrified her as much as they had that day, and she went to move behind a nearby fern only to have him look up and lock eyes with her.

He smiled, and she felt as if his eyes bore into her soul. For a moment she stood there frozen in place as he began to walk toward her, but she somehow found the courage to turn and run away.

She hurried past the stairs and slipped into the servants' hallway. The area was dark, and she had to run her hands along the walls to make her way through in order to not trip along the way. How did the servants find their way? She could not stop the tears from sloshing over her lashes. What if he saw her enter the otherwise hidden hall? Would he pursue her once again?

The hall led to a door that opened to the small room where the servants rested and ate. It was empty now, as all the servants were otherwise engaged in serving the guests, but she hoped Forbes was still here.

"Forbes?" she called out in a loud whisper. *Oh, please be here!* "Forbes!" Her toe bumped against something, and she covered her mouth to stifle her cry. Just enough light came in from under the doorway for her to find a long table with heavy wooden chairs settled around it. She made her way toward the door but stopped when she heard footsteps coming from behind her.

A cool breeze washed against her arm, and she turned to see the outline of a door that led outside. Returning down the dark hallway was out of the question; who knew who had followed her? She could either go to the door with light trickling beneath it, which would startle the poor servants and force her to admit she had run when she should have gone straight to Isabel, or she could run outside and wait until the threat left. No one would be outside that she could frighten with her sudden appearance. Whoever was following her—she was certain someone *had* been following, and more than likely it had been Connor—that person would not believe she would have gone outside alone. Her reasoning made as much sense as a dog riding a horse, but it was the best she could do when her mind was in a panic.

With her heart racing, she slid the door open and slipped out into the chill night. A moon just shy of being full gave enough light to see despite the fact she stood in an alley, and she pressed an ear to the door she had closed behind her. Trying to control her breathing, she listened until she heard the telltale sound of footsteps. Connor had found her!

In a panic, she glanced around her. The alleyway was long and foreboding despite the moon's attempt to maneuver around the nearby buildings. When the footsteps stopped, she pressed her back to the wall, and counted to twenty before letting out a sigh of relief. Connor must have done as she had expected and gone through the other door. She was safe.

She rubbed her hands over her arms to warm them in the cold night air. Looking first in one direction and then the other, she considered her options. She could chance walking around and reentering the house from the safety of the front door. However, too many shadows hid unknown threats, and furthermore, who would hear her cry for help if she was accosted? None had heard her in broad daylight when Connor had accosted her before! Yet, what if Connor was waiting for her when she returned to the room on the other side of that door?

In that moment, Hannah wanted nothing more than to have John by her side. He would see her protected from any harm, and he would love her like no other man could. However, he was not here, so she took a final deep breath. The safest option was to return to the servants' room, and once inside, she would alert Laurence and Isabel. She would tell them what he had done before, and they would remove him from the house.

As she turned to head back inside, a figure appeared in front of her. She went to scream, but a hand covered her mouth, and an arm wrapped around her waist.

"Come with me," a man's voice whispered in her ear. "Your mother is in danger."

***

"I am sorry," John said as he shivered from the cold. "I am sorry for having to approach you in such a manner, but there was no other way. You must understand that I love you, and nothing will stop me from telling you so."

He let out a sigh and shook his head in frustration at his words. "Let me try again." He cleared his throat. "I am nothing without you. A former rogue who has been set free from his foolishness by you. Do you understand? I cannot allow you to not hear what my heart feels for you."

He groaned and pressed a hand to his forehead. He sounded like a fool! He began his harried pacing once again from his place across the street from Laurence's townhouse, where he had been for the past ten minutes trying to build up the courage to approach Hannah. However, each attempt to speak the words sounded more awkward than the prior, and he did not know what to do. He had only one chance to make things right with Hannah, and he would not fail!

As each moment passed, he grew colder and realized that he needed to speak with her whether his words were foolish or not. Therefore, resigning himself to the fact that his words would not be any more elegant with more practice, he straightened his coat and began what seemed a great distance to cross the street.

Halfway, his feet gave pause as two figures emerged from the alley that snaked between Laurence's townhouse and the one belonging to the neighbors. The woman in the blue dress was no doubt Hannah, and an older man held her hand. They moved quickly as they turned and hurried away from him, and his heart filled with dread.

He was too late. Hannah had been driven into the arms of another man. In her heartbreak, she had made the decision to steal away into the night as a way to ease her pain, and he could not blame her. Yet, she had not mentioned any gentleman who had caught her eye. Therefore, this man had no doubt leapt at the opportunity to gain her trust while she was reeling from her heartbreak over what John had done to her. If that was true, then this man would use her for his own pleasure only to leave her even more heartbroken than before.

The question was, would Hannah, even in sadness, run off with another man, any man? Surely she would not do such a thing, and certainly not so soon after what she had endured. Even if she was hurt, which she most certainly was, would she sneak off into the night during a party where her sister and mother were in attendance? It made no sense no matter how he considered it.

"What will you do?" he asked himself.

Something was not right; he was certain of it. Therefore, he decided to follow the couple. He would follow close enough to not lose sight yet keep his distance so they would not see him. If Hannah had indeed found another man, at least John would have his answer, and he no longer had to rehearse what he would say to her. If she was being taken against her will, he would never allow that to happen.

John had seen the man look over his shoulder more than once, forcing John to scurry to one doorway or another to hide in the shadows. At the next alleyway, John came to a stop and pressed his back to the front wall of the building, hoping they had not seen him. This was the moment, he was certain of it. He would learn if she was a willing accomplice or a hostage.

The moment when he heard Hannah scream, he realized he had his answer, and John bounded around the corner only to find the alleyway empty. He had waited too long.

He shouted her name, and when no reply came, he cursed himself for not going with his instincts sooner. Now he had no way to find her, and he was certain she was in peril.

Chapter Twenty-Five

Hannah had never been more terrified in all her life. Her heart threatened to leap from her chest as she was led away, and she made an attempt to escape only to have a hand clamped over her mouth once again and she was dragged into the deep shadows of a thick hedge in the alley.

"Hannah!"

She fought against the arm that held her tight. That was John! However, try as she might, she could not break free. Tears ran down her face and her head grew light as the hand covered not only her mouth but her nose, as well. Tears ran down her cheeks. She would die here in this alley, and whatever she might have been able to rectify with John would be gone forever. For he had come to save her! However, her rejoicing turned to torment when he ran past where she stood in the shadows with her captor.

Before she could blink, she was dragged through a narrow space between the hedges, the branches tearing at her gown, pulling at her hair, and scratching the exposed skin on her arms. They came out on the other side in a clearing, her slippers dragging across the grass of the small park she had visited often when she wanted time away from the townhouse.

She managed to glance around and was dismayed to find thick trees and other shrubbery provided concealment, and with the late hour, no one was about who would be able to see her. Her first thought was to scream again when he released her, but the knife he withdrew from his pocket negated that idea.

Her captor removed his hand, and she shivered from cold and fright as she turned to face her assailant. "Why...?"

"I have missed you," Albert Moore said with a wide grin. "When you sent me that letter, I knew it was untrue, for you would never refuse to marry me."

Hannah wiped the tears from her face, praying that John would think to look in the park. The entrance was on the opposite side, but from where they stood, she could not see it, for the that side of the park was as deep in shadows as their current location.

How had Albert, a man she thought a friend, tracked her down in London of all places? The look in his eyes told her he had an objective, and she was it.

"You said my mother is in danger. Is she safe?" Hannah could not keep her voice from trembling.

Albert nodded. "Your mother," he said, tapping the breast of his coat, "has many secrets, all of which she wrote down. You never told me your mother was a writer."

"I did not know," Hannah said, barely listening as she glanced around for any way to escape. She sucked in her breath as Albert placed a firm grasp on her arm.

"It is true," he said. "And I know how to protect her."

This caught Hannah's attention. "Protect her from what?"

"Secrets," he replied. "Secrets I am certain she does not wish others to know." The look in his eyes was that of a madman, and Hannah knew her days were nearing their end. No man such as this made plans to keep a woman such as she alive, at least not long. And she refused to be used. She would take her own life before she allowed him to touch her in that way.

"I know secrets that will destroy her, your sisters, your brother, and everyone else you love."

The man made no sense whatsoever. "How could my mother being a writer destroy her?"

His laugh made the hair on the nape of her neck stand. "That is nothing compared to what else I know." Then he told her things that made her stomach churn, things that could not be true. However, if she stated she did not believe, who knew what he would do?

"How will you protect her?" she whispered again.

"Why, by not revealing what I know, of course," he said, tapping his breast again. This time she heard a deep thumping, as if he had something hidden inside his coat. "You will inform her that it is your desire to marry me, and I, in return, will keep her secrets. It is quite easy, really. What a heroic way for you to save your family's reputation, would you not say? You leave with me tonight." He stepped in closer. "I have secured payment for a vicar to perform the ceremony. It was expensive, but well worth the cost. Then we will return together to Scarlett Hall."

Hannah thought she would bring up every meal she had ever eaten. "I-I cannot marry you," she said. The man's smile faded. "I do not love you, and I must return to the party before my mother worries."

"Your mother will be hurt," he hissed as he tightened his grip on her arm. "Unless you leave with me, I will see her suffer. I have spent countless hours scouring every corner of Scarlett Hall. Many nights over the last year, I have watched you and Juliet, even your mother, sleep at night."

How could this be? she thought, her mind whirling at the thought of this man gaining access to her home without anyone knowing. Then horror struck her. "Juliet? Is she...?"

"Safe for now," he replied, his smile eerie in the light of the moon. "As long as you do as I say, she will remain so. I will ask one last time, and I would answer wisely. Will you leave tonight with me and become my bride?"

What if he was lying? What if he had never been inside her house? Should she ask him to prove what he said?

As if reading her thoughts, he reached into his pocket and produced a bracelet she immediately recognized. "As easy as I have taken this is as easily as I could slip into her room and..." He lifted the knife to show what he would do.

"No!" she gasped as tears streamed down her face. To imagine her mother or Juliet hurt by this man was more than she could bare. "I will leave with you now."

"Good," he said. "Once we are wed, we will return to Scarlett Hall where I will rule over the house. I will be the master there..." His ramblings were those of a lunatic, and Hannah cringed as he pulled her to him and pressed his lips to hers.

Disgust and shame rushed through her, and she pushed against his chest with her hands.

A low groan erupted from his throat. "Do not..."

A light rustling caught their attention, and Hannah turned to see a man emerge from the shadows.

"John!" she cried.

Albert made to grab her, but at the last minute, Hannah turned and leapt to her side, the knife whizzing past her, missing her cheek by mere inches.

"Hannah, leave!" John shouted, running toward them as Albert grabbed at her arm once more. It was in that heartbeat that Hannah realized how much she loved John.

Albert, who she thought was a friend, was in fact a man who meant to hurt everyone she loved. It was that thought that replaced her fear with anger, and she brought her foot down as hard as she could onto his.

Albert cried out just as John crashed into him, sending them both to the ground.

"Run!" John shouted as he scrambled to his feet. Hannah's feet refused to move, and he shouted at her again, "Go! Get help!"

Albert struck John in the jaw, causing him to stumble back with a grunt, and Hannah turned and ran, not only for her life, but for that of John, as well. The branches tore at her dress, arms, legs, and face, but she did not care. She had to find someone, anyone, to lend aid.

She emerged back in the alley, her breathing painful, but she did not pause. Instead, she ducked her head and ran as fast as her legs would carry her, praying that John would be safe.

As she turned the corner on the street that led to Laurence's townhouse, she caught sight of two figures ahead.

"Help me, please!" she cried, forcing the words with what little breath that remained.

"Miss Hannah!" Forbes shouted, followed by a cry from her mother as the two came rushing up to her.

"What is wrong?" her mother asked. "Where did you go?"

"John," Hannah gasped. "He needs help. Albert is hurting him! This way!"

She did not wait to see if they followed her as she rushed back to where the narrow opening between the hedges sat. She forced herself through the branches once again and stopped when she spotted John staring down at Albert who was lying on the ground.

"Oh, John!" Hannah said as she rushed forward, but John raised a hand for her to stay back.

"Ah, the good Lady Lambert!" Albert said with a laugh as he rolled to his side. He reached into his pocket and produced a book of some sort. "I have been wishing to speak to you, for I know your secrets."

"Mother?" Hannah said when she saw the look of worry on her mother's face. Was all that this man said true?

Her mother shook her head. "What do you want?" she demanded. "Do you want money in exchange for my journal?"

Albert laughed and wiped at his nose. The air grew colder, and Hannah shivered as she wondered at what Albert had told her.

"I want Hannah," he said as he rose to his knees, a smug smile on his lips. "I want you to give me her hand. Then I want your money, your home, and your land." He laughed as Forbes approached him and took the journal from his hands. "You believe I care if you take the book? I have memorized every word, every name, even the name..."

Forbes sent the man flying backwards as his foot struck him in the face, and Albert lay silent. "It appears this man will need to be taken to the magistrates," the faithful butler said. "I will take care of this problem, my Lady, Miss Hannah. You should return before you catch your cold and worry your guests."

Her mother took a step forward. "Forbes, I believe..."

What happened next was etched into Hannah's memory for years to come. "Eleanor," he said in a stern tone Hannah had never heard the butler use with her mother, "attend to your daughter and leave this matter to me."

The manner in which her mother merely nodded in obedience further surprised Hannah. Her mother turned, slipped her arm in Hannah's, and led her toward the hedges. "Come. Let us go."

Forbes turned to John. "My Lord, please make certain the ladies arrive home safely. Your noble deeds are done for tonight."

John stared at the older man for a moment before nodding and joining Hannah and her mother, and soon they were on the other side of the hedges once again.

As they made their way back to the townhouse, Laurence met them on the footpath. Her mother did not give him the opportunity to ask any questions before she said, "We will enter through the servants' entrance and go straight to the drawing room, is that clear?" Her voice was firm and brooked no argument.

"Yes," Hannah whispered.

"If anyone asks," she continued, "John caught a thief near the window attempting to gain entry into the house. John and the thief fought, and Hannah, fearful of what she had seen, ran and hid in the bushes." Hannah and John nodded their agreement. "We will never speak of Albert or this evening to anyone besides ourselves, is that clear? No one!"

Her mother did not wait for their response, but instead turned and headed down the street and to the door Hannah had used to escape when she believed it was Connor who was pursuing her.

Hannah's mind was still reeling from what had transpired, but as they entered the house—lights now blazing in the servants' hall—she felt safe inside its walls, and, more importantly, with John by her side.

***

Hannah sat beside John on the couch in the drawing room, her mother across from them. Isabel had come in earlier to see how they were doing, and their mother relayed the story of the thief and John's heroics in stopping him. Isabel did not stay, however, for there were still guests in the ballroom, and she promised to make excuses for the three who now sat alone in the room.

Remorse over all that had happened coursed through Hannah. "I am sorry for the fiasco I caused," she said with tears rimming her eyes once again. "It was never my intention…"

Her mother lifted a hand, and Hannah clamped her mouth shut. "You have done nothing wrong. It was that…animal…who is to blame."

"May I ask who that man was?" John said.

Hannah glanced at her mother, who gave her a nod. "He was a friend, or rather an acquaintance, from a society of writers I met last year. I learned before coming to London that he became enamored with me, and he asked me to marry him. I did not give him an answer at the time, although I did not wish to marry the man." She looked down at her hands in shame. "I sent him a letter explaining that I did not wish to marry him, but he said he did not believe it." She looked up, first at John and then at her mother. "I am so sorry…to both of you."

"It is as your mother said," John replied. "You are not to blame. I am glad I decided to follow you."

"Why did you leave with him?" her mother asked.

"I saw someone here…"

The door opened and Isabel entered once more, this time followed by the very man she was going to mention—Connor Barnet. Fear gripped Hannah, and she clutched her skirts in her hands as if readying herself to run once more.

"My apologies for interrupting," Isabel said, "but Connor wishes to say something."

The man stepped forward, his hands rigid at his sides. "Miss Hannah," he began as if rehearsing lines, "I came to apologize for my behavior the last time we met."

John shifted in his seat and shot the man a glare, but he said nothing.

"You see, I was so excited to see you that I acted in a manner that is not befitting of a gentleman. I have replayed that scenario in my head time and again since, and I handled myself rather brashly. I make no excuse for my actions, mind you, but if I caused you any fright, or made you feel uncomfortable in any way, I beg your forgiveness."

Isabel smiled at him. "It was Connor who told Mother about seeing you in the hallway. When he tried to apologize tonight, he said you ran off in fright."

Beside Hannah, John mumbled something she could not quite make out.

"I knew I was the cause of your fear, and so when I saw your mother, I explained what had happened before. Lady Lambert has been gracious enough to pardon me for my actions that day, but I hope you can find it in you to forgive me, as well." He finished with a deep bow.

"So, you were not angry with me that day?" Hannah asked.

The man gasped. "Angry? Absolutely not! I could never be angry with you. I had rehearsed often what I would say when I saw you again; however, when I did finally get the opportunity to share my feelings for you, I muddled it up so much I was angry with myself. You most certainly did nothing wrong, and I would understand if you never spoke to me again."

"Thank you for explaining," Hannah said. She looked up at the man who had given Isabel much support when Isabel's husband died. A man who had remained a friend to the family after. "And I also forgive you. It is clear that it was all a misunderstanding."

The rigidness Connor had been carrying disappeared. "Your kindness is appreciated," he said with an eager bow. "I wish you all a pleasant evening."

"Come, we will return to the party," Isabel said, taking Connor's arm as if he had offered it to her. "I have guests to attend to."

He gave her a wide smile, and the two left the room.

Hannah felt a small part of the fear and worrying she had been carrying leave her. Connor had meant her no harm, and Albert was being delivered to those who would do whatever needed to be done. She and her family were safe.

"Connor is a good man," her mother said. "I am thankful he came to me, for it was his information that led Forbes to go out in search of you."

"He is a good man," Hannah replied. "I am embarrassed now of being frightened of him." She shook her head and then looked up at her mother. "I imagine now would be a good time to explain my reasons for leaving the house."

Beginning with her previous encounter with Connor, she explained how she had lied to Isabel about the dog and ended with how she found her way to the alleyway this night to find Albert waiting in the shadows.

"I do not know how he came to be in the alley," she said. "Or how he knew I would go outside."

"He was wearing servants clothing," John said thoughtfully.

Hannah's eyes widened. "Then it was he who was pursuing me through the servants' hall and not Connor," she exclaimed. "I wondered how it was the staff had no lights lit; he must have snuffed them all out beforehand." She shivered at the thought, and John placed a hand on hers.

"I overheard a footman mention the lack of lighting," John said. He sighed. "As I said before, I am glad I decided to follow you."

"You were about to explain how that came about," Hannah said.

"Oh, yes. I saw you and he walking down the footpath, but it did not take me long to realize that you were not pleased to be in his company." His face reddened. "I must admit, it was not until you screamed that I made that realization, and for that I am truly sorry. I should have known immediately that something was amiss, something far more sinister than you running off with another man." He turned to Hannah. "I was not aware of the passage through the hedges, so when I found you both had disappeared, I ran past it. I found the main entrance to the park, and it was only luck that I had decided to enter."

Hannah shuddered at the memory of Albert and his actions. "When I heard you call my name, I could not believe you had found me. I thought I would never see you again."

"I would never let that happen," John said.

Her mother cleared her throat. "Seeing how the night's events are most unusual," she said as she rose from her chair, "I shall allow the two of you to speak in private. For a few minutes only, mind you. I will be outside the door."

When the door clicked closed, John took her hand in his. "Before you say anything, I have a confession to make. I must explain about the person I was."

"There is no need," Hannah replied. "I know who you are now."

"No, there is a need. You see, I was a rogue and cared for the feelings of no one. I never thought I would fall in love, or attend the theater, or bother to read a book. Until I met you." He kissed her hand. "When I told you I loved you, I spoke the truth. The woman you met the other night, Mary? I swear she has no more feelings for me than I have for her. She will return to the man she does love, Lord Laskey, which in turn has allowed me to return to the woman I love. If she will have me, that is."

Hannah could not stop her heart from soaring at his words, and she nodded. "I was angry about your past, to be sure, but that night, you admitted what had happened, and I ignored it. I believe now that you have changed and the man before me is the man I love. The man who protects and cares for me. I can imagine myself with no one else."

"Nor can I." He reached into his coat pocket. "I know it may not be the most appropriate place, such as the circus..."

Hannah laughed and then gasped when he produced a small box. She inched it open, her hands shaking in the process, and inside she found a ring.

"This ring symbolizes my love for you. The woman I wish to marry and with whom I wish to spend the rest of my life."

Hannah was so overcome with joy, she could only nod, and then he slipped the gold ring on her finger.

"I do love you, Hannah."

"And I love you," Hannah replied. She held her breath as his hands encircled her waist, and for the second time, they kissed. This time, however, it held more passion and confidence, for the man she kissed was the man she loved and who would soon be her husband. In his arms, she felt their love grow, if that were possible, and she had never felt more secure than she did at this moment.

Sadly, the kiss broke, and John smiled as he brushed back a strand of her hair. "I think it would be appropriate if you told your mother," he said.

She nodded. "Yes, I believe it would be."

As they rose, however, the door opened, and her mother entered. There was much more to tell this night, and as they shared the good news with her mother, Hannah could not help but be astounded about the upheaval of the day. What had begun as a night of horror had ended in love, and Hannah knew with all her heart, love would always remain.

***

Hannah studied her reflection in the large standing mirror. How strange to feel as if she had aged years in one single night. Even the face that stared back at her seemed older somehow. A girl one day and a woman the next. A woman who had misjudged not one, but two men. Nay, three. Connor, who only wished to express his regrets for his previous treatment of her. John, who had a past that haunted him but who had changed significantly because of her.

And Albert, who she now realized did not truly love her but loved the idea of being a wealthy man of the *ton*. She suspected that he chose her simply because she would be an easy prey. A weak woman who desired a life that was not her own. She had been just as willing to use him as he was her, that was what saddened her the most. And terrified her.

No, she could not concentrate on the past, for it was gone. Connor had set straight his part and had thankfully bowed out, and Albert would pay for his crimes. He would not enjoy prison, and she hoped they would never release him.

Now was the time to consider the future. A future with John. She would be married soon, and her family would be happy for her. A smile formed on her lips as she thought of what would be and the celebrations they would share.

A knock at the door had her throw her dressing gown over her nightdress, and her mother entered the room.

"How are you feeling?" her mother asked with a smile.

"Much better, thank you," Hannah replied. "I am safe." She held up her hand to show the ring. "And engaged to be married."

Her mother gave a small laugh. "So you are." She sighed. "Come. Sit with me."

They walked to the chest at the end of the bed and sat down on it together. Hannah could not help but eye the journal her mother held in her hand.

Her mother seemed to notice, for she placed the book in her lap and patted the cover. "Albert mentioned this to me. Did he tell you what it contained?"

"Secrets," Hannah replied. "He said the secrets inside would destroy you and everyone in Scarlett Hall. I know it is a lie."

Her mother sighed. "I'm afraid it is not a lie. Our home holds many secrets, and although I have tried desperately to keep them close to my heart in order to keep them from you and your siblings, it seems they have a way of breaking free."

Hannah frowned. "I do not understand," she said. "What secrets could there possibly be? What Albert said cannot be the truth."

Her mother closed her eyes and took a deep breath. When she opened them again, she said, "You recall I told you of my love of writing?"

Hannah nodded. "I do."

"It was that love of writing that I see in you, but it is the reason I wished you to keep your distance from Albert." She shook her head and stared across the room with unfocused eyes, as if staring into the past. "There are many like him in this world—men who are evil. I have kept this secret close to my heart for so long, but now I must share it with you."

Chapter Twenty-Six

Scarlett Hall, July 1791

Every Tuesday during the summer months was exactly the same, which was perfectly fine with Lady Eleanor Lambert. The day began with Priscilla, the nanny, taking the three girls out for an afternoon walk and a picnic lunch. The servants were in town completing whatever errands that needed to be done, and her husband, Charles, was off attending to business. This left Eleanor alone to do what she loved best - writing.

It had not been easy to convince Charles to allow her to take on such an activity, for no lady of the *ton* would ever admit to writing anything beyond a few lines of poetry. However, after promising the man countless times that she would never tell a living soul about how she enjoyed spending her time alone, he allowed it.

It had been her dream since childhood to put to paper the many stories that swirled around in her head, and this book would be her first of many. She hoped to publish her stories—under a pseudonym of course. Perhaps she would even see her story in a bookstore in London one day!

"Eleanor."

She started and turned to see Charles standing in the doorway, Forbes, their young new butler at his side. Charles had a temper, which seemed to grow shorter each day, but she could not help but still adore the man.

"Forbes will accompany me into town today," Charles said. "Do not forget dinner will be an hour later than usual."

She nodded. "I will not."

"Good. The professor has arrived, as well."

Eleanor smiled. Professor Archibald Downing, a man nearing forty years of age, was tall and thin and had a regal stance about him, as if he knew his worth. He had been employed as Eleanor's writing tutor, a gift from Charles several months earlier as a means to keep her busy when he was away on his many excursions for business.

"Lady Lambert," the man said with a stiff bow, a book clutched in his hand at his side. "Have you read the poetry I requested?" His voice reminded her of a headmaster demanding the best from his pupils.

"I have," Eleanor replied with a wide smile. "It was beautiful."

"It takes a special person to see such things," he said. "I am pleased with your progress thus far."

Eleanor could not help but beam at the man's words, but Charles simply snorted and left the room, Forbes following behind him.

"May I sit?" the professor asked.

Eleanor shook her head to clear her thoughts. "Forgive me," she replied. "Please, sit wherever you wish." She went to the couch, and her heart skipped a beat when Professor Downing took the place beside her. Typically, he sat in the chair across from her, or stood over her as she sat at the writing desk. In honesty, she found the closeness a bit awkward; however, she said nothing, for he was her tutor, not some suitor who had come calling.

"Now, let us continue where we left off last week," Professor Downing said. "Recite."

Eleanor nodded, took a deep breath, and began to recite the poem they had been learning. "'My heart is consumed with passion for my love.'"

"No, no, no," the professor shouted. "That will not do. You speak as if you are bored of my selection of material."

"It is a beautiful selection," Eleanor said, shocked at this sudden burst of anger. "I can assure you I believe so."

"A writer must *feel* the words in order to write them. Do you understand?"

"Yes, I do," she replied. She, in all honesty, did understand, for that was how she felt as the words poured from her heart onto the page every time she wrote. "I am sorry."

"This time," he took her hands in his, "speak the words as though you feel them."

Eleanor's heart quickened. Why had this man deemed it appropriate to take her hands? She did not like it, not one bit. "I-I do not believe this is acceptable behavior…"

"It is simply to help you," the professor said as he looked down at her hands for a moment. "We are adults rehearsing lines, just as those at the theater. If you wish to consult another tutor, then I shall inform Lord Lambert immediately…"

"No!" How would she ever explain to Charles her reasons for wanting a new tutor? He would take any excuse as suspect, and she certainly could not tell him the truth. No, her husband had been in a foul mood as of late; he would use any excuse to take away the one thing she cherished most that was all her own. "I apologize. Please, forgive me."

Rather than commenting, the man simply nodded, and Eleanor began again. With each word she spoke, the smile the tutor wore grew wider. Soon, his thumbs were brushing the backs of her hands, and she closed her eyes and pictured it was Charles to whom she was reciting those lovely words.

Then she reached the final line. "'Shall my love kiss me until the sun rises?'"

Then her heart rose to her throat when she felt lips upon hers as Professor Downing pushed her back into the couch. She placed her hands on his chest and pushed him away. "What are you doing?" she demanded.

"I see the way he speaks to you," the professor said, no longer the dry headmaster. "And the way you look at me."

"I do not see you…"

The man lunged forward, his hands taking hold of her arms, and he kissed her face, her neck, and to her horror, moved downward. Terror raged through her, and she fought, but the weight of his body upon hers made attempts at movement mute.

"Our love for one another is special. We share a passion we can no longer deny!"

Eleanor tried in vain to push him off her, and when she tried to scream for help, his lips silenced her. Her vision shimmered as tears filled her eyes, but the man would not remove himself from her.

Then the man's eyes went wide before he rolled off her onto the floor, and over her stood Charles, a look of such rage as she had never seen before in her life, a bronze statue that once stood on a nearby table in his hands.

"You!" he shouted. "I come home to retrieve my purse, and I find you in the arms of another man!"

"Charles!" Eleanor wailed. "It was not I..." Her head flew back and her cheek burned from the impact of his hand on her face.

"Quiet," he seethed. "After all I have done for you, and this is how you repay me? By seeking the admiration of another?"

"It is not as you believe," she cried.

Forbes entered the room, and his eyes widened. Eleanor followed his gaze. Professor Downing had not moved since Charles had struck him, and she detected no movement from his breathing.

Charles also turned and squatted beside the man, his hand on his chest. "My wife," he said, "has been in an appropriate relationship with her tutor. Were you aware of this, Forbes?"

Forbes shook his head. "No, my Lord. I have seen no such thing."

"I suppose you would not," Charles snapped. "Like me, you are not here when my wife is alone with the man. What a fool I was to not see what was happening right under my own roof!"

Eleanor rose from the couch and stepped over the professor, wondering when the man would awaken. "Charles, please. If you would simply listen..."

Her husband turned so quickly, Eleanor thought he would strike her again. "You will listen to me," he said, a finger poking her chest. "I will not have my family name ruined, nor have my daughters living in shame when they learn their mother is a harlot! The man is dead, Eleanor. Do you realize what that means?"

Eleanor covered her mouth as she turned to look at the lifeless form. "No," she whispered.

"Yes!" Charles said through clenched teeth. "I will not take responsibility for this murder. It will be *you* who stands trial; I will see to it."

"But Charles..." Eleanor cried as she reached for her husband.

He slapped away her hand. "No. You will bear the consequences for your actions."

Sobbing, Eleanor imagined the magistrates taking her away from her children and the sentence of death that would await her.

"Go on," her husband shouted. "Cry for the death of your lover all you want; I care not!"

Eleanor shook her head. How had the man come to hate her so much? Could he not see that the professor's advances had been unwanted? Did he not see how she struggled beneath the man's body?

Then a thought struck her. Perhaps she had not fought hard enough. Perhaps this had been all her fault after all.

"My Lord," Forbes said, breaking Eleanor from her horrible thoughts, "there is a ravine at the edge of your property."

"Yes. What about it?"

"Allow me to dispose of this problem there. If Lady Eleanor were to stand trial, it would ruin your family name forever."

Charles rubbed his chin. "And if someone comes across the body? Will they not come to me asking questions?"

"I am certain Lady Lambert has already written a letter to the professor asking why he did not keep his appointment. Of course, we were both here this day, for you had reprimanded me in the dining room just next door as I cleaned the silver."

How casually these men spoke of disposing the body of a man they knew! It was as if they made plans for organizing a gathering that was of little consequence!

Charles turned to Eleanor. "You must thank our butler for saving you," he hissed. "I will tell the driver to return to his quarters. We will place the body in the carriage and take it tonight to the ravine." He stormed from the room.

Eleanor stared at Forbes. "I did not...It was he who..."

"I understand what happened, my Lady," Forbes said, his voice kind. "There is no need to explain the truth to me. I must ask you to leave, for you do not want to witness what I do. You must prepare the letter and send it immediately."

Wiping at her eyes, Eleanor nodded and hurried from the room. The fear and sickness of what Professor Downing had done combined with his demise and her husband's accusations were all too much to bear, and she collapsed in her bed, sobbing until her chest hurt.

***

That evening, under the watchful eye of the moon, the body of Professor Archibald Downing was buried in the ravine. Although Forbes had requested that Eleanor not be in attendance during the ordeal, Charles insisted, for, as he mentioned, "She is the cause of all this!".

Eleanor had never felt number in all her life. She had trusted the professor, had such expectations of what he would do for her, she never considered his feelings for her. As Forbes threw the last piece of driftwood over the freshly turned dirt, she stood watching, Charles at her side.

"We shall never speak of this again," he said. "You will never be allowed alone with a male caller, and you are no longer to work on that accursed book again. Do you hear me? Never! I no longer trust you, nor will I ever again. You will attend to our children and keep producing children until you produce an heir. A harlot is not worthy to remain with me, and therefore you will move into your own quarters this night. Never again will you ask me for anything because you deserve nothing. Is that clear?"

"Yes," Eleanor whispered as tears streamed down her cheeks and her heart shattered.

Charles turned to Forbes. "Do you wish for money? Land? How do I repay you for what you have done tonight?" He reached into his coat pocket, but Forbes stopped him.

"Allow me to continue to serve you and watch over your family." His eyes met those of Eleanor for a brief moment, and she saw kindness in them.

"Very well," Charles replied. "If that is what you wish." He turned and opened the carriage door. "Let us leave this unpleasant night behind us." Without waiting for Eleanor to enter first, he jumped inside the carriage and plopped himself into the seat.

Eleanor whispered two simple words to Forbes, words of gratitude, for although she had lost a husband, she had been able to keep her children.

"Thank you."

The man said nothing but instead gave a nod before she entered the carriage. He closed the door behind her and climbed up into the driver's seat.

As they rode back to the house, Eleanor realized that her life was forever changed and would never be the same again.

Chapter Twenty-Seven

That is the reason I was in fear for you concerning this man, Albert," her mother said as she finished her story.

"What a horrendous experience for you, Mother!" Hannah said, holding her mother tight against her as tears streamed down her cheeks. "Never again will I refuse your words of wisdom."

Her mother kissed her head before their embrace broke. "That is the secret I have kept for so long," she said as she pushed a strand of hair behind Hannah's ear. "You must never reveal it to anyone, not even John."

"I promise I will not," Hannah swore. In her heart, she knew it would be the only thing she kept from him, but it was an important secret to keep. What good would come from revealing such information? Her father was now dead, and it had been he who had caused the death of the professor.

Her mother smiled and wiped a tear from Hannah's cheek. "Many times, as I watched you read beneath that tree in the garden, or as you scribbled in your book, I knew my old dream had been replaced by a new one. I wanted you to enjoy what I once had, and I hope you will continue with completing your book."

"I will," Hannah replied. "More than ever, I wish to finish it and realize my dream. I'm sorry for the words I said before I left. My behavior toward you over the last year was atrocious. I love you, Mother."

"And I love you. I know that, for a period of time, I was not available to you when you needed me the most. However, I have some issues with which I am dealing." Her mother sighed and rose from the chest. "Let us just say that I will continue to deal with them."

What her mother said made no sense, but Hannah decided not to question her. The woman had earned her right to secrecy.

"Get some sleep."

"I will," Hannah replied.

When her mother was gone, Hannah walked over to the vanity table and picked up the hair clip Forbes had given her. She had always cared for the man, and now she realized she truly loved him, not as she loved John but rather in the way a woman loves an uncle or an older brother.

Smiling, she set the pin down and went to lie on the bed. She pulled the blankets over her and reviewed the story her mother had told her. Never in her life would she have expected to learn her family held such secrets, that her father would have taken the life of another and be so callus in doing so.

However, as she considered it all, she realized that it revealed who her mother truly was—a strong woman who cared for her children and continued to do whatever it took to keep them safe. At one point, Hannah had held such anger at the woman, but that was now replaced with an admiration she had never thought possible.

As she closed her eyes, the fear finally gone, she pictured John, and her heart was at peace once more.

***

Eleanor sat in the servants' quarters, the candle on the table beside her flickering in the chill draft and a cup of tea her only companions. It was late—the party had ended hours earlier and the sun would soon rise—however, she refused to go to bed until Forbes returned. What was taking him so long?

Her mind reviewed the events of the night, and she struggled to quell the fear she had felt when Hannah's safety had been compromised, and the fear in revealing a secret she had hoped would be buried with the man in the ravine.

Scarlett Hall had born witness to many generations, and each had secrets of their own, much like the ones Eleanor bore. Many of those secrets had been collected in journals, which Eleanor had secreted away, some she had written while others had been written by its former residents. However, it was the one journal she had thought well-hidden that had almost destroyed her family that made sleep illusive. How could she have been so careless!

Sharing her secret with Hannah had lightened her burden somewhat, although the guilt still lingered after all had transpired this night. Hannah was safe, but she could not eradicate the memory of that crazed man hurting her beloved daughter who was so much like her mother and did not realize it.

For a moment, she closed her eyes, imagining her children as they once were. They were in the garden at home, none of them over the age of eight at the time, and Isabel was instructing Juliet on how to be a lady as Hannah sat beneath her tree with a book in her hands. Nathaniel was no more than a dream at the time.

Such lovely memories were threatened in times past, as much as the present, wishing to bring an evilness to her daughters that Eleanor would never allow. That is why she had sent Nathaniel off to boarding school as soon as he was able, so he would be safe from the secrets his legacy carried, at least for now. She would see him protected from that which he had no reason to know, and she would continue to protect him for as long as she possibly could.

Opening her eyes, she took another sip of her tea, although it had grown cold. When the sounds of footsteps came to her ears, she rose from the chair just as Forbes entered the room. She hurried over to the butler.

"Is he...?" she whispered as she gazed into the man's blue eyes.

"He has been delivered to the justice he deserves," Forbes replied. "As I promised."

She reached up and placed her hand on the side of his face. "You are a good man, and I thank you." It was then that she noticed the rust-colored stains on his usually stark-white shirt. "Were you hurt?"

"I am no one for whom you should be concerned," he replied as he took her hand in his. "It is Hannah for whom I am worried. Has she recovered from her ordeal?"

"She has," Eleanor replied. "But what of Mr. Moore? What has…"

"There are matters with which you should not concern yourself," he said in a tone that brooked no argument.

She glanced down at his hands and realized that they, too, had that same rust color splashed on them.

"It appears the man has made quite a few visits to Scarlett Hall," Forbes continued. "He has been collecting trinkets with each visit." He pulled out a bracelet that belonged to Juliet, as well as an ornamental hairpin belonging to Hannah. The last made her breathing catch, for it was a ring she knew should have been in a box on her vanity table.

"My ring. I remember the day…" She could not complete the statement lest she be overcome with pain. Shaking her head, she put the items in her dress pocket and looked back up at Forbes. "To think that man was in my home," she said, her stomach churning. "While my daughters slept, he was in their rooms! Oh, the things he could have done!"

"He will never hurt any of you again," Forbes said. "Ever."

Eleanor gazed into the face of the man that had saved her before. It was Forbes who believed that it had been the fault of Professor Downing that day and not her, and he had kept her, and her children, from heartbreak by offering a way to rid the family of the problem.

"I will never be able to thank you," she whispered.

"Knowing you and your family are safe is all that matters."

"I know this," she said, her voice trembling. "I have always known this."

Then Forbes rolled his hands into fists and raised them above his head, the blood on them and the sleeves of his shirt even more prevalent. "For a hundred and fifty years, Scarlett Hall has stood far above everyone else, just as have those within it. As long as I draw breath, I will see that the children and their heirs reign for a hundred more."

Nothing more needed to be said, for Eleanor knew what had taken place since she and Hannah left Forbes in the park earlier. It was as he had done before when they stood beneath the moonlight near the ravine as she spoke her words.

"Thank you."

To many, those words were simple and meant to compliment the receiving of a gift. However, to Eleanor, they signified far more, and she knew Forbes understood her meaning. And just as many years ago, the man simply replied with a nod.

In silence, she stood looking at the man, thankful for him being a part of her life, and she felt at ease in his presence.

"It is time for you to sleep," Forbes said. "Hannah and Isabel need a mother well-rested to continue to care for them as you do."

Eleanor gazed at him a moment longer and then replied, "As always, you are right."

She walked to the door and paused. Turning, she looked back one more time, her heart going out to the man. She reached into her pocket and removed the ring given to her so long ago. With a smile, she slipped it onto her finger, returning it to where it belonged.

Chapter Twenty-Eight

S everal months had gone by since Hannah's first arrival to London, a place she had once loathed but had come to love. Since that fateful night in the park, John had not only saved her from Albert, but he had changed her life by proposing marriage, and from that day forward, their love nearly doubled each day that passed.

The plan was that she and John would marry by special license, with Laurence and Isabel to witness, and then they would return to Scarlett Hall as a married couple. However, she would only return for a visit, for they were to make London their permanent residence.

From the first night after leaving her home, she had experienced a gamut of emotions and events that allowed her new ideas for her book. However, it was the love that she had for John that gave her the courage to finish her story. She was no longer a spectator of love, but rather a willing participant, and it allowed her intimate knowledge of what her characters endured and what they needed in order to continue.

Tonight, they sat in the home of Connor Barnet, who had made a point of offering her and her family a special invitation as a way to apologize once again, although Hannah had told him on numerous occasions there was no need.

She smiled. How could she have missed the fact the man had feelings for her? How could it ever have come to be that she had *three* men who had developed an affection for her? It was all very strange to a woman who had not wished to love any man!

Her eyes fell on John, who stood speaking with two other men across the room. It did not escape her attention that other women had looked at him, as well, but that fact no longer caused her concern. The man he once was now was gone, and the smile he gave her in return did away with any doubt that might have risen in the past.

Sighing, she took a sip of her wine as her gaze went to her sister, engaged in conversation with Connor. Laurence joined them, and soon the three were laughing.

Hannah was so caught up in her thoughts that the movement beside her caused her to start.

"Hannah," the woman said, and it took a moment for Hannah to recognize her, "I am so happy to see you."

"Lady Ellen," Hannah replied with a wide smile. "My apologies. Ellen, it is wonderful to see you again."

The woman wore her customary red dress, which emphasized her large bosom a little more than Hannah thought appropriate. However, if Ellen did not mind, who was Hannah to judge? "I'm sorry I did not return to the writing group," she said. "I found myself pursuing a different dream altogether." She could not help but smile as she looked over at John.

"You were right to do so," Ellen replied. "I was wrong in my advice."

"You meant no harm," Hannah said. "And I know this."

Ellen took a step closer and lowered her voice. "The night you left, I stayed awake for hours thinking of how pure your heart was and how you saw the world with such innocence."

"That was simply the ideals of a naive child," Hannah said, feeling embarrassed.

"No. It was a woman who knew her heart and would not accept anything less than what she wanted. What I mean to say is that your actions inspired me."

Hannah raised her brows. "Oh? I am pleased to hear I was of help, but I cannot imagine how."

"I had long given up on love," Ellen said with a sigh. "After Patrick's passing, I found myself withdrawn. However, that night I met you, I took out my manuscript for the first time in years."

"That is wonderful," Hannah exclaimed. "Have you completed it?"

The woman gave her a single nod. "I have. Therefore, I must thank you for helping me."

"Of course," Hannah said.

"And your book? I understand it is to be released tomorrow."

Hannah felt that now familiar excitement whenever she thought of that finished work. "It is. I still cannot believe that I found someone willing to publish it."

Ellen shook her head. "You are a strong woman," she said. "I wish you all the best in life. Promise me that next season you will come see me?"

"I will call well before the season begins if you allow me to do so," Hannah said with a laugh. "We are to return to Wiltshire to my childhood home to celebrate our wedding, and then Cornwall, but our plan is to maintain residence in London."

"That is wonderful!" Ellen said.

A man approached, and Ellen held out a hand to him. "Donald, may I introduce Miss Hannah Lambert." It did not escape Hannah's notice the man had not released Ellen's hand. "Hannah, this is Lord Donald Peters. He and I are courting." Her eyes lit up as she said this, and Hannah's went wide.

"It is a pleasure to meet you," Lord Peters said. "However, my love, I only popped by to inform you that I will be meeting with a few friends in the other room; in case you came searching for me." His eyes twinkled as he spoke.

"Of course," Ellen replied.

When Lord Peters kissed Ellen's cheek and then walked away, Hannah gave her friend a tiny smile. "He seems quite nice."

Ellen laughed. "My dear, he is young and handsome, but he is good to me. I am happy to have found love again."

After a short conversation, the two parted ways with promises that Hannah would inform Ellen when she returned to London, and John joined her. It was much like when they were at the circus, when time seemed to stand still, as he came to stand before her.

"Was that Lady Ellen?" he asked. "The one you pointed out earlier?"

"It was," Hannah replied. "She is wonderful, and like us, she is in love." She glanced around the room. "I wonder at times what it must be like for others who are not lucky enough to share what we have."

"You know, I have wondered the same," he replied. "It is a sad notion, but one about which we will never need to worry again."

"Indeed," Hannah replied, her heart flying above the clouds. "We never will."

***

Hannah stood outside Martin and Sons Publishers as Laurence, Isabel, and John waited in the carriage. The day was warm, as it was this time of year, the sun as bright as her future. Her dream of publishing a novel had finally come to pass, and today was a day of celebration. Many years of frustration, joy, tears, heartache had led to this point, and she regretted none of them.

With confident steps, she walked to the door and entered. Albina Bragg met her with a welcoming smile.

"It is so good to see you," Albina said as she kissed Hannah's cheek.

"You are too kind," Hannah replied. "I wish to thank you for all you have done for me. I can never express my gratitude enough."

Albina clicked her tongue. "Oh, pish-posh!" she replied. "It is your writing, and your tenacity, that led to this moment. Never forget that."

"I will not," Hannah replied with a smile.

Albina took her hand, led her to one of the bookshelves, and then took a step back. "You have done well," she said. "Not many women can say they have been published. I'm sure your book will be read for generations to come."

Hannah nodded as she blinked back tears. She reached out and picked up the book and ran her fingers over the embossing.

"This story comes from the heart," Hannah said, almost to herself. "With so much love, a dream that was nearly never completed." She drew in a deep breath and turned to face the woman again. "I must return home for a short time, but I will come see you upon my return."

"See that you do," Albina said. "And give my best to Lord Stanford."

"I will."

Hannah left the shop but closed her eyes once she was outside. Some women had dreams but were never given the opportunity to experience them. Others might fulfill their dreams but never cherish them. However, as she opened her eyes and saw John emerge from the carriage, she knew how fortunate she truly was.

For she had fulfilled not one, but two dreams—one of publishing a novel and one of finding love. A love which she never thought existed outside of books. A love she had denied herself from ever experiencing. However, just like a good book, love had found its way to her and brought John to her. Although Hannah still had much to learn in life, she knew in her heart that, what love had brought together could never be torn apart.

***

The joy of having her dream of publishing fulfilled was just the beginning to the wonderments of the day, for when they returned to the townhouse, the vicar was already waiting.

No guests were in attendance, no feast had been prepared, but Hannah did not care about any of that. They would have plenty of celebrating when they returned to Scarlett Hall, where her family could be with her. And as Hannah looked into the eyes of the man she loved with every ounce of her being, she spoke the vows that brought them together as man and wife.

The season had come to an end, but a new season was to begin. A season like none she had ever experienced; one she looked forward to enjoying with John.

"May the blessings continue to enrich your lives," the vicar stated, and John smiled down at Hannah, his eyes sparkling with unshed tears.

Then he leaned down and kissed her, and she felt the passion behind it, the wanting that matched her own. When the kiss ended, he whispered, "I am happier than you can imagine. I cannot wait to begin this new life with you. It will be a story we will work on every day together."

"We will," Hannah agreed. "For we will write a story that has a beautiful ending."

"I think," he said so quietly only she could hear, "our story will continue on forever and have no ending."

Hannah nodded as her eyes filled with tears. How right he was!

He took her hand and they turned and faced Isabel and Laurence. It had been her sister who had always looked after her and guided her through life, and it was Isabel who, like Hannah, had sought refuge away from love. And, although Hannah had once thought she could never compare to her sister, she now realized she was very much like Isabel, for her eyes shone with a love that would remain forever, much as Hannah knew her own did, as well.

Chapter Twenty-Nine

Scarlett Hall stood tall and proud upon the hills of Wiltshire as the carriage carrying a newly married Hannah pulled up the drive.

"I must admit," John said, his eyes wide with awe, "although I have seen Scarlett Hall once before, I still find it a magnificent place."

Hannah smiled as she turned to her husband. "It is a place filled with love, and now ours will be added to it."

Their plan was to visit Hannah's childhood home for several days and then head off for their honeymoon in Cornwall. Hannah had never been to that area of England, and she could not wait to see the great open lands and dazzling cliffs she had only read about in books.

Once they had endured two celebrations of their wedding, they would return to London where they would set up their home together. Well, perhaps endured was a bit harsh, but although Hannah had grown more accustomed to being in the company of others, it did not mean she did not enjoy time alone with the man she loved wholeheartedly.

The front door of the house opened and her mother exited, followed by Forbes. Hannah was overwhelmed with pleasure at seeing them again, and she had to fight back the urge to rush to embrace them as she and John walked toward them. She was now a married lady, after all.

"Miss Hannah," Forbes said with a deep bow, "it is so wonderful to see you."

She could not keep up the pretense any longer, and she ran up the stairs and embraced the man who had been so wonderful to her for so long. "It is so good to see you too, Forbes," she said into his coat. When she released the poor man, she took a step back. "Forbes, I would like to properly introduce my husband, Lord John Stanford, Marquess of Greyhedge.

Marquess? she thought as she froze in place. She was a marchioness! The thought never occurred to her, for John never made much of the fact he held such a title, and she found the idea a bit overwhelming. She had no idea how to be a marchioness! She would have to speak to Isabel about proper conduct.

Then she looked at John. No, she would ask John, but for now, she would simply be herself.

"It is my honor and my pleasure to meet you, my Lord," Forbes said with another bow.

"As am I," John replied as he offered the man his hand. "Any man who would do what you did for my wife, deserves a decent handshake."

Forbes shook John's hand, but Hannah could feel his discomfiture from where she stood. "I only do what is required of me, my Lord."

"My daughter has returned." Hannah could hear the strain in her mother's voice as she fought back tears. "A woman married to an honorable man. It is so wonderful to see you both."

Hannah nodded to John, and he handed her a book wrapped in brown wax paper. "Thank you. If you would like, you may go inside. Forbes will have tea sent up; I will join you in a moment."

He took her hand and kissed it before following Forbes into the house, leaving Hannah and her mother alone.

"Is that what I think it is?" her mother asked, looking at the package. "Is that your book?"

Hannah nodded as she handed it to her mother. The woman eased back the paper as if what was inside would bite her hand if she removed it too quickly, and Hannah wanted to reach out and rip the paper away. Once the book was revealed, her mother ran her hands over the cover. "The binding is beautiful, and the..." Her words trailed off and she brought her gaze up to Hannah. "I thought you chose another title for your book?"

"Read the first page."

Her mother nodded, opened the cover, and read the page.

"This was my..." Her mother was unable to complete the thought as tears flowed down her face.

"Your dream," Hannah said. "A dream you once had and that was unjustly taken from you."

"But what of your book?"

Hannah laughed. "I will finish that story soon enough, but, you see, I finished your novel in order to fulfill that dream we shared."

Her mother embraced her, and the two women held each other for several moments.

"I can never thank you enough," her mother whispered. "This has brought me happiness I have not felt in many years."

"I knew it would, Mother. I have been fortunate in having seen two dreams fulfilled, and I could not think of you not having yours."

Her mother placed a hand on the side of Hannah's face. "You are a good child," she said. "Or rather a good woman. I forget sometimes, even when you stand before me to show me the beautiful lady you have become."

"I will always be your child," Hannah said. "As all your children will forever be."

"I only ever wanted you all to be happy."

"And we are, Mother." Hannah took her mother's arm and led her toward the front door of Scarlett Hall. "We most certainly are happy."

Epilogue

That night, Hannah waited patiently with Isabel in the drawing room. John and Laurence were in the study, as Hannah's mother wished to speak to them privately. Although Hannah did not know about what the woman wished to speak, she could not stop a wave of concern from flowing over her. She had expected a giddiness, a sense of comfort at returning home, but the air was filled with anxiety, like a heavy blanket suffocating everything beneath it.

Isabel seemed to feel it as well, for she sat more rigid than normal, and she, just as Hannah, kept glancing up at every sound. Even the chimes on the clock made them both jump.

Footsteps in the hallway had them staring at the door, and Annabel entered, followed by their mother, both wearing a strange look of sadness.

"Remain seated," their mother ordered before either Hannah or Isabel could stand. Annabel joined Hannah on the couch, and their mother stood before the empty fireplace, her back to them.

Hannah shot a glance at Isabel. Something was most definitely wrong. She gave Annabel a questioning glare, but the girl wrung her hands in her lap and refused to look up.

"Mother?" Isabel asked. "What is it?" Their mother's shoulders shook, and Isabel jumped to her feet. "What is it? What is wrong?"

When she turned, tears streamed down her face. "Juliet," she whispered.   "My   sweet   Juliet."

Author's Note

I hope you have enjoyed the Secrets of Scarlett Hall thus far, beginning with Isabel's Story in *Whispers of Light*, followed by that of Hannah, *Echoes of the Heart*.

More secrets are revealed in the next installment of the Secret of Scarlett Hall Series, *Voices of Shadow*, which will recount Juliet's story.

Jennifer

Regency Hearts Series

The Duke of Fire
Return of the Duke
The Duke of Ravens
Duke of Storms

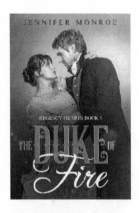

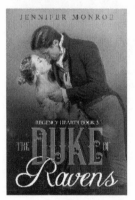

The Defiant Brides Series

The Duke's Wager
The Spinster's Secret
The Duchess Remembers
The Earl's Mission
Duke of Thorns

OR
Get all 5 in one boxed set!

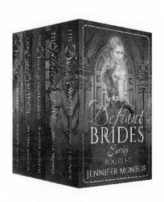

Made in the USA
Coppell, TX
15 October 2021

64123772R00141